There came a cracking sound, loud, and Conan jerked his gaze away from the recalcitrant horse and stared at the lake. The surface of the frozen lake burst asunder, and chunks of ice the size of large dogs flew through the air before smashing back down. As Conan watched, beings began to clamber from the fissure onto the surface of the lake. And what beings they were! Each was man-sized, but shaped like a great ape. They were pure white, without facial features – no mouths or noses or eyes – and each was as smooth as polished crystal.

The white monsters shambled toward him with hands outstretched, reaching.

Conan the Fearless

Steve Perry

SPHERE BOOKS LIMITED

SPHERE BOOKS LIMITED

Penguin Books Ltd, 27 Wrights Lane, London W8 5TZ (Publishing and Editorial)
and Harmondsworth, Middlesex, England (Distribution and Warehouse)
Viking Penguin Inc., 40 West 23rd Street, New York, New York 10010, USA
Penguin Books Australia Ltd, Ringwood, Victoria, Australia
Penguin Books Canada Ltd, 2801 John Street, Markham, Ontario, Canada L3R 1B4
Penguin Books (NZ) Ltd, 182–190 Wairau Road, Auckland 10, New Zealand

First published in the USA by Tom Doherty Associates 1986
First published in Great Britain by Sphere Books Ltd 1988

Publisher's Note. This is a work of fiction. All the characters and events
portrayed in this book are fictional, and any resemblance to real people or
incidents is purely coincidental.

Set in 9½/11 pt Times
Printed and bound in Great Britain by
Richard Clay Ltd, Bungay, Suffolk

For Dianne, as ever:
And for Carl, Ruth, Ken and Ella

ACKNOWLEDGMENTS

In the writing of this novel, there were people who aided, by word or deed, or sometimes simply by being. I can hardly list them all, but I would be remiss if I did not mention those who were most helpful. Thanks, then, to: L. Sprague and Catherine de Camp, who might well be termed Conan's step-parents – no one knows the Cimmerian better than they; thanks to Harriet McDougal and her husband, Jim Rigney, certainly; and, finally, thanks to Michael Reaves, for his reading and critical help, which added much flavor to this fantasy.

PROLOGUE

The chamber exuded cold, but a kind of coldness deeper than that offered by the damp and mold-speckled gray stone walls. It was an unnatural chill, a thing of the soul as well as of the air, a frigidity of ancient bones interred in the heart of a glacier old when Atlantis still rode the oceans. In the center of this coldness stood wrapped its cause and its focus – Sovartus, Mage of the Black Square, delving into an arcane spell forged with warped and stained essences of evil.

The magician's body swayed with the forces flowing through him, and his voice was deep and powerful when he spoke. 'Come forth, child of the gray lands. Come forth, spawn of the pits. Come forth by my command!' Sovartus then intoned the Seven Words from the Parchment of Slicreves, being careful to pronounce them precisely. To do less was to court instant death – a word misspoken would allow the demon he conjured to tear free of the diagram sketched exactingly upon the flagstones.

From deep within the body of the castle a terrible shriek issued forth, made as if by some unearthly beast being dipped slowly into boiling lead.

In the center of the drawn pentagram smoke boiled forth from a tiny vibrating point, expanding outward in malignant waves of dark purple mixed with hard yellow, as a fresh bruise upon the air of the chamber. There came an eye-smiting flash of infernal light, and the smell of burnt sulphur claimed the room. A demon suddenly stood within the confines of the pentagram, dripping black slime and exuding the stink of Gehanna from every pore. He was half again as tall as a man, with skin the color of fresh blood; he stood naked and hairless, and only a blind man could have failed to see how awesomely male he was.

1

'Who dares?' the demon screamed. He lunged toward Sovartus, seeking to wrap his taloned hands around the throat of the man with jet hair and pointed beard who grinned at him; but the demon slammed into the wall of force that bounded the pentagram. Giant muscles bunched in the monster's arms as he pounded his fists against the invisible barrier. He screamed, a sound that carried the rage of Hell, and he bared long ivory fangs at the man. 'You will beg a thousand days for death!' His voice screeched like sheets of thick brass being sundered.

Sovartus shook his head. 'Nay, hellspawn. I have summoned you and you shall serve at my command.' The mage grinned, then laughed. 'You shall serve indeed, Djavul.'

The demon recoiled, holding his clawed hands in front of him. His face held horror. 'You know my name!'

'Aye. And thus you will do my bidding or remain bound in my pentagram until time's end.'

Black slime oozed from Djavul's body and dripped onto the floor. Where it touched, tendrils of smoke spiraled up from the flagstones. Pools of sludge formed, but stopped at the outline of the magic diagram Sovartus had drawn. Djavul stared at the man. 'You are a Wizard of the Black Ring?' the demon asked.

'Not the Ring, night-child. I am Sovartus of the Black Square, adept, and soon to be master of the Four Ways. I do not delude myself with the scarlet dreams of the black lotus, nor dabble in base necromancy such as those inept Stygian pretenders. It is not the Ring but the more powerful Square that binds and now commands you, Djavul. Know you of the Square in the pit?'

Djavul gnashed his fangs. 'We know of it.'

'Ah. And shall you serve as I bid?'

'I shall serve,' he said. He flashed his teeth yet again at Sovartus. 'Yet take you care, man, for if you should make the smallest mistake –!'

'Threaten not, demon. I can bind you to a rock and have you carted to the Vilayet Sea to be tossed in to contemplate the bottom muck, should I so choose!'

Djavul's eyes flared redly, but he spoke not.

Sovartus turned away from the demon and looked to the wall nearest him. Three children languished there, two boys and a girl, bound as was the demon, but by more mundane means: they were chained to the gray wall. The children seemed beyond fear; they stood or sat staring at nothing, as if drugged. There were three of them – only three.

Sovartus turned back toward the demon. 'Look upon these children,' he commanded.

The demon beheld the three. He nodded. 'I see them.'

'Do you know them?'

'I know them,' Djavul said. 'They are Three of the Four. The girl is Water, the boys are Earth and Air.'

'Very good. So you would recognize the Fourth if you beheld her?'

'I would know her.'

Sovartus nodded. He smiled, his own teeth flashing whitely in the frame of his black mustache and beard. 'I thought as much. Here, then, is your task, demon. To the south and east lies the city of Mornstadinos; within that city, the Child of Fire abides, but hidden. You will find her and bring her to me, alive and well.'

Djavul glared at the wizard. 'And then?'

'And then I will release you to return to your pleasures in Gehanna.'

'I shall look forward with great joy to seeing you there, human.'

Sovartus laughed. 'Of that I have no doubt; but when I arrive in Hell, it will likely be as your master, demon. More, you shall help me to achieve it; best, then, you take care not to offend me meanwhile.'

Djavul's sharp teeth grated together and he started to speak in his metal-shredding voice. 'I see –' He stopped.

Sovartus's black eyes gleamed in the light of the guttering lamps lining the walls. 'Yes? Speak.'

Though the demon was obviously reluctant, he nodded and said, 'As I saw the Essence of the three children, so, too, I see your Essence, sorcerer. There is power in you, much power, and the promise of greater forces hangs upon you like a malignant shroud.'

3

'Ah,' Sovartus said, nodding in return, 'you are perceptive for one born of the pit. You recognize how well-served you would be to avoid antagonizing me, then?'

'Aye. The Black-Souled Ones allow many things in their dealings with men. You may well do as you speak. I shall serve you, human. I have no desire to spend ten thousand years buried in black mud at the bottom of the Vilayet Sea.'

'You are wise for a mere demon,' Sovartus said. 'When I arrive in Hell to rule after a few thousand years – after tiring of my rule here – mayhap I shall need a wise assistant such as yourself. Consider such as you do my bidding and so serve me well.' He stroked his pointed beard with one slender hand. 'For now, I bid you leave. Accomplish your mission and return quickly.'

The demon gathered himself. 'I hear, O master,' he said, 'and I obey.'

Gigantic muscles flexed and bunched as the inhuman thing squatted and prepared to spring. He leaped, and another bruised flash lit the dank chamber; when it dimmed, Djavul was gone, leaving only the pools of sludge staining the floor where he had stood.

Sovartus laughed again, and stared at the three children. Soon he would have the Fourth; soon he would bring together the energies each held. Then, ah, then, he would command all of the Four Elements and not merely the undines and wind-devils; not merely the salamanders and flames; not only the demi-whelves. No, when he at last had all Four of them, he would be able to create and unleash the Thing of Power, a force so awesome even Black-Souled Set himself must take notice.

Sovartus spun away, and his black silk robe flared about him. He was the most powerful of all the Black Square, and save for Hogistum, he always had been.

Hogistum had sought to keep the power from him by hiding it. The old one had ensorcelled a maiden, and then impregnated her. The maiden had birthed four children at once, quadruplets, and each child carried within it the lines of power for one Element. They had been separated at birth and scattered, to keep Sovartus from them.

4

Thirteen years he had searched, thirteen long years, and all the while he looked, he studied the arcane, to improve his skills. He had traveled to the corners of the world, seeking the children and knowledge. In the far-eastern jungles of Khitai he had dealt with the frozen-faced and yellow-skinned wizards; in the ruined temples of Stygia he had learned the skills of the Black Ring. Too, the mage had seen with his own eyes the emerald-skinned alien monster with the misshapen head of an elephant enshrined in Yara's tower in Arenjun, the Zamorian City of Thieves. Yes, he had learned his evil lessons well; even without the power of the Four, Sovartus was a force to be reckoned with, a sorcerer second to none in all of Corinthia. Such power was not enough, of course, not when he could be the supreme power in all of the world.

Sovartus smiled as he stalked forth from the chamber and walked down the dark hallway toward the main hall of Castle Slott. Rats chittered and fled from his passage, and spiders climbed higher in their webs when he passed them.

Hogistum was dead, poisoned by Sovartus's hand, and the slain magician's plan was no more than a fading memory. The children had been gathered, save the one, and he possessed them. Sovartus had spent fortunes to obtain the first three. His henchmen had found them in Turan; in Ophir; in Poitain; how ironic that the last one would be in Corinthia, practically upon his own doorstep! He had three of them, and the bodies of those mortals who had aided or known of his quest now fed the fishes or more unspeakable water creatures, or lay moldering where no man's eye would ever behold them. When his demon collected the last, he would triumph. Too bad the old man was dead; Sovartus would like him to see the victory. Perhaps he would bring Hogistum back to life. He would have that power. Yes, that would be a fine jest, to bring the old mage back long enough to savor his failure and Sovartus's victory. He laughed loudly at the thought. He would do it, by Set he would. It was not every man who could bring back his murdered father from the gray lands.

CHAPTER ONE

In the nameless village at the foot of a pass from Zamora through the Karpash Mountains into Corinthia, a ramshackle inn squatted forlornly. To this rickety and dilapidated place rode a tall and muscular young man, astride a fine buckskin horse for which he seemed ill-suited. The deep-chested horse carried a fine saddle and exotic silk blankets, and had bridle fittings of silver cast in the shapes of cranes and frogs; obviously, this was an animal belonging to a rich man.

The rider, however, wore a harbergeon of old and cracked leather, sans both mail and basinet, and his half-breeches appeared supple, but well-stained with age and sweat. His cape was ragged about the edges, if well spun. Strapped to his forearm in a sheath rode a long and wicked-looking dagger; and by his side a great broadsword with a plainly wrapped grip nestled in an even less ornate leather scabbard. The evening winds blew the young giant's black hair into an unruly mane about his head, and his deepset eyes cast back the setting sun's fiery glare almost as if those eyes held blue fire of their own. He was Conan of Cimmeria, and if any man noticed the discrepancy between horse and rider as the pair approached the inn, none made so bold as to speak of it.

A boy of ten stood near the doorway of the inn, which, like the village, boasted no name that the rider could see. The man leaped from the back of the horse and observed the lad.

'Ho, boy, have you a stable in this place?'

'Aye.' He stared at Conan's attire. 'For those who can pay.'

The boy's look amused Conan. He laughed and fished

around inside the pouch on his belt, producing a small silver coin, which he tossed toward the boy.

Deftly, the boy snatched the coin from the air. He grinned widely at the man. 'Mitra! For this you could near own the stable!'

'Food and water and brushing for my horse will be sufficient,' Conan said. 'And there might be another coin such as that for you on the morrow if my horse's coat gleams.'

'It will outshine the sunrise!' the boy avowed. He leaped to catch the proffered bridle.

'Bide a moment,' Conan ordered. He lifted a pair of heavy bags from the horse, being careful to keep the gold coins within from clinking as he did so. Those bags would better pass the night undisturbed next to him and not in some stable; Conan knew about thieves, for he was one himself. He watched the boy lead his horse away, and then turned to enter the inn.

The inside of the place certainly did not belie the promise of the exterior; the main room was dirty and enshrouded in smoke that curled from a sputtering fire in a blackened fireplace at the far end. There were no windows; the only other light came from cracks in the low roof and a few smoky oil lamps set on several of the rough wooden tables.

A fat man in a stained apron scurried toward Conan, his gapped smile displaying much blackness and rot. 'Ah, good evening, my lord. How may I serve?'

Conan looked around. There were ten people in the room, and those he saw seemed as disreputable as the place itself. There were dark-skinned Zamorians, of course; two short and slant-eyed men who looked as if they might be Hyrkanians; a pair of sad-eyed and weary-looking women in torn pantaloons who could only be plying the oldest of all trades; finally, perched on a stool was a short and round man with gray hair, who watched Conan as a hawk might watch a serpent.

Conan turned back to the innkeeper. 'Would you have other than moldy bread to sup upon in this wretched place? And wine less sour than vinegar?'

'Of course, my lord –'

'And a room for the night,' Conan interrupted. 'A room with a door and bolt.'

'Mitra has blessed my establishment with such things as you seek,' the fat innkeeper said, showing his blackened teeth again.

Conan grunted. 'Fetch me food then, and we shall see if Mitra's blessing extends to the cook. And wine, your best.'

The man appeared to appraise Conan shrewdly; but before he could speak, the wide-shouldered youth flipped a coin at him. The fat innkeeper's eyes widened as he caught the reflection of dim lamplight on yellow, even as the disk flew through the air. He snatched the piece from its flight faster than a falcon slays a thrush, then opened his fingers carefully, to keep the coin hidden from the curious stares of the others in the dank room. But the flash of gold would not be denied.

'Gold!' The fat man's whisper spoke at once of greed and lust, and reverence. He made as if to bite the gold, to assure its purity, but apparently considered the state of his teeth and only weighed the money in his palm. He clamped his fingers tightly around the shining disk and glanced around at his patrons, seeming, as he did so, kin to some wily rodent.

Conan chose that moment to stretch his mighty frame. Sinews cracked and joints popped as he rolled his massive shoulders and flexed his thick arms. The sounds and motion seemed to startle the innkeeper from his greed-fed trance. He bowed, mumbled, and hurried away. He was back in a moment bearing a wineskin and cup, which he fawningly placed on the table nearest Conan.

'Your meal will be prepared at once, my lord.'

Conan grinned, aware that the riffraff of the tavern were staring at him. Disdaining the cup, he snatched up the wineskin and lifted it over his head. The stream of thin red wine tasted slightly bitter; but it was cool enough. Thrice Conan filled his mouth and swallowed before he downtilted the skin for breath. He stretched again, his muscles dancing like tame beasts under his deeply tanned skin, then sat upon the rude bench next to the table.

Around him the inn's customers turned back to pursue their own business – save the rotund man, who continued to watch the young giant from the corner of one pale eye.

The innkeeper returned in a short while bearing a wooden platter covered with a slab of steaming beef. The meat was as thick as Conan's hand and dripping blood, being only lightly seared, but the Cimmerian fell to eating, using his razor-edged Karpashian dagger to hew great chunks from the steak. He chewed lustily and washed the half-raw meat down with streams of the thin wine. It was not the best meal he had ever had, but it would suffice.

When he finished the meat and most of the wine, Conan turned to search for the innkeeper. Before he could do more than glance around, the obsequious man with the black-toothed smile appeared at Conan's elbow. 'My lord?'

'I am no man's lord,' Conan said, feeling sated with food and wine. 'But I am tired and would see the room Mitra saw fit to bless in this . . . establishment.'

'At once.'

The innkeeper led Conan from the smoke-filled room, through a narrow corridor, to a steep set of wooden stairs. Each step creaked as Conan trod upon it, so that his ascent reminded him of a twittering flock of feeding birds. He grinned. Good. No thief could climb these steps to take a man unawares in the night.

The room was scarcely an improvement on the scene below, save that it was empty of anything but a pile of clean straw and a rough wool blanket. There was a round hole cut in the outside wall – window enough to admit air or moonlight, but too small for a man to enter. The door seemed solid, and there was a well-oiled brass bolt that slid easily in its recess to seal the portal. Odd, that. The bolt was the best-kept part of the room. Conan waved the innkeeper away, bolted the door, and tossed his leather bags full of loot into the corner near the mound of hay.

Something scuttled away from the solid thump of the gold and silver, chittering unseen in the dimness. Conan pulled his dagger and crept closer to the rude bed, his blue eyes alert. When he was ready, he rustled one edge of the hay.

The rat burst forth, fleeing, but he moved too slowly. Conan stabbed with remarkable speed and impaled the brown-furred rodent on his dagger.

Conan grinned. That one would not be nibbling at him this night. He stood and flicked the dagger toward the small window, flinging the dead rodent from the blade, outside into the deepening evening. He wiped the dagger on the hay, sheathed the knife, and settled himself for sleep.

A whisper of a noise came in the hours before false dawn. It was so faint that it would have seemed to be hidden from ordinary ears by the night-creaks of the inn growing older. Conan awakened instantly, his senses alert.

Skritch. Skritch. It was a tiny thing, this aural intruder upon his rest; but it boded ill, for Conan detected in the noise the scrape of metal upon metal. Only a man used instruments of iron or brass, and a man at this hour meant danger.

Through the hole in the wall a faint beam of sinking moon and starlight entered the room. This was hardly enough for a cat to navigate by, but the Cimmerian's vision was sharper than other men's, and honed by many past dangers. He swept his gaze around the room until he focused upon the cause of the nocturnal sound.

In the pale glow Conan saw a thin wire sliding between the door and its jamb, a hooked bit of copper that tugged at the well-oiled bolt.

For a moment Conan felt a prickle of fear along the back of his neck. No man born of woman had mounted the stairs that he had climbed earlier – this he would wager. He reached for his sword.

Suddenly, the greasy bolt slid free and the door burst inward. Three men rushed into the room, each wielding a dagger raised to strike.

Conan leaped up, jerked his broadsword free of its scabbard, and lunged for the assassins. If they thought to slay a sleeping man, they were sadly mistaken, for the Cimmerian attacked.

The first man was spitted before he saw his mortal danger.

11

Conan ripped his sword free as the man fell gargling in his death throes. The Cimmerian instantly swung the heavy blade with a force denied all but the most powerful of men. The second assassin half-turned and managed to raise his dagger in defense, but his effort counted for naught. Sparks flew as the broadsword mated with the dagger and swept it aside as if it were no more than a feather. Conan's blade bit deeply into the villain's side, shearing ribs and organs alike, and the man screamed in his final agony as he fell, to lie prone upon the filthy wooden floor.

The third man backed quickly away into the tight corridor, fear staining his features.

The wall across the corridor kissed the would-be assassin's back. He looked frantically to the right and left, but seemed to know that if he turned to flee, the berserk giant would be on him instantly. He switched grips on the dagger, holding it like a sword, and jabbed the point in Conan's direction.

Just then, from the stairs came a cacophony of screeching footfalls. Flickering tapers threw ghostly fingers of yellow light ahead of their bearers. Conan did not take his attention from the dagger-bearing thief; however, the man must have thought it so. He lunged at Conan, seeking to bury the point of his weapon in the Cimmerian's groin. Conan leaped lithely to one side, fast for so large a man, and swung his sword overhead and downward with all his might. The sharp edge connected with the villain's head and bisected it, as a cook might split a melon. Gore splashed patterns upon the walls of the corridor, now better-lit by the innkeeper and the roundish man Conan had seen earlier in the common room. Conan turned toward these two with the point of his bloody sword aimed at the innkeeper's heart, a heart hidden under a grimy nightshirt.

The innkeeper went deathly pale and began to sweat profusely. 'Pl-pl-please, sir, I have a family!'

Conan fixed the man with an unblinking stare, with eyes blazing like two glowing blue coals. He looked away, finally, at the mortal remains of those men who would have killed him had he been less vigilant. 'Who were these scum?' he asked, pointing his blade at the nearest corpse.

'I – I – I know them not, sir,' the innkeeper managed to stammer. Sweat rolled from him in fat, greasy drops that plopped onto the floor by his bare feet.

The short rotund man spoke. 'Zamorian cutpurses, it would seem. They arrived at the inn only earlier this day.'

Conan regarded the man. 'I am called Conan of Cimmeria, but late of Shadizar. Who might you be?'

'I am Loganaro, friend, a merchant from Mornstadinos, in Corinthia. I am returning there from a visit to Koth, where I have – ah – business interests.'

Conan nodded and turned his gaze back to the innkeeper. 'How came these carrion-feeders to my room, owner of this Mitra-cursed dog barn? Not by way of those stairs.'

'G-g-good sir, there is a second set of stairs at the far end of the corridor. B-bet-better-constructed ones.'

'Aye. Now explain the reasons for the oiled bolt, dog.'

'B-b-bolt? It – it was but recently installed, sir. The craftsman would have oiled it.' The innkeeper swallowed and nodded as though he were a puppet with a loosened string. 'Yes, that must be it; the craftsman must have done it.'

Conan shook his head. 'A likely story. I am disposed to look up this craftsman and ask him.'

The innkeeper turned an ashen hue. 'B-b-but he is no longer in our village. He – ah – left – for Turan.'

Conan spat at the floor. He squatted and used the ragged cloak of the dead cutpurse to clean his blade, then inspected the steel for nicks. There were no fresh marks on the blade; the thief's dagger must have been of poorly made steel.

Smoothly, Conan rose to tower over the trembling innkeeper. 'Drag this offal away from my room,' he ordered the innkeeper. 'I would return to my disturbed slumber.'

'S-s-sleep?' The fat man seemed horrified at the idea.

'What else? No cock has crowed, and I am tired. Be quick, and I may overlook the matter of the oiled bolt.'

Conan grinned as he ate portions of the breakfast the innkeeper had laid before him. The food was well-prepared and hot. If he belched, the owner of the dog kennel called

13

an inn came running to inquire if he could be of service.

As Conan sat there the short merchant approached him. He addressed the Cimmerian. 'Do you travel west, by happenstance?'

'Aye. To Nemedia.'

'Then you will ride the north fork of the Corinthian road through Haunted Pass.'

'Haunted Pass?'

The merchant smiled. 'A name to scare children, no doubt. The wind sings strange songs as it makes its journey over the rocks. There are hollow places that give back sounds some men find unnerving.'

Conan laughed, and tore a final chunk of fresh bread away from the third loaf the innkeeper had brought him. He washed the bread down with a sip of wine. 'In the land of my birth we know of such wind-flutes,' Conan said. 'Even small children in Cimmeria have no fear of such sounds, much less a man of eighteen winters.'

Loganaro shrugged under his dark brown robe. 'There is also a haunted lake, called Spokesjo, near the summit of the pass.'

'And do fish blow bubbles at unwary travelers from this haunted lake?' Conan laughed again, amused by his own humor.

The merchant's face grew serious. 'Nay, no fish swim in this lake. Those things which do are better left unmentioned, save to say one should avoid the shores of the place in which they dwell.'

Conan shrugged. 'I travel through Corinthia to Nemedia, and this pass is the route by which I go, wind-noises and wives' tales notwithstanding.'

Loganaro grinned. 'Ah, a brave man. As it happens, I will also be returning to my country by this route. Perhaps you would care for a companion?'

Conan shook his head. 'Nay, merchant. I travel better when I travel alone.'

The merchant shrugged. 'As you wish. I shall be before or behind you, in any event. I would not startle you should you note me upon your trail.'

14

'It would take more than a single merchant on the road to startle me, Loganaro.'

The short man nodded and said no more, but there was a look of amusement about him Conan did not care for. It was as if he withheld some deep and dark secret from the young Cimmerian.

CHAPTER TWO

The snow lay like a thick and crusty blanket on the rocks girding the pass. The breath of Conan and his buckskin horse fogged the freezing air as they wound along the trail. Conan took no notice of the temperature, save to pull his fur cloak a bit tighter about him.

The buckskin mount picked its way slowly along the rocky path. There was little wind, but Conan heard a distant howling of air across some hollow. He grinned. Wind-flutes might scare the timid, but not a Cimmerian. The slow clop-clop of the horse's hooves accompanied the faint echo of the wind playing its ghostly tunes.

Ahead, Conan saw the surface of the small lake of which he'd been told. He shook his head, and his square-cut black hair moved stiffly in the cold. The lake was frozen from shore to shore, and Conan would wager half the gold in the sack mounted behind him that the ice was as thick as his own well-thewed leg. It was less than likely any evil spirits would be emerging from *that* lake.

The trail passed within a few yards of the lake's frozen edge. The horse picked its way along in a lazy fashion, lulling Conan with the motion.

Halfway along the length of the lake the horse stopped suddenly and turned its head sideways to stare at the giant slab of ice.

Conan looked, but saw nothing. He dug his heels into the beast's sides. 'Move,' he said.

The horse whinnied and shook its head, almost as if answering him. The animal snorted and began to sidestep away from the lake. 'Foolish fly-brain!' Conan said. He kicked the horse harder. 'I will feast on horseflesh this night if you do not move!'

There came a cracking sound, loud in the silence, and Conan jerked his gaze away from the recalcitrant horse and stared at the lake. A long, jagged fracture appeared on the surface of the ice; quickly, another appeared, then a third. It was almost as if something were *pushing* up from under the ice.

The surface of the frozen lake burst asunder, and chunks of ice the size of large dogs flew through the air before smashing back down. As Conan watched, beings began to clamber from the fissure onto the surface of the lake. And what beings they were! Each was man-sized, but shaped like a great ape. They were pure white, without facial features – no mouths or noses or eyes – and each was as smooth as polished crystal. A dozen of the creatures scrambled from the ice and began to run. For an instant Conan thought them pursued by something and uninterested in him, for they ran at angles away from him. Then he realized what they were doing: cutting off his escape!

Conan dug his heels into the horse's ribs hard, and slapped the beast's rump with one hand, trying to force it to flee. The horse, however, was possessed by primal terror; it reared and bucked, trying to throw its rider. Conan clamped his knees against the sides of the panicked beast, and by sheer force of his massive strength managed to hold on. The horse stopped bucking, but then seemed to freeze in its terror, becoming as a statue in the cold air.

The white monsters shambled toward him with hands outstretched, reaching.

To Gehanna with the horse! Conan leaped from the animal and drew his broadsword even as he flew through the air. He landed solidly, never pausing as he charged the nearest of the white monsters. When he came within range, he swung the sword hard.

The blade sheared one of the ice-beast's hands from its arm, and the hand fell to the ground with a thump. But no blood circulated in that frigid body; from the stump of the icy arm there issued instead a gush of clear liquid, a stream as clear as water!

Cold fingers bit into Conan's shoulder and he spun to

17

face another smooth beast. His sword sang as desperation drove his slash. Luck guided his aim: his blade lopped the water monster's head from its neck. The thing spasmed, then released its hold on him as it fell. Another fountain of crystal fluid jetted from the falling body.

By Crom, the abominations could die well enough! But there were more than ten against him; bad odds, and Conan was no man's fool. He needed a path out, and he would have to carve it quickly!

Muscles of striated flesh flexed and bunched, driving sharp steel against the denizens. Thrice, cold hands were laid upon him; three times did Conan chop the offending hands away. He slashed, cut, stabbed, and kicked, showering the frozen ground with shards and watery chunks of the faceless monsters. They were many, but they were clumsy compared to the whirling, leaping man. Conan raged against them, destroying three more. The fluid of their bodies steamed and froze in the hard chill as Conan continued to weave his pattern of steel-laced death.

It was a fight that could have but one end, he knew, if he stayed and tried to slay them all. He was tired; the sword was heavy in his hands, and there were still eight of the shambling monsters trying to kill him. Time to depart.

Conan turned and ran in the direction from which he had come. The eyeless beasts followed him, stringing themselves out into a line. Conan managed a grin even in his exhaustion. Good. They were not only clumsy, they were no tacticians.

Abruptly, he stopped and turned, then ran back at the monsters. They were too far apart now to reach him in force; he faced a single creature, the largest of the group. Conan ducked the wild swing of the monster's fist. He raised his sword and brought it down smartly. The ancient steel bit through the thing's leg and slashed the limb away from the body. The water monster fell in silence, blocking Conan's path behind him. Conan sprinted away in the direction he had been heading when first attacked. Now, if he could only collect his cursed horse!

A sharp whinny pulled Conan up from his run. He turned and observed his mount being dragged toward the rent in the lake's surface by several more of those things that harried him. Still more of the evil spawn emerged from the lake to help clutch at the horse. There must have been at least twenty of them now. Half of them subdued the horse, while the others turned toward Conan.

His horse, all his food, and the stolen sack of gold were being dragged down into Spokesjo Lake! For an instant Conan chased them, his sword held high and rage befogging his mind. He stopped. No horse was worth dying for. There were thousands of horses and many rich men whose gold he could steal, if he lived.

'Crom take you all!' he yelled at the crystal-clear bloodless monsters before he turned and loped away.

On the road descending from the pass Conan spied a mounted figure in the distance. Though he increased his speed from a walk to a trot, then to a run, the figure grew no closer. He shouted a greeting, but received no answer; the rider never paused. Could this be the merchant he had met in that dog kennel of an inn earlier? If so, why did the man seem so intent on maintaining the distance between them? Cursing the watery attackers who had drowned his horse, Conan kept on.

After a weary day's walk Conan sighted the city of Mornstadinos, the first Corinthian city he had seen. True, there were no towers or tall spires such as graced Shadizar or Arenjun, but the settlement boasted a high wall and many buildings, even if most seemed more squat than those in other cities he had known. It would serve. If he hoped to continue his journey to Nemedia, he would have to obtain another horse and more silver or gold, and here of necessity would be the place to find both.

As the ground passed steadily under his boots Conan realized he would be at least another day on the road. From a vantage point on a foothill he could see a large forest on the far side of the city, and what seemed a vast plain beyond that. No travelers came toward him from the town, which was unfortunate. A fat merchant would no doubt be carrying exotic foods and valuables of which Conan could avail himself. Aside from his sword, his Karpashian dagger, and his clothes, the Cimmerian had nothing but a purse bearing a few coppers, enough for perhaps one meal and a few cups of bad wine. An unpleasant prospect, but one he had learned to accept; it was not the first time going hungry had been his lot.

Well. The city lay ahead and his belly would manage on roots and stream water until he reached its gates. Conan trudged stoically onward.

Loganaro judged that the tall barbarian was now an hour behind him, thanks to the gallop into which he had forced his horse. The beast was lathered with sweat, but this was of little importance: What mattered was that there be time for Loganaro to contact one of his patrons. Or, in this case, a patroness.

While the horse wandered along eating sedge grasses the man began his preparations for far speaking, a magic of no small power for which he had paid dearly. Even so, there was another price to be paid for each use of the talent. Loganaro pulled a short fat-bladed dagger from beneath his robes and clutched it tightly in his right hand. Clearing his sleeve away from his left arm, he revealed a forearm covered with thin scars. Some of these were old and faded by sun and age; others lay fresh upon his flesh, in shades ranging from angry red to pale pink. Loganaro picked a spot between two of the younger lines and laid the tip of the dagger against it. Gritting his teeth, he pressed the needle-sharp tip into his flesh.

Blood welled as he drew the blade downward, scoring tanned flesh with a thin line of living ruby liquid. There was some small pain, a necessary portion of the spell; more, there was the salty fluid itself, the major ingredient. The dagger's chore finished, Loganaro laid it aside, to replace the steel with his middle finger. He gathered the blood on the finger's tip until that member was fairly coated; raising the finger skyward, the man intoned a phrase he'd been taught: '*Hematus cephil augmentum sichtus.*'

Quickly following the words, Loganaro drew upon his

forehead in blood the three arcane symbols that completed the spell: the adulation rind, his own personal chop, and the double curve that represented his patroness. Then he waited.

Five minutes pounded past, on their way to join the uncounted lines of time that had marched before them. On the birth of the sixth minute a voice came to Loganaro – a woman's voice. Scarcely above a whisper, the voice carried intensity and power within its folds.

Why have you called?

Loganaro spoke to the evening air. 'Mistress, I may have found that which you seek.'

I seek many things, insectus minor. Which thing in particular do you pretend to have discovered?

'That which will complete your Incantation of Animation for your ebon simulacrum, the Prince of the Lance.'

Many have offered that final ingredient, servant. All have been found wanting.

'I think not this time, Mistress. I saw this man slay three experienced cutthroats with as little effort as a man takes to wipe wine from his lips. More, he traveled through Haunted Pass unaided by any conjur or cantrip.'

A lucky man to move while the undines slept.

'Nay, Mistress, those creatures slumbered not under the ice of the haunted lake. They came forth in great numbers and tried to carry this mortal to their watery mansions. He slew many of the monsters. His horse was taken, and I thought for a moment he would follow them under the ice to retrieve the beast.'

He accomplished this unaided?

'Indeed. I thought it best to remain unseen.'

No doubt. I have never thought you a candidate for my Prince's assemblage. This man, however, interests me. Continue to observe him. I shall make contact with you with instructions when I deem it should be so.

'And my reward . . .?'

Fear not, low one; the gold you value shall be yours if the heart of this man be sufficiently brave. The word of Djuluva the Witch is her bond.

'To doubt such never entered my mind, Mistress.'
Has this man a name?
'He is called Conan, Mistress. A barbarian from Cimmeria.'

Within her manse in Mornstadinos, Djuluva sundered the magical link with Loganaro and leaned away from the polished steel mirror that gathered her focus of mystic energies. She beheld her image: a fire-haired woman of thirty whose face appeared ten years younger smiled back at her. Her thin gown of raw silk revealed a shapely body lush of hip and breast and much experienced in carnal ways. The image held within the steel reflected the wicked smile of the comely witch as it seemed to mirror her thoughts and feelings. No man born of woman was a match for Djuvula in the arts of lovemaking, she knew. Many had tried; all had failed.

Realizing that no mortal man would ever be able to keep her pleased, Djuvula had decided to undertake the creation of an ersatz-man, a simulacrum she could hold in perpetual thrall, to satisfy her every whim. It had been simple enough to begin the undertaking. Her magic was particularly powerful when it came to such things. Unfortunately, some of the components of the assemblage were less simple to obtain. Her ebon-skinned Prince of the Lance lay in all his perfection in her bedchamber, yet unable to function without the final ingredient required for her witchery: the fresh heart of a truly brave man. Dozens of organs had been tried; all had failed to animate her lover. The so-pronounced brave hearts had done nothing whatsoever. Djuvula's disgust was profound.

Despite his obsequiousness, Loganaro was usually reliable in his dealings with her; perhaps, just perhaps, he had finally found what Djuvula needed. Such a thought was worthy of the smile she shared with her mirror. She would prepare her potions, just in case.

A tall man stood next to a much-scarred log, which leaned against a granite wall. The place was a remote corner of the

22

estate of Lemparius, Center Strand of the Senate's Treble Whip, and the man none other than the owner of that vast acreage. In his long-fingered hands Lemparius held a device of brass and gold, shaped like a ball within a cube, but twisted in some perverse manner that was easy to see but difficult to describe. A voice issued from the device, that of Loganaro the free agent, speaking to the witch Djuluva. The conversation was not meant for Lemparius's ears, but such privacy was beneath the senator's consideration. He listened as he chose, using the *storora*, the 'magic ear' constructed by some nameless Stygian artificer dead a hundred years.

'– called Conan, Mistress. A barbarian from Cimmeria.'

Lemparius laughed, the sound much like a growl, as he adjusted some small subdivision of the device he held. The voices of the fat agent and the witch dwindled and finally vanished. Carefully, the senator bent and placed the mechanical miracle behind the man-thick log that formed an oblique angle against the massive granite wall. There was a special recess designed for the *storora* there, cut into the stone. The senator did not want anything to happen to the Stygian magic box; it was most useful, and, so far as he knew, it was unique.

Satisfied that the arcane device was safely nestled away, the senator turned around. A warm wind ruffled his long blond hair, giving his head almost a tawny glow. The sun glinted from his eyes as he moved, and that glint showed strangely shaped pupils more akin to a creature designed for predatory attack from above than to a man. Methodically, Lemparius removed his clothing. He stripped away his tunic and silken underbreeches first, then his sandals, until he stood naked on sandy ground bounded by a wall as tall as three men. He was alone in the vast clearing, so none beheld his nakedness.

None saw what followed.

Lemparius began to change. His contours altered, the skin and muscles flowing like fresh potter's clay. Bones crackled; cartilage tore asunder; the blond hair of a man thickened and turned into the tawny pelt of an animal, the hair sprouting as might weeds in some hellish garden. Lemparius's face seemed to sink. His nose flattened and broadened at the nostrils; his mouth stretched and his teeth fused and grew until the canines became fangs.

What had been a man groaned as it dropped onto all fours. Claws replaced nails, paws metamorphosed from fingers and toes. The man's form shrank in places, stretched in other places, and when at last the metamorphosis was complete, the sthenic form that stood there was no longer any design of ape.

That which prowled the estate of Lemparius, one of the Treble Strands of the Senate Whip, was the spawn of cats: It was Lemparius, panther, one of the werefolk.

And the cat-beast was hungry.

CHAPTER THREE

The sun had made but a small part of its journey across the morning sky when Conan entered the city of Mornstadinos. From a distance the Cimmerian had been unable to perceive the convolutions of the narrow streets. He now traversed myriad alleys, cul-de-sacs, and cobbled roads which appeared to have been laid out by someone besotted, blind, or mad. If a pattern existed to the maze, Conan was unable to discern it. Here sat a stable full of horses and stinking of dung; next to the stable stood a temple replete with cowled oblates; beyond that edifice an open air market dealt in fruit and baked goods.

The barbarian's stomach rumbled, insistent in its hunger. He strode to the market, attracting more than a few stares at his muscular form. From a woven basket Conan extracted a loaf of hard black bread. He poked the loaf with one finger, then waved the bread at an old woman. 'How much?' he said.

The woman named a figure: 'Four coppers.'

Conan shook his head. 'Nay, old one. I do not wish to buy your house and grandchildren, only this loaf of stale bread.'

The old woman cackled. 'Since it is obvious you are a stranger, I shall make you a bargain. Three coppers.'

'Again, I have no desire for the entire basket of these rocks you would sell as bread, only the one.' Conan waved the loaf and scowled.

'Ah, you would cheat an old woman of her hard labor? Very well then, I will accept two coppers and the loss so that you may think us hospitable in the Jewel of Corinthia.'

'Where is your dagger, old woman? Surely a cutpurse who would steal my money must need a blade. Though I will allow that your tongue and wit are sharp enough.'

The woman cackled again. 'Ah, you're a handsome boy; you remind me of my son. I could not see you starve for want of a copper. One will buy you the best bread on the street.'

'Done, Grandmother.'

Conan reached into his pouch and retrieved one of his few coins. He handed it to the old woman, who nodded, smiling.

'One other favor,' Conan said. 'You are right in calling me a stranger. Where might a man find an inn and some wine with which to wash down the best bread on the street?'

'A man of means might find a number of places. But a man who would haggle over a few coppers with an old woman has fewer choices, meseems. Down this road, two turnings to the right and one to the left, such a man could find the Milk of Wolves Inn. And if this man was some outlander who might not be able to read civilized writings, he might look for a picture of a wolf *salient* above the door.'

'A wolf what?'

'Standing on her hind legs about to leap,' the old woman said, cackling again.

'Well met, then, mistress baker. And farewell.'

Conan located the Milk of Wolves Inn with no difficulty and, bearing his loaf of black bread, strode inside. The youngful hour seemed no barrier to the fair-sized crowd standing or seated at long wooden tables around the room. Most of the men appeared to be locals, judging from looks and clothing; several women were serving steaming bowls, and others offered hints of pleasures other than food or drink. He had been in many such places, passable, for the most part, and cheap.

The Cimmerian found a vacant place at one end of a table and seated himself. He looked around the room, scrutinizing the patrons. Most of the men were probably poor but engaged in some honest trade: coopers, smiths, tradesmen, and the like. To his left Conan saw a group of four men who looked more unsavory, probably cutpurses or strong-arm thieves. The largest of the four was of medium height, but very broad and heavily muscled, with dark eyes and blue-black hair; further, he had an enormous hook nose, which resembled a bird's beak. Conan had seen men with similar countenances before, men bearing a mix of Shemite and Stygian blood. This beak-faced one looked dangerous, not a man to turn one's back on.

Seated near the four was an odd pair: an old man with white hair and the weight of a good sixty or seventy winters riding his stooped shoulders, and a girl, a child of twelve or thirteen. The old man was dressed in a long robe with full sleeves. The girl, auburn-haired, wore blue hose and boots and a short jerkin of supple leather. Additionally, she carried a short sword under a broad belt, in the Turanian style.

'Your pleasure, sir?'

Conan looked up at the speaker, a fat wench draped in a shapeless dress much stained by food and drink. The barbarian fetched out one of his last three coppers and held it up. 'Would this buy me a cup of decent wine?'

'It will buy you a cup of wine. How decent such a beverage is I leave to your judgment.'

'That bad, eh? Well, I am in no position to be choosy. I shall risk the vintage.'

The girl left, taking Conan's coin. The Cimmerian half-turned, to study the old man and the auburn-haired girl.

Conan quickly became aware that he was not the only person regarding the pair. The four Conan had marked as strong-arm thieves were also taking an uncommon interest. Such did not bode well for them, Conan figured. But it was not his business. He turned his gaze back toward the serving girl, who approached bearing an earthen mug brimming with dark red liquid. Some of the wine sloshed over the lip of the cup as she set it onto the table. Without saying anything, the girl moved off to see to other patrons.

Conan tasted the wine. In truth, it was not bad; certainly, he had drunk both better and worse. It would wash the bread down and help fill his belly for now. Later he could worry about his next meal. He broke a chunk of the black bread and tore off a mouthful of it with his strong teeth.

27

The bread, too, was passable. He chewed slowly, savoring the taste.

Nearby, Beak-nose gestured at the old man and girl with a quick movement of his head. Two of his companions rose from the table and began to sidle toward the pair. One of the men toyed with the handle of his dagger; the other man merely scratched at his scraggly beard.

Beneath drawn brows Conan watched, interested. He took another bite of the bread.

When the two men were a few steps away from the old man, several people seated or standing near the inn's doorway gasped. Conan glanced toward the door and saw men scrambling to get out of the way of something. He could not see what caused the commotion, but it was as if a wind cut a path through a field of tall grain. As the crowd rippled aside, the cause became apparent.

Scuttling across the sawdust-covered floor was a spider. This creature was like none the Cimmerian had ever gazed upon before. It was the size of his fist, covered with fine hair, and glowed like a lantern inlaid with rubies: indeed, the thing *pulsed*, as might a throbbing heart.

Without hesitation the spider ran to the table at which the old man sat; in an eyeblink it scuttled up a table leg; another second saw the glowing arachnid leap in a graceful arc to land squarely in the mug of wine the old man held in one gnarled fist. The wine emitted a loud sizzle, a pop, and a small cloud of red vapor suddenly floated above the mug.

With every eye locked into a stare upon him, the old man smiled calmly, raised the cup to his lips and drank.

Beak-nose's two minions suddenly decided they had business elsewhere, that they were late for such business, and that further delay would be disastrous. At least it seemed that way to Conan as he watched the two men scramble over each other in order to be first to reach the door.

Behind Conan someone uttered an oath and muttered, 'Magic!'

At that moment the girl seated next to the old man leaped up. She tossed a moldy sunfruit into the air. Conan saw her

28

set and guessed what would happen. A heartbeat later the girl pulled the short sword from its sheath smoothly and slashed it back and forth at the falling fruit. At first it might have appeared she had missed with her strokes, but Conan's sharp eyes beheld the truth and he grinned even as the fruit continued its fall – now in four pieces instead of one.

The Cimmerian chewed another bite of bread. Here was a message for all who chose this particular morning to breakfast at the Milk of Wolves Inn: this old man and girl were not so helpless as they might appear; best to tread elsewhere for easy pickings.

Beak-nose was not amused. He glowered at the old man, his own cup of wine clutched so tightly that the knuckles of his dark hand were chalk-white.

Someone at the door gasped again. A second spider appeared, this time heading for the foot of Beak-nose's table. Without preamble the hairy arachnid scrabbled up onto the rough wood and leaped into the man's wine.

Conan laughed. A challenge! Would he dare to drink?

Uttering a cry of wordless rage, Beak-nose leaped up and tossed the mug away with a backhanded flinging motion. The mug and its contents flew straight at Conan's face.

There was no danger, Conan knew. He raised one muscled arm to bat the mug away; unfortunately, the hand he chose contained the loaf of bread, the better part of which was as yet uneaten. The wine drenched the bread as the mug struck it, knocking Conan's breakfast onto the filth of the much-trodden sawdust floor. Conan stared at the bread as it rolled over three times, covering itself with a layer of grime.

In better times, such an occurrence might be amusing, especially were it to happen to someone else; but at the moment Conan failed to see the humor. First his horse and all his gold had been lost; now his food. The Cimmerian took a deep breath, and the air fed his quick rage as wind feeds a hot fire.

Beak-nose had drawn his own blade and was advancing upon his intended victims. The child bravely pulled her own small sword and moved to cover the white-haired man, who tried to pull her back to safety. Conan's broadsword hissed as the leather sheath stroked it in its passage. Conan raised his blade and clenched the handle with both hands.

'You – you *filth*!' Conan roared.

The man turned in surprise. What he saw must have surely alarmed him, for he spun and tried to position his sword for a block or parry. At the same time, he tried to backstep away. He managed neither. Conan's sword caught Beak-nose in the middle of the breastbone and a hand's span of sharp steel sliced its way downward, opening the man as might a vivisectionist, from sternum to crotch. The man's face contorted in shock as his entrails spilled through the massive rent in his body. He fell backward, his spirit already on its way to join his ancestors.

Conan's rage was only partially spent. He looked around for the fourth member of the band. That one, however, was not in evidence. Conan glared at the inn's patrons, who all shrank away from the big youth with the bloody sword. All save one.

The young girl approached Conan, smiling. She had sheathed her sword, and when she drew near, Conan saw that the girl barely reached his chest in height. With great reluctance he lowered his broadsword. He stared at the child. 'Well?'

'Thank you, sir, for saving us.' Her voice was warm. Indeed, the very air seemed to grow warmer as she stood there staring up at the Cimmerian.

'Do not thank me,' Conan said, his voice still rough and angry. 'The scum destroyed my breakfast. Would that he had put up a better fight, so that I might have made him suffer for it.'

The girl's mouth opened into an *O* as Conan spoke, her face filled with shock and puzzlement.

The murmur of voices began to rise to fill the inn.

'– you see that strike? Such power!'

'– split him like a chicken –'

'– foreigner from some backwoods –'

A thin man with a jagged scar that lifted both his lip and left nostril came closer, warily watching the Cimmerian's unsheathed blade. He wore a splattered apron that might have once been white, but now displayed the remains of too many spilled wine cups and meals to be more than a splotched gray. Likely the owner of the inn, Conan judged.

The innkeeper glanced down at the dead man. His perpetual sneer seemed to increase a bit. 'So, Arsheva of Khemi has finally picked the wrong victim.' The man looked up at Conan. 'Few men deserve such an exit from this life so much as he; he shall not be missed, and no mistake about that.' Pulling a rag from the pocket of his apron, he tendered it to Conan. 'Here, wipe your blade, sir, lest Arsheva's gore chew upon the steel with teeth of rust.'

Conan took the greasy rag and methodically cleaned his sword.

'Still,' the man said, 'the Senate's Deputation will no doubt eventually arrive for an investigation of Arsheva's passing. I trust you had sufficient reason to dispatch him to the next world?'

Conan slid his sword into its leathern home. 'Aye,' he began, 'my reasons were just. This offal –'

'– intended to attack myself and my assistant,' the old white-haired man said. 'This man is our bodyguard; he was merely performing his job in protecting us.'

Conan stared at him. What was he about? He started to speak, but the old man interrupted again. 'We shall finish our breakfast whilst awaiting the deputies. If you would bring my friend here a tray to replace the meal he lost, along with a bottle of your better wine, I should be most grateful.' Here the old man raised a wrinkled and age-twisted hand bearing a small coin of silver. 'And the balance of this for your trouble in this matter.'

Scar-face took the coin, and nodded. 'Aye. Obviously, a gentleman of means such as yourself will have no difficulties convincing the Senate's Deputation of your position in this matter.' He drew back a chair at the old man's table for Conan. 'I'll tend to your meal, sir.'

Seated with the old man and girl, Conan waited for answers to his unasked questions. Earlier, he had held his tongue, reasoning that the old man had some purpose in coming to his aid. Perhaps it was merely to thank him for

31

splitting the blackguard who would have attacked the girl. While unintentional, Conan had served them, certainly. But the barbarian now suspected there was more to be said than words of thanks.

The old man waited until the inn's patrons focused their attention elsewhere before he spoke. 'I am Vitarius and this' – he waved his arm in its voluminous sleeve toward the girl – 'this is Eldia, my assistant. I am a conjurer of small talent, an entertainer of sorts. We wish to thank you for taking our part in this matter.'

Conan nodded, waiting.

'I sensed you were about to speak of your true reason for slaying our would-be assassin – he who slew your loaf of bread – which is why I injected my remarks.'

Conan nodded again. The old man was not without sharpness of sight and wit.

'The deputies who will come to speak with us are corrupt for the most part. A few pieces of silver will expedite the resolution in our favor without a doubt; still, carving a man for knocking a loaf of bread to the floor is hardly considered just punishment in the minds of the Mornstadinosian Senate. Protecting a patron from attack by a cutthroat thief is sufficient reason to draw steel, however.'

The young giant nodded. 'I am Conan of Cimmeria. I have done you a favor and you have thus returned it; let us then consider the scales balanced.'

'So be it,' Vitarius said. 'After breakfast, at least.'

'Aye, that I will allow.'

A serving girl arrived with a tray of hard rolls, fruit, and a greasy cut of pork, along with another cup of wine of a vintage better than the first drink Conan had partaken of. He ate with gusto, and washed the food down with gulps of the red liquid.

Vitarius watched Conan intently. When the Cimmerian was done with his meal, the conjurer spoke. 'We are quits on debts; still, I have a proposition in which you might find some merit. Eldia and I demonstrate our simple illusions at street fairs and market gatherings, and we could use a man such as yourself.'

Conan shook his head. 'I truckle not with magic.'

'Magic? Surely you do not think my illusions are magic? Nay, I work with the simplest of the arts, no more. Would I be in such a place as this were I a *real* magician?'

Conan considered that. The old man had a point.

'Still, of what use could I be to a conjurer?'

Vitarius glanced at Eldia, then looked back at Conan. 'That blade of yours, for one. Your strength, for another. Eldia and I are hardly capable of protecting ourselves from such as the one you slew. She is adept with her own sword for demonstrating speed and skill, but hardly a match for a full-grown man in a duel. My illusions might scare the superstitious, but in the end can hardly sway a determined assassin, as you have just seen.'

Conan chewed on his lower lip. 'I am bound for Nemedia.'

'Surely such a considerable journey would be easier were you mounted and well-appointed with supplies?'

'What makes you think I lack such things?'

Vitarius peered around the inn, then back at Conan. 'Would a man of property be spending his time in such a place?'

That reasoning was sound, but Conan followed the line a step further. 'Then, good conjure artist, why are *you* in such a place?'

Vitarius laughed, and slapped his thigh. 'Ah, forgive me for underestimating you, Conan of Cimmeria. That a man is a barbarian does not mean he lacks wits. As it happens, we are conserving our money for supplies; we, too, intend to leave this fair city, to travel westward. Our path will veer southward, toward Argos. We wish to – ah – travel in some style, in an armed caravan, and thus avoid possible encounters with the bandits along the Ophir road.'

'Ah.' Conan studied Vitarius and Eldia. He was a thief, to be sure, but he had nothing against honest work for a brief enough time. Besides, he was in no great hurry to reach Nemedia. In any event, the journey would be a great deal easier astride a good horse than on foot.

'A silver coin a day,' Vitarius said. 'We shall be ready to

leave within the month, I should think, and surely such a short diversion would not inconvenience you greatly?'

Conan considered the sorry state of his money pouch. A good horse and supplies could be had for twenty or thirty pieces of silver, certainly. And such work, guarding a conjurer and his assistant from sneak thieves for a moon or two, could not be too taxing.

Conan smiled at Vitarius. 'Master of glowing spiders, you have engaged a bodyguard.'

From under the cowled robe of a priest, Loganaro watched the Cimmerian talking to the old man and the girl. Djuvula's agent smiled to himself. The barbarian's speedy and fearless assault upon the would-be assassin was impressive. Such convinced him he had discovered the man he sought to complete the witch's spell. Here was a brave man, to be sure. Visions of gold danced in Loganaro's thoughts as he leaned back against the wall of the inn and sipped his wine. Before long, the heart of that giant barbarian with the fire-blue eyes would animate the witch's simulacrum for her carnal pleasures.

CHAPTER FOUR

The young Cimmerian and the conjurer's assistant followed Vitarius through a throng of brightly clad people come to celebrate the arrival-of-age party of a local winemaker's daughter. As the conjurer wended his way through the crowd, Conan decided there was more to the man than he pretended. He had seen too many older men make fools of younger ones to feel that an aged man was helpless; what a man lacked in muscle he could sometimes make up for in wisdom.

'We shall try to find a spot near the winemaker's stall,' Eldia told Conan. 'There the richer friends of the wine-maker's daughter will gather, and there our performance will be better rewarded.'

Conan said nothing. He saw a stalwart lad minding the reins of three horses, one of which resembled greatly the animal he had lost to the water-dwelling creatures only a few days past. The flame of fury in his eyes burned brighter at the sight.

Vitarius chose that moment to turn and observe Conan. 'You seem troubled, Conan,' the conjurer said.

'Nay, Vitarius, only by a foul memory. I once had a horse, the twin of one of those we just passed. He was taken from me.'

'I find such a thing difficult to understand. I would not like to be the man foolish enough to try to relieve you of any of your possessions, much less a horse of good breeding.'

Conan grinned ruefully. 'No man did the deed. I rode through a snowbound passage in the mountains east of here. While so doing, I was attacked by some water-dwelling beasts, the likes of which I have never before encountered.

White they were, and faceless, with blood as clear as pure water.'

'Undines!' Vitarius's voice carried both surprise and a touch of fear.

'You know of the monsters?'

'Aye. They are water spirits.' Vitarius exchanged glances with Eldia, and something of import passed between them. After a moment the old conjurer looked back at Conan, and seemed to be weighing and measuring the Cimmerian's observation of them. That peculiar warmth Conan had noticed earlier seemed to emanate from Eldia as she stood next to him; indeed, the air seemed to smolder. The sun was high and its rays drew sweat from most of the throng, but this new warmth was hotter.

Finally, Vitarius spoke. 'It is said that the undines are now controlled by Sovartus, Mage of the Black Square. He is an evil sorcerer who, so it is rumored, seeks something – or someone – within the city of Mornstadinos. To this end, Sovartus attempts to cut off the city. Aside from the undines, there are other inhuman creatures held in thrall by this villain, aiding him in his quest.'

'Sovartus, eh?' Conan rolled the name from his tongue and tossed it around in his mind. 'Well, if this magician indeed controls the things that stole my horse, then he owes me a replacement.'

'It would not be wise to try to collect such, Conan. Sovartus is a man without conscience and possessed of great magical powers. He kills without compunction and without regret.'

'Nonetheless, I am not one to forget a debt, whether incurred by or owed to me.'

'Some things are better forgotten,' Vitarius murmured as he continued to weave his way through the crowd.

Loganaro stood uncomfortably before the tall rostrum and chair of Senator Lemparius, the most powerful politician in Mornstadinos, perhaps in all of Corinthia. The short man's discomfort was not made less by the two senatorial deputies who flanked him, each with a dagger pointing toward Loganaro's throat.

'There must be some mistake, Honored Senator. I have done nothing to contravene the laws in the Jewel of Corinthia –'

Lemparius laughed, showing very white teeth. 'You should have been a jester, Loganaro. If your crimes were divided equally among the population of the city, it is likely our dungeons would burst. You could be condemned a hundred times on what I personally know, thrice that number if half what I suspect could be proven.'

Loganaro swallowed dryly. A vision of himself dangling on the gibbet made the bones of his legs feel rubbery. This encounter was unexpected, and it began to look as if he would not survive it. What had he done to so arouse the Senate Flail? A more important question was: how had he been discovered doing it?

Lemparius waved his left hand languidly. 'Leave us.'

The pair of deputies bowed slightly, sheathing their daggers. They spun on the balls of their feet, and, as one, marched from the chamber. Loganaro felt the cold beads of sweat rolling down his spine, but he tried to maintain a calm appearance.

'While I could have you flayed and dipped in boiling salt water, such is not my intent – at the moment anyway.' Lemparius arose from his chair with fluid grace. He toyed with the handle of a knife ensheathed at his right hip.

Loganaro stared at the senator's long fingers as he caressed the weapon; the short rotund man felt as if he were snared in some spell, for he could not take his gaze from the almost sensual stroking.

Lemparius laughed again. 'You admire my steel tooth, eh?' The tall blond man pulled the knife from its leather holster and raised it to chest level. The weapon was curved from the butt to the point, like a bow. It conjured up ugly images: pictures graven of fangs or talons, set for ripping. The handle was of some dark wood, likely ebony, close-grained and highly polished. Loganaro could see that the knife was full-tanged, with brass rivets mating the wood with the steel. There was a brass cap where the blade proper began, not so much a guard as a break in color from black

37

to silver. The blade itself was short, perhaps twice the length of a man's little finger, but tapered along a wicked steel curve to a needle's tip. The outer side was thick and serrated for a quarter of its length; the inner curve alone bore the sharpened edge.

'Have you ever beheld a great saber-toothed cat?' Lemparius queried. 'No? A pity; they are magnificent beasts, though their numbers are declining. Each of these cats bears a pair of tusklike fangs, shaped just so' – the senator waved the steel blade back and forth – 'so that they can slay nearly any beast that walks or crawls. I used one of these ivory wonders as the design for my own steel tooth. It allows me to feel a certain . . . kinship with the great cats.'

Loganaro nodded dumbly.

'Ah, but you wish to see it demonstrated, do you not?'

'M-most Honored Senator, it is not necessary –'

'Certainly it *is* necessary, Loganaro. Follow me.'

Lemparius led the shorter man down a narrow corridor lined with flickering tapers, then descended a steep flight of stone steps into the anteroom of what was obviously a dungeon. Loganaro began silently imploring each god he could remember for his life.

In a filthy cell hardly bigger than a coffin, a disheveled man of indeterminate age was pent. The man's hair was matted and unruly, his beard unkempt, and madness lit his wild eyes.

Standing in front of this cell, Lemparius turned to Loganaro and smiled. 'You have a dagger. Give it to me.'

Loganaro quickly complied, tendering his fat-bladed weapon to the senator. The Flail of the Senate then tossed the dagger into the cell through the slats of rusty iron. The man snatched up the knife in an instant and lunged at the pair outside his cell, stabbing through the bars as far as he could reach, but his efforts fell short. The attack drove Loganaro back in a startled leap. Lemparius moved not a hair.

'This man is condemned to die,' the senator said. 'For crimes too boring to enumerate. He has an appointment with the hangman on the morrow, but I feel that he may well be unable to keep his date with the gibbetmaster.'

With that, Lemparius flicked the tip of his knife at the wrist of the prisoner. The movement was deceptively easy, Loganaro thought, but of such a speed that the creature within the cell had no time to move his arm from the strike. When he did jerk his hand back inside the bars, blood was already welling from a thumb-length cut upon his wrist. The man howled wordlessly.

Lemparius then threw the bolt set above the door and opened wide the entrance to the cell. He took two steps back in Loganaro's direction. Loganaro himself scrambled backward twice as many paces. Was the senator mad? The condemned man had nothing to lose by attacking and killing them both!

The prisoner leaped forth from the cell, grinning like a living skeleton. He paused for a moment to suck the blood from his wrist, then spat the collection onto the grimy flagstones under his bare feet. He howled again, then charged for Lemparius, the short dagger held low to gut the senator.

In all his travels, Loganaro had never seen anyone move quite as the senator did then. He was preternaturally fast, and he leaped like a cat at the prisoner. In his right hand Lemparius held the steel saber-tooth like a sickle. The knife blurred, and struck the condemned man on the side of the neck. Before the man could react, the knife based on a predator's tooth was jerked back and swung again, cutting this time into the opposite side of the already gravely wounded neck. Lemparius leaped away from his victim.

Loganaro had some experience with observing and even inflicting mortal wounds, but he had never seen anything like this. The great vessels carrying blood from the body to the head were cleanly sheared; crimson gouts pulsed from the arteries with each pump of the man's heart. The dying man stood for an instant as if he'd grown roots, unable to move. Then he fell abruptly. In only a few seconds he paled to a ghostly hue as his blood pumped away. Dead.

Lemparius wiped the blood from his knife with the thumb and forefinger of his left hand, then cast the gore off with a slinging motion. He smiled at Loganaro. 'Did you know that by reversing the grip on my beauty thus' – he flipped the knife up, caught it as it twisted, so that he held the weapon with the handle pointing toward the ceiling and the point down – 'I can effect a strike between a man's legs in much the same manner as the neck cut? Such a stroke does not kill, but does leave a man somewhat less . . . of a man.'

Loganaro swallowed as if his throat had suddenly been filled with desert-baked sand.

'You seem quiet, free agent. Lost your tongue?'

Loganaro licked lips as dry as bleached bones. 'Wh – what would you have of me, Honored Senator?'

Lemparius sheathed his knife and laid an arm around the shoulders of the other man. 'You are in the employ of Djuvula the Witch. Did you know she has a brother who is a demon? Ah, no matter. Currently, you shadow a barbarian called Conan. Yes, that is the name. Our witch wishes this man's heart to enliven the simulacrum she has designed.'

'H-h-how can you know this?'

'I am not without my ways. Suffice it that I *do* know. I, too, have an interest in this barbarian. When the time comes, I would greatly appreciate your aid in capturing this man for my own.' Lemparius smiled widely.

'I – I cannot.' Loganaro's voice was barely a whisper.

'Your pardon, friend Loganaro, for my bad hearing. I thought for a moment I heard you say that you would not help me in this matter.'

'Honored Senator, Djuvula would have my head mounted on a pole in the pit of her outhouse!'

'Dear little man, what I will do should you refuse my simple request would make you beg for such a fate. I shall protect you from Djuvula's wrath, you may be assured.'

Loganaro swallowed again. 'Might I know why you wish this thing?'

'I see no harm in such, now that you are in my employ. Djuvula, as you may know, no longer takes lovers from

40

among men. I would have her take one more before she animates her simulacrum.'

'You, Honored Senator? But – but I thought...' Loganaro's speech dribbled away as he realized what he had been about to say.

Lemparius laughed, apparently undisturbed. He finished Loganaro's thought for him. 'You thought that I had already partaken of that dubious honor, and, like all the others, had been found wanting?'

'Your pardon, Senator –'

'Nay, you would be correct in your assumption. That was the case; however, this was some time ago. I have since become imbued with certain vigors of, shall we say, an animal-like power. With this new energy I feel certain my – ah – performance in that arena in which Djuvula so rightly claims mastery will be vastly improved.'

'But if this is so, why not merely tell her this?'

'You have little understanding of women, it would seem. She has set her mind and it will not be changed without a great deal of determined effort. If I cannot instill belief beforehand, I shall have to have something with which to bargain. If I should hold this barbarian, I could extract a price for him. Should I fail in my ministrations, then Djuvula will have her simulacrum. I must confess, I foresee this as unlikely; still, it is the kind of bargain that should appeal to her; after all, she cannot lose either way.'

'I see. And you shall then assume a position in which you can protect any of your agents who might have caused her distemper in this matter?'

'Of course.'

Loganaro considered his options. In truth, he saw no other choice than to agree with the senator's wishes. If Lemparius's plan somehow failed, likely as not Djuvula would seek revenge upon the man who betrayed her; on the other hand, if he refused the senator, he was a dead man for certain. Better to risk the unhealthy future than the unhealthy present.

'Naturally, since you have explained your reasons, I could do nothing less than offer my services wholly to you, Honored Senator.'

41

'I thought you might come to see it that way, Loganaro. My instructions are simple: go back to your dogging of the barbarian. Say nothing of this to Djuvula, but rather continue your communication with her. When she orders the taking of this man Conan, you will inform me and receive my instructions.'

'As you wish, Honored Senator.'

'You must address me as Lemparius henceforth, free agent. After all, you are now a respected employee, one who will be paid well for his services.'

After Loganaro had gone, Lemparius went back to the body of the slain man and stared thoughtfully at it. He smiled. Djuvula would certainly forgive him, could he make good his boast of renewed vitality; it was unlikely that she would ever forgive Loganaro his devious switch in alliance. Too bad; the little weasel was very adept at spying and other criminal activities. He could be useful if he did not have to die to satisfy the witch's anger. Better him than me, Lemparius thought.

The senator stared at the body on the floor and felt a rumble in his belly. Well. There was no point in wasting such fresh meat.

There was no one to see the thing that Senator Lemparius became then, nor what he did. The guards would have less to toss upon the offal pile than the gibbetmaster's work would have left, though. And the panther would sleep with a full belly this night.

The evening shadows played across the thinning crowds as Conan watched Vitarius perform his conjures for the winemaker's party. The old man was good, Conan noted. He pulled live birds from a lady's dress, changed a glass of wine into vinegar, made an empty bottle spew ribbons of bright silk. Eldia ran about, collecting coins from the laughing crowd, stopping now and then to perform a trick of her own with her sword. She would slice a single button from a tunic, carve a loaf of bread into fancy shapes, even hold the blade in her hands and leap back and forth over it.

It was a good show, and the coppers collected rapidly in the cup that Eldia rattled at the gathering.

Conan had little to do save watch. No cutpurses stalked the duo, though several pickpockets moved here and there. As long as they did not bother his charges, Conan bore them no malice. Being a thief made him tolerant of such things; after all, a man had to eat, and these folks would not miss a few lifted coins.

As with most street magicians, Vitarius seemed to be saving his best illusions for last. He had better hurry to finish, Conan thought, before everyone went home, taking their money with them.

A hush fell upon the people watching Vitarius as he drew himself up and began preparing for his final trick. Some of the crowd smiled and nodded. Conan heard a woman near him say, 'His last one is the best; wait until you see it.'

The old man gestured this way and that, mumbled incantations, and hopped about from foot to foot in a kind of dance. The watchers laughed, and Conan smiled with them.

Finally, Vitarius was ready. He motioned for the people around him to move back, and with a final dramatic wave of his arms, Vitarius said, 'Now!'

There was a flash of bright light, and a cloud of dense white smoke filled the space; as the smoke began to thin, Conan discerned an enshrouded figure within. A large, dark form loomed ominously.

The crowd gasped as one voice as the smoke disappeared – to reveal a demon! The thing stood half again as tall as a big man, and Conan judged that, were it real, it would scale twice his own not-inconsiderable weight. The demon was bright red, massively male, and his grin showed teeth from a nightmare. Conan felt a chill frost his shoulders. Vitarius's other illusions were as nothing compared to this; the Cimmerian was impressed. When he glanced at Eldia, who stood an armspan away from him, Conan felt a jolt as she tore her gaze away from the demon to look at Conan. For the girl said quietly but quite clearly, 'He did not bring it, Conan. It is *real*!'

The demon took a step toward Vitarius. He spoke then in

43

a voice reminiscent of metal tearing. 'Where is she, White One?'

When Vitarius made no answer, the demon scanned the crowd with eyes that glowed with infernal light. His sweeping gaze alighted upon Eldia, and he grinned widely. Dripping slime, the demon turned away from the conjurer and started toward the girl.

Eldia drew her sword and faced the monster.

The crowd, sensing malpractice in the apparition, began to scatter as leaves before a storm.

'Hold!' Conan yelled.

The demon glanced down at Conan. 'Bespeak you to me, gnat?'

'Aye, demon. But rather this gnat is a wasp, with a stinger.' Conan jerked his broadsword free and gripped it easily in both hands, to point at the demon's belly.

'I have no quarrel with you, wasp,' the demon grated. 'My business concerns this female human child and is none of your concern.'

'Wrong, hellspawn. She stands under my protection; menace her at your peril.'

'My peril? You are amusing, wasp, but I grow weary of you. Fly away and avoid being crushed.'

Conan raised the broadsword and sighted along the edge at the demon's malefic face. 'Conan of Cimmeria does not fly from the likes of you, beast.'

'Then pray to your gods, insect, for your time is come.'

The demon extended his black-taloned hands towards Conan, and the sound of his giant muscles cracking rent the air as he crouched and sprang.

CHAPTER FIVE

As fast as the demon was, Conan was faster. The Cimmerian leaped, as did the blood-red pitspawn, but to the side; the demon's initial rush bypassed the man. Tortuous veins stood out on Conan's brawny arms as he swung the sword, aiming for the demon's neck. The force of Conan's strike sheared the air, moving so fast, the blade cried out a note somewhere between a moan and a whistle.

The demon, however, did not stand idle, awaiting decapitation; instead, he leaped high into the air and tucked his massive body into a tight ball, performing a somersault as neatly as an acrobat might. Before Conan could recover to bring the blade back for the return stroke, the demon regained his feet and danced lithely away.

'Where is your stinger, wasp?' The demon laughed in his grating way.

Conan gave no answer, but instead rushed forward, mighty legs pumping and his sword held ready for another slash.

The demon backstepped quickly, knocking a fruit vendor's stall askew as if it were no more than cobwebs. He might be laughing, but he moved readily enough from the cold steel Conan bore.

From the corner of one eye Conan saw Eldia dart forward with her blade upraised, only to be stopped by the hand of Vitarius. 'Not that way!' the old conjurer yelled.

There was no time for a lack of attention, Conan knew. The demon might fear steel, but he was big, strong, and hellishly fast; his claws would gut a man as easily as a handful of daggers would, and Conan had no intention of allowing the inhuman creature to lay those talons on his own hide. The Cimmerian whipped his sword back and forth, creating a deadly fan that sought the red flesh before him. The thing kept moving backward through the ruins of the fruit stall, and Conan followed, concentrating fully upon the fiend.

That concentration was a mistake. Conan stepped upon a crushed section of some greasy fruit and his leading foot shot out from under him. He lost balance and nearly fell. Only his quickness saved him then, for the demon reacted far faster than most men could have, lunging at his attacker with his giant right hand, the talons set to rend Conan's throat.

Even as he fell to one knee, Conan snapped his blade up in a short arc, releasing his grip with one hand to keep what balance he could. Man-made steel met inhuman flesh and black bone, and . . . the ancient broadsword cleaved through the demon's wrist. A hellish right hand fell to the ground, smoking and dripping acidic ichor as it did so. The fingers of the severed extremity spasmed and relaxed several times, as if still somehow connected to the demonic muscles that previously controlled it.

The demon roared, a terrible noise that shattered nearby wine bottles and blew all other sounds from Conan's ears. As Conan sought to regain his own stance the maddened creature seemed to explode into motion: the now-handless arm swung at Conan, splattering the man with gore as the stump brushed aside the upraised sword, knocking the weapon from Conan's grasp. The barbarian managed to dive into a roll away from the demon's onslaught, and he came up with his own powerful arms widespread, ready to grapple with the one-handed attacker. Conan felt the foul breath of doom in his face; he knew he was no match for the demon with his bare hands, but he did not back away. By Crom, he would meet his end head-on and fighting!

As the demon gathered himself for his final lunge at Conan, a stream of blue fire suddenly splashed over his back and shoulders, blending with his red skin to form a purple haze. The child of the pit roared again, but the supernal glow only increased around him, sending ragged trails of smoke skyward as his skin began to char. Conan twisted to see the source of this blue fire, and beheld Vitarius, one hand extended towards the demon, the other laid upon the bare head of Eldia, who also glowed with essence of blue flame.

'No!' the tortured monster screamed. There came an eye-smiting flash of yellow and a danker shade of purple, and the demon vanished as abruptly as he had come.

Left behind was the demon's right hand, which twitched fitfully upon the cobblestones near Conan, as if still trying to reach the one responsible for its destruction.

Vitarius came to stand next to Conan, to stare down at the demon's hand. For a time neither man spoke. It fell to Conan, finally, to break the silence. 'I think your explanation about being a simple conjurer is somewhat flawed, Vitarius. No small spell called that thing, nor did any *illusion* drive it away.'

'True enough,' the old man answered, looking tired. 'An explanation is owed you, and I shall provide it. Were it not for you, Eldia would have been taken by Sovartus's enthralled one and the consequences of that do not bear contemplation.'

'I await your tale.'

'Aye, you shall have it. As you have surmised, Eldia and I are not precisely what we pretended upon our meeting in the Milk of Wolves Inn. I –' The old man stopped and jerked his head around. Save for Conan and himself, the road and stalls were empty. 'Eldia! She is gone!'

Conan spun in a quick circle, looking for the girl. She was not to be seen. 'The demon –' he began.

'No. He left alone! We must find her, Conan! If she is taken to Sovartus, she is doomed, as likely are many more. I swear to explain all this fully, but we must first retrieve the girl. You must trust me.'

After the briefest of pauses, Conan nodded. He had no reason to believe Vitarius, since it was obvious the man had lied to him before; still, Conan was a man of action and so trusted his instincts more than his reason. No evil stench lurked about Vitarius and Eldia, and the demon would likely have killed him without their help. Conan retrieved his sword and waved it to point down the street. 'I will take this direction; you go that way.'

Vitarius nodded, and Conan loped off. He glanced back, to see the old man pause long enough to collect the demon's hand and drop it into his belt pouch.

The bedchamber of Djuvula the Witch exploded into a cloud of bruised purple and yellow, leaving Djavul amid the smoke, clutching at the stump of his right arm with his remaining hand. The door to the chamber opened and the witch rushed in, alarmed by the sudden intrusion into her sanctum. 'Demon-brother! What has happened?'

Djavul cursed with the power of Hell in his words. On the witch's bed the dark form of the unanimated simulacrum tossed from the force of those curses. Then the wounded demon said, 'My hand!'

Djuvula seemed to relax somewhat. 'Brother mine, why fret over such a thing? Another will grow to replace it –'

'Fool woman! It is not the hand, but the way in which it was lost! I am bound to Sovartus, a Mage of the Black Square –'

Djuvula sucked in a quick breath, startled.

'So, you know of this one,' Djavul said, staring at his sister.

'Aye. A man of no small power, he.'

'As I am in his thrall, I am well aware of that, flesh of my damned father. And I have failed in my attempt to do his bidding. That which I sought was guarded by a man of supernatural abilities. Instead of my taking his charge, he took my hand!'

'What would you have me do, brother-mine?'

'I must return to report my . . . difficulty to Sovartus. He will not be pleased. It would behove me to be able to indicate I have some assistance forthcoming, perhaps even another plan for obtaining that which he seeks.'

'We are blood-tied,' Djuvula said, 'and naturally I will aid you as I can.'

'Good. Sovartus wishes to collect a girl-child known as Eldia – she is one of the Four, as you will know when you behold her. He already has the other Three. This one travels in the company of one of the White Magicians, possibly of the White Square, though I could not be certain. And there is a large man of origin unknown to me with them. 'Twas he who cost me this.' Djavul waved the handless stump. Already the wound had sealed itself into a smooth black glasslike stub.

Djuvula nodded, but the implications of what her demon brother had just spoken were not lost upon her. If Sovartus managed to hold sway over all of the Four children imbued with the power of the Four Ways, he would be the paramount force in magic upon Earth. If she could somehow strike a bargain with Sovartus for delivery of the remaining portion of his magical spell – this girl, Eldia – she could bask in some of his thus-earned power. And the man who separated Djavul from his hand, well, he sounded very much like a candidate for a spell of her own. She looked at the somnambulent form of her simulacrum, her Prince of the Lance.

She considered these things in a few heartbeats and then smiled at Djavul. 'I will help you capture this child,' she said. 'Tell me, where did you leave her?'

Loganaro crouched under the cover of a fallen awning and watched the muscular barbarian run down the nearly empty street. The agent had arrived in the vicinity just in time to see the finish of Vitarius's performance. More than ever, Loganaro was convinced that Conan was the man for animating Djuvula's dream-lover. Certainly, this barbarian from far Cimmeria would be worth admittance to the witch's bed, if Senator Lemparius held him. Capturing him might be less than easily accomplished, however. It could be an expensive undertaking, Loganaro thought, and some of the coin needed would certainly find its way to his pouch.

The barbarian was too fast for him to follow, especially without cover to shield him from a casual backward glance, so Loganaro decided to append himself to the old magician instead. He felt certain that Conan would return to the white-haired one before long.

*

49

The sound of Conan's boots was loud upon the rough cobblestones of the street. It was growing darker as evening stole upon the scene, casting her nightly net. Conan's sharp blue eyes sent his penetrating gaze down each alley he passed, covering such passages from top to bottom with a single glance. Eldia was not to be seen.

As he ran past yet another of the building-bounded paths filled with the detritus of city life, Conan blinked and skidded to a halt. He raked the alley with a second look. Nothing moved in that dark rectangle; of that he was certain. Here stood a mound of trash – rags, scraps of animal skins, broken pottery – there, a stack of firewood. He beheld an alley like a dozen others he had passed in his run, and yet, something within struck him as different. Some small thing intruded upon his senses, untouchable and yet somehow *wrong*.

There! A tiny flash of whiteness against the dark backdrop of the woodpile! Instantly, Conan knew it for the eye of a man, reflecting the now-risen moon's soft glow. He drew his sword and moved into the alley, the point of the heavy blade held aimed at the darkness-hidden bearer of the eyes he had seen.

As the barbarian's own sharp vision adjusted to the greater darkness of the alley, he made out a form squatting next to a pile of split kindling. The form arose and there shone the glint of moonlight upon steel as a short blade came up to point at Conan.

'Wait!' came a girlish voice. Eldia. 'It is Conan, a friend.'

The form grew yet clearer in Conan's sight: a woman, her body nearly covering that of Eldia, standing behind her. The woman held her knife – a wavy-bladed dagger – aimed at the approaching man.

'Eldia, come forth into the light,' Conan called.

'No,' a woman's voice replied. This voice had the sound of honey upon steel, smooth and yet backed by hardness.

Conan stood motionless for a moment, then decided there was no danger here for him. He sheathed his blade and held his hands out to show their emptiness.

The woman took a step forward and the pale moonlight

caressed her gently. She was perhaps eighteen, Conan judged, with jet-black hair that hung unbound to her waist. Her form was covered by a silken shirt and thin leather breeches, and upon her feet she wore thonged sandals of a fine cut. The body covered by these items was of a cut much finer than the sandals. The woman was lush of hip and leg, and beneath the thin blue silk of her shirt her breasts were full and heavy. There was something about her face, which was in itself flawlessly detailed, that seemed familiar to Conan. He knew he would hardly forget such a lovely woman had he seen her before, yet he was certain he knew that face . . .

Eldia moved into view, and Conan knew where he had seen the raven-haired beauty before: she was Eldia grown up into full womanhood. The woman was too young to be Eldia's mother, so she must be –

'You are her sister,' Conan said, voicing his thought as it came to him.

'Aye,' the woman said. 'And come to reclaim her from the villains who took her from our home.'

Conan shrugged, his massive shoulders rising easily as he found it within himself to grin at the woman. 'I took no one anywhere,' he said. 'And it seems to me Eldia travels with Vitarius of her own accord.'

The woman glanced toward the mouth of the alley, then back at Conan. She raised the dagger a bit higher, clutching it tightly. Conan could see her knuckles whiten upon the haft of the weapon. 'She was dragged screaming into the night,' the woman said. 'My father was slain, as was my mother. Before my mother died, she told me that Eldia was special, that she had brothers and a sister – my half-brothers and sister – of whom she had never told us. That whatever I did, I must find Eldia and hide her from those evil ones who desire her for their own wicked purposes.'

Conan glanced at Eldia, who seemed content to allow her sister to speak. 'And is Vitarius one of those evil ones?'

Eldia shook her head. 'N-no but –'

'It is all right, Eldia,' her sister said. 'You do not have to explain anything to this – this barbarian.'

'Someone is going to have to explain it,' Conan said

evenly. 'I am tired of being made the fool in whatever games Vitarius and you two have mounted. We shall go back to this "conjurer" and hear this tale outlined in its fullness.'

'No,' the woman said. 'We are going home!'

'After I am satisfied with explanations of why I was attacked by a demon in a public square,' Conan said, the anger rising in his voice.

'Now,' Eldia's sister said, pushing her knife toward Conan. 'Now, or I'll spit you and leave your carcass for the rats.'

Without another sound Conan leaped at the woman. He caught her wrist as she tried to impale his throat upon her blade; he twisted the woman's arm hard, and she exclaimed and dropped the dagger.

Suddenly, the alley seemed to come to life. Small bodies slithered over the trash and woodpile; the scratchings of hundreds of tiny feet could be heard along with the gentle rasp of small forms moving everywhere. Conan saw that the very walls and ground seemed to undulate in small waves.

'Crom!' He released the woman and moved back a pace, drawing his sword in a fluid and well-practiced move. But there was no single enemy to be faced here. Something touched Conan's boot, and he turned his fiery blue eyes downward to stare at the thing.

It was a salamander. The creature was no longer than Conan's middle finger, but it mounted his footgear with a kind of determination Conan found hard to credit. Such lizardlike things usually ran at the sight of men, but to judge from the sound, there must be hundreds of the things here in this alley. How had they gotten here? Why were they advancing upon him?

'Hold!' Eldia said. The rustle of tiny feet stopped instantly. The single salamander upon Conan's boot froze as if transmuted into stone.

Eldia looked at her sister. 'He saved my life on two occasions,' she said. 'And Vitarius means only to help me. We must allow him to have his explanation.' She nodded toward Conan. 'And you must hear what Vitarius has to say, sister, before we can go home. I was frightened by the demon earlier, otherwise I would have had you stay then.'

Eldia looked at the salamander on Conan's boot. 'Away,' she said.

Obediently, the creature turned and wiggled away. Around them the sounds of other scurryings touched the night air; in a moment all was quiet again.

Conan stared at Eldia.

'Shall we go?' she said.

Conan and Eldia's sister looked at each other, and nodded. But Conan was not pleased with any of this. Not at all.

'Fool!' Sovartus screamed. 'To be thwarted by an ordinary man!'

Djavul stood within the bounds of the black magician's pentagram, drawn up to his fullest height. 'Nay, human mage, this was no ordinary man. In a thousand years I have faced hundreds of men in mortal combat. Their bones lie moldering in graves the world over. Never have I lost a death fight to any man. This man was more than most; more, he had magical help, else I would have triumphed over him despite his strength and skill. You face one of the White, Sovartus.'

'Vitarius!' Sovartus's voice was filled with anger.

'I know not his name, but he focused the power of Fire upon me, and the heat was not that which I could withstand.'

'Damn you!'

'You are too late, magician. But all is not lost. I am brother to a human witch who has no small influence in the city that hides your quarry. You will have your child; I will have the man who did this.' Djavul raised his right arm and stared at the stump where his hand had been.

In the far depths of Castle Slott something screamed in hideous anticipation.

CHAPTER SIX

The patrons in the Milk of Wolves Inn gave the four people seated at the table nearest the fireplace a wide berth. Conan suspected that some, if not all, of the people pretending to look everywhere else save at him and his companions had been present at the conjuring exhibition earlier. The Cimmerian did not blame them for being nervous; he himself felt no joy in the presence of those steeped in magic. The lethal flame in Conan's eyes burned low, but burn it did, as he listened to Vitarius's tale.

'... Eldia was one of four children. Her mother, your mother, as well' – Vitarius pointed with his nose at the young woman seated across from Conan – 'was ensorcelled by a powerful magician during her conception by him.'

'You are saying I have a father other than the one I have known all my life?' Eldia's gaze was sharp and much harder than that usually seen in a child of her age.

'Aye. At your birth your mother was allowed to retain only one of her brood. Your father was Hogistum of the Gray Square, and he took the others and had them scattered across the world.'

'Why?' Conan, Eldia, and the woman – Kinna, she called herself – all spoke at the same instant.

Vitarius sighed and shook his head. 'It cannot be understood so easily. Hogistum uncovered some ancient sorcery, weathered runes that came from a more primal time. He managed to decipher these writings and so learned how to link each of the Four Elements to a living soul. He was not an evil man, Hogistum, but he was curious. Of the Gray, he could work magic for black purposes or white, and usually, he tended toward the White. The Spell of Linkage was, in itself, neither good nor evil; it depended upon how it was used, once invoked. Hogistum had no intention of using it; he wished only to see if he could accomplish it. At least this was what he claimed.'

'How do you know this?' Kinna's voice was no less silken than Conan had noted before.

The old man hesitated for a moment, pausing to wet his lips with the wine cup in front of him on the rough table. 'Hogistum had two students,' he began. 'One was his natural son, the other a pupil who had demonstrated magical aptitude but was of a low caste.' Vitarius looked at each of the three faces in turn. 'I was the low-caste pupil.'

Conan nodded. No surprise there. Vitarius's attack upon the demon was explained, then.

Vitarius continued. 'Since his own wife had died, Hogistum chose a young woman of his household, daughter of an old retainer, for his new bride. Upon this girl Hogistum worked his spell even as they lay together on the nuptial bed.'

'How . . . vile!' Kinna said.

'I can see how you would think it so,' Vitarius said. 'In time, the birthing of four children occurred. Each of these babes was filled with power.'

'I find this all hard to believe,' Kinna said.

The old magician blinked like some ancient owl at the young woman. 'Do you? In your life with your sister, have you not noticed certain . . . abilities in her? Can anyone be cold in her presence? Is not her bed always warm, even on the coldest winter nights? And, of coure, there are the salamanders.'

The fire in Conan's eyes leaped a bit at this last statement. Aye, the girl had some truck with such creatures. Conan looked at Kinna, and saw that she nodded in spite of her obvious reluctance to believe what she was hearing.

'Eldia is one corner of the Square,' Vitarius said. 'She is the Child of Fire, flameweaver and Mistress of its beasts, the salamanders. Her sister, Atena, is the Child of Water, and through her the undines serve; her brothers are Luft, Child of Air and the wind-devils, and Jord, Child of Earth,

Master of the demi-whelves and trolls. I did not make it so, but I speak it as it is.'

Something had been gnawing ratlike at Conan's mind, something Vitarius had said earlier. The young man voiced it. 'You spoke of another student, the natural son of Hogistum. Who is he? What has happened to him?'

Vitarius nodded as if expecting the question. 'We speak of one you have had contact with, albeit indirectly. He owes you a horse.'

'Sovartus?'

'Aye. He poisoned his own father and has spent the years since tracing and recovering the children Hogistum so carefully hid. He now has them all save Eldia.'

'Hogistum was less than careful, it would seem.' Conan toyed with his own cup of wine. 'He is dead and his son's goal nearly accomplished.'

'Aye. I managed to thwart him by taking Eldia from her captors before she could be tendered to him. I was too late for the others. Through them, he now influences three of the Square's Four Corners: Earth, Air, and Water. If he should complete the Square, he would have at his bidding a beast greater than the sum of the parts, a synergistic force Hogistum called the Thing of Power. This would be such a monstrous happening that even the gods would turn their faces away from it.'

Conan shifted upon the bench, suddenly uncomfortable. Talk of magic always made him feel thus; such things as this men should leave alone.

Kinna leaned across the table, one more-than-ample breast brushing against the back of Conan's hand as she moved. 'What are your intentions, then, Vitarius?'

The old magician sighed again. 'I must protect Eldia, keeping her from Sovartus's clutches; more, I must somehow find a way to free the three children he holds.'

'Can you do it?' Eldia said quietly. 'Can you save my brothers and sister from my – my . . . half-brother?'

Vitarius shook his head. 'I do not know. He is of the Black, and so wields powers I cannot; too, he commands the forces of Three Corners and I only One. I fear he is stronger than I. Sovartus, so it is said, even dares to practice base necromancy in his sorcery, calling upon the legions of the dead for certain spells. All I can do is try. I can do no more, and I will do no less.'

Kinna leaned back and nodded. 'Very well. I shall help you in any way I can. As long as Sovartus lives, Eldia is endangered. We must destroy him.' Kinna looked at Conan. 'What about you?'

Conan crossed his thick arms upon his chest and stared at the woman. She was beautiful, but he wished no part of this.

'I travel to Nemedia,' he said. 'And I paused only long enough to earn an easier passage. I have been misled. I am not fond of liars, especially those who risk my neck without warning me, and I have less liking for practitioners of magic. I wish you well in your undertaking, but I am no longer a part of it.'

Kinna glared at Conan, but Eldia only nodded, as did Vitarius. The mage said, 'I cannot blame you, Conan. You have behaved bravely and we returned falsehood for it. We thank you for your help and wish you well in your journey.'

Conan nodded and started to rise.

'But stay a moment,' Vitarius said. 'We owe you something for your trouble. There is the silver for this day's work, and a few coins besides, well-earned. And since I have held two rooms for this evening's rest, you are welcome to one of them, in further gratitude.'

Conan took the coins, transferring them to his own pouch. 'Aye, I'll use the room this night, deservedly.'

The young Cimmerian turned and walked toward the doorway leading to the stairs and the lodging above the inn. The day had been long and he was tired.

The room was somewhat better appointed than the last in which Conan had slept, but not by much. A pallet stuffed with straw lay upon a much-worn and ratty carpet; a shuttered window could be opened out so that the room's occupants could behold the maze of streets three flights below. A nub of a taper burned in one corner of the room, sending the remains of smoky tallow toward the dark ceiling, but little light into the rest of the darkness. At least there were no rats buried within his bed, Conan noted. He pinched the candle wick and extinguished the small flame, then sprawled upon the pallet, his sword nearby. Sleep fell upon him like a cloak.

Like a cloak jerked away, sleep left the prone form of Conan a scant two hours later. The blue eyes flashed out a gaze that swept the dark room, but there was nothing to be seen, for the blackness was too thick even for the Cimmerian's sharp vision. He held his breath so that his hearing would work yet better, but the only sound was that of a small wind playing around the edges of the shuttered window and the creaks of the aging wood of the inn. And his own heartbeat sounded in his ears. No danger was apparent, yet Conan trusted his instincts too well to ignore his wakefulness at this hour. He reached for his sword, feeling better once the stained leather handle was in his grasp.

Perhaps it was only the wind after all, he thought as he lay there. When nothing else moved for a long time, Conan again slept, his hand still locked upon the hilt of his sword.

The darkness in Castle Slott was complete save for a musty yellow glow cast in a single room by a single lamp. Revealed in the fitful light stood Sovartus, his thin-fingered hands digging cruelly into the shoulders of one of three children chained to the damp and moldy wall. Presently, a faint glow began to surround the bodies of the magician and his captive. At first the glow merely shimmered dimly; after a short while, however, the gleam of pale yellow light began to rival that of the lamp on the wall. In a few moments the boy and magician produced a source of illumination too bright to gaze upon without squinting. As Sovartus felt the boy's energies suffuse him, the magician laughed. Yes!

Wrapped in the folds of darkness outside the Milk of Wolves Inn, Djuvula the Witch felt the wind tug at the edges of her black silk veil, stirring the cloth gently. She had determined that the child she sought was ensconced within, along with him of the White Square who was her protector. All it had cost her was money; a few silver coins spread around could oft work more miracles among men than could magic. Aside from the girl, Djuvula also sought some sign of the barbarian who had injured her demon-brother. Surely such a one must be a man with a powerful spirit. And a powerful heart.

The rising wind also tangled itself about the short form of Loganaro, hiding in the lee of an outhouse close to the inn in which Conan the Cimmerian slept. Loganaro impatiently awaited the arrival of the six cutthroats he had hired, paid for with gold from Senator Lemparius's bountiful purse. Surely the big youth could be taken by six men, no matter that some of them might be lost in the process. Such had been Lemparius's decision when Loganaro had reported that Conan had seemed upon the verge of departing the company of the old man, girl, and newly arrived woman. It had been hastily arranged; Loganaro would have preferred a longer time to select his crew, but one worked with what one was given. His major worry concerned not the taking of Conan, but the displeasure of Djuvula when she learned of his switch in allegiance, no matter he had little choice in the matter. This above all played upon his fears, and he wondered where Djuvula might be at the moment. And where those dimwitted cutthroats dallied.

On a dark street overshadowed by cluttered buildings and unkissed by the light of moon or man, a tawny shape walked. Dogs barked fearfully at the passage of the shape, perhaps startled by the scent of what was far too huge to be any street cat, though cat it surely was. Within the mind of the werepanther a laugh was formed, but when it erupted from between sharp white fangs, the laugh was something else entirely. The dogs of Mornstadinos went silent at the sound, as if they were afraid to draw the attention of the thing by further outcry.

The dogs need not have worried; the cat-which-was-also-a-man stalked a different prey than dogs: He had grown fond of the taste of a two-legged animal. The city was full of such. Six of those particular animals passed the cat in the darkness, blind to his presence. The werepanther allowed these six to move by unmolested, for beneath the feline brain the mind of the man knew they were about on his business. And such business would bring him a different kind of pleasure than eating.

The normally peaceful slumber of Conan of Cimmeria was disturbed this night, and the powerful form of the barbarian turned restlessly upon the pallet of straw upon which he lay. He came to wakefulness once again, but once more could identify no threat to him. A dream, he thought, must have infiltrated his sleep. As he fell back asleep the second time that night, only the sound of the night wind came to his ears. Outside, it sounded as if a storm were rising.

CHAPTER SEVEN

The wind howled through the streets of Mornstadinos, seaching out every hollow that could announce its passage. Gusts of damp air rattled loose objects and sent trash flying before it. The rain, when it came, exploded upon the cobblestones in fat drops, immediately drenching anything or anyone unprotected from the storm. Lightning turned the night into day in a series of instants; thunder followed in the darkness, booming like the angry grumbles of some irritated god. The storm, undetected by the bone aches of the weather-sayers, unleashed its torrents upon the city with a rare tropical fury usually unknown to the region.

'Mitra curse this rain!' said one of the cutthroats standing in the scant shelter of a roof overhang across the street from the Milk of Wolves Inn. Three or four of his companions echoed his comment before Loganaro silenced them with a withering glare.

'Are you cakes of spice who will dissolve under a little rain?' Loganaro said.

'Nay,' the cutthroat answered, 'but this be no small shower, pursemaster. The rats'll be drowning this night.'

'Concern yourself not with rats,' Loganaro said. 'You are not paid to worry over them, but to fetch me the man who lies sleeping yonder.' Loganaro pointed toward the inn.

The cutthroat, a swarthy man of Zamorian ancestry with a patch of leather covering one sightless eye, nodded. 'Aye, that be true,' Patch said. 'But my mates and me would have words wi' ye regarding our ... arrangement.' The man spoke in a heavy foreign accent laced with a polyglot patois.

Loganaro regarded the man. 'Words? What words?'

'There be a story that this 'un you wants be the same man

who played sword against the red monster some seen in the square during the winemaker's party.'

'And what if he is? Do the six of you fear one man?'

'Nay, man, not fear; respect it be. They say this 'un be devil quick and strong as a bear to boot. If these things be true, my mates and me figures it be likely this 'un won't go easy. So maybe there ought to be a bit more grease.'

Loganaro ground his teeth together. 'How much more?'

Patch grinned, showing his own crooked yellow teeth. 'Ah, a gold piece each would sit well.'

'No doubt it would. We have an agreement for twelve gold solons for the job.'

'That be before. Now we figure eighteen.'

'Impossible. I might manage another two silver pieces each.'

Patch shrugged. 'The rain be cold; just as well we're shut of it.' Patch started to turn away.

'Two gold coins more,' Loganaro said, angry with the man.

'Five,' Patch returned.

Loganaro thought of the man he had seen slain in the dungeon under the Senate, and swallowed. A hard gust of wind blew rain against his back; cold water trickled down under his collar and along his neck. He thought about trying to bargain further, hating to lose more of his money to this thug, but decided against it. All the gold in Corinthia would be worthless were he not around to gloat over it. He took a deep breath. 'Done. Five solons more. When you deliver the barbarian.'

Patch showed his crooked teeth again. 'Aye.'

The fury of the storm seemed to wane for a moment. Loganaro waved toward the inn. 'Do it, then. Now.'

The six men darted from under the overhang and ran toward the inn, splashing through puddles already as big as small ponds.

Djuvula hurried toward her manse, cursing the rain. She hated to leave the surveillance she had undertaken upon the inn, but she could not abide the rain. There was no chance the old man and girl would be going anywhere in this night, in any event. She could return on the morrow.

The panther snarled, but the sound was lost in a giant's drumbeat of thunder. His fur was rain-matted, and the cat was not happy. Such weather kept his prey indoors and well-shuttered against intrusion. Those unable to afford inns or houses were more difficult to locate, since the torrential rain washed much of their scent from the air. Prowling under the downpour was a muddy business and less than enjoyable.

The panther turned away from his hunt and scurried toward one of many places especially prepared for his night roamings. This one was no more than a shed for storage of wool, but it offered shelter and a hidden cache of clothing suitable for a senator wishing to be incognito.

In the privacy of the shed, that which was a cat growled as it began to stretch joints and ligaments unnaturally, altering itself from a beast that walked on four legs to one of those who, moments earlier, had been its prey.

Conan had no fear of storms, but once again he lay awake, gripping his sword tightly. This time a sound in the corridor outside his room was apparent even over the tempest raging outside the inn. A soft footstep upon a loose board.

The barbarian came lightly to his feet and moved quickly toward the door. He threw the simple latch up, jerked the door open, and, in a single bound, leaped into the hall, sword held ready to strike.

Conan found himself facing a single figure wrapped in a thin blanket. Kinna.

Conan lowered the sword, staring at the young woman. The blanket she wore covered much of her, but allowed most of her long legs freedom in the night air. Most shapely legs, Conan saw, with an underlying muscle he found instantly attractive.

Kinna seemed to note Conan's interest and tried to move the blanket to cover her limbs; this action allowed more of her upper body an air bath, however, including a glimpse of her full breasts before she hurriedly recovered them.

Conan grinned. 'Why are you about at this hour?'

'I – I heard a noise at my window. A strange sound.'

'We are three floors from the ground,' Conan said. 'It is less than likely anything could be playing at your shutters. The wind, no doubt.'

Kinna nodded, sending a ripple through her long black hair. 'So I thought. Once awake, I could not find sleep again. So I came out here to . . .' She trailed off and looked embarrassed.

'To what?' Conan asked, curious.

Kinna glanced down the hallway toward the night chamber, colored briefly, but spoke not.

Conan followed her gaze, then understood. Ah, women. To be embarrassed by such a thing as a visit to the night chamber was a thing he had never understood. Everyone had the same natural need; why should it bother anyone?

The silence between them grew, stretching to awkwardness. Conan felt no need to fill the quiet with words; still, he was awake and fully alert. So he said, 'This noise did not disturb your sister or Vitarius?'

'No. She sleeps the sleep of the innocent, and he rests as though practicing for his Final Slumber.'

'Ah. Since I am up, perhaps you would like me to examine your window for the source of this noise?'

Conan saw sudden relief in her eyes, but it was quickly replaced with a more cynical glint. 'Nay. Do not trouble yourself on our account. I would not delay your journey to Nemedia.' She sounded angry.

Conan shrugged. 'As you wish.' He turned to go back into his room.

'Wait,' Kinna said, touching his shoulder with one hand. Her touch was warm against his skin. 'Forgive me. I offer rudeness where none is deserved. Eldia told me how you saved her from the assassin in this place earlier, and I myself saw you stand between her and the demon. I cannot blame you for wishing to go about your own life instead of continuing to risk it for our sakes.'

Conan looked at her. She was a most attractive woman; she also kept her hand on his arm.

'I would like you to inspect my window after all.' She smiled. 'And, perhaps, afterward, we might also inspect the shutters in . . . your room?'

For a moment Conan failed to understand. He nearly blurted out that nothing was wrong with his shutters. Then he saw Kinna's smile, and he understood. He returned her grin. 'Aye,' he said.

Conan stepped lightly over the recumbent form of Eldia and around that of Vitarius, using the light of the taper Kinna held. He reached the shuttered window and looked at it. Nothing amiss there. He turned toward Kinna, already anticipating the short trip across the hall to his room. 'Shield the flame,' he commanded in a whisper. With that, Conan opened the shutters and stared into the rainy night.

Lightning flared twice in quick succession, driving away the darkness and giving the barbarian a good view of the walls and lower rooftops nearby. Save the storm, the night was empty as far as he could tell. He started to close the slatted wood strips.

The inn began to rattle, as might a wall under a barrage of rocks by small boys; Conan felt his hands and arms pelted, and he muttered a quick oath.

Startled, Kinna said, 'What –?'

'Hail,' Conan answered. 'As big as grapes.'

The clatter increased, and a sudden fierce blast of wind and ice tore the shutters from Conan's loose grasp. 'Bel's eyes!' Conan leaned out and reached for the free-swinging shutters, receiving a pounding of hailstones for his trouble. He managed to snare one of the shutters and was reaching for the second when the wind slackened and the hail stopped. The rain continued to fall in heavy sheets, and there came a sound, louder because of the relative silence following the stoppage of hail. At first Conan thought the new sound thunder, but he quickly discarded that notion; the noise was continuous.

Kinna joined the Cimmerian at the window. 'What is that?'

Conan shook his head. 'I know not –' he began. Then the lightning flashed again and revealed the source of the rumble: a tornado approached, twisting through the city, destroying everything in its path. The rampaging funnel looked to be heading directly toward the inn.

Someone moved behind Conan. Vitarius's voice cut through the wind and rain. 'What do you see out there?'

Conan pointed wordlessly. The lightning seemed to have stopped for the moment, but there was no need of it; within the funnel of the tornado discharges played almost continuously, giving the twirling wind a bluish-yellow glow of its own, a ghostly, eerie luminescence unlike anything Conan had ever observed. 'Crom,' Conan said softly, 'a devil-wind.'

Vitarius took in the sight. 'Of that you may be certain, but it is no natural thing. Watch how it moves in a straight line along its path; no ordinary spinner does that. What you see before you is Sovartus's doing. He unleashes the power of Air against us. Fire will not stop it. We must flee, or when the storm leaves, it will bear us with it!'

Kinna leaped to rouse Eldia while Vitarius gathered up his pack containing his magical gear. Conan continued to watch the tornado cut an arrow's line toward the inn.

'We need a cellar or sewer,' Conan said.

'Not for this storm,' Vitarius said, shouldering his pack. 'It will simply stand and dig us out like moles. Our only hope is to get behind it; even Sovartus and his control of Air cannot reverse the direction of a storm so easily. We must move at angles to the wind and then into it before the funnel can tack to find us.'

The four made their way down the dark stairs and into the main room of the inn. A pair of guttering fat lamps cast their luminous flux over the dank walls, giving enough light for Conan to see the exit. 'This way,' he commanded.

At that instant the door opened and a half-dozen men burst into the room. Each was armed either with a sword or long dagger; several of the rough lot bore ropes as well. The man leading wore an eyepatch, but there was nothing wrong with his remaining eye, for he jerked to a halt and pointed at Conan. 'There he be, boys. Come to save us a climb, I reckons.'

Blades flashed in the faint lamplight as the six men moved apart from one another and toward Conan. The Cimmerian never paused to wonder at the cause of this new danger; he merely drew his own broadsword and moved to meet it.

'Time, Conan, we do not have time!' Vitarius waved his hands vaguely in the air.

Conan grinned tightly, but did not look away from his adversaries. 'I shall hurry as best I can.'

Two of the men blocked the exit; the rest fanned out, trying to encircle Conan. The barbarian grinned. This was his kind of fight, steel and muscle, not magic. He picked a target, a wolf-faced man bearing a short sword. Conan hesitated not an instant, but sprang with feral grace at the man, swinging the broadsword in a two-handed sweep across his body. Wolf-face raised his blade, but too slowly; Conan's cut tore a furrow across the man's throat which showed for an instant the villain's spine. The man gurgled and fell backward.

A second man attacked Conan from the rear, swinging his sword overhead in a body-splitter strike. Conan turned and blocked, tensing the sinews of his thick arm. Steel kissed steel, and the two blades sang together; Conan's arm moved not at all, and the man lost his balance as he recovered from the failed stroke. Conan slid forward, the point of his weapon leading, and skewered the back-striker just under the breastbone. Conan raised one foot and shoved the falling body from his blade with his boot. He spun, to face two more attackers moving in together. Conan set himself to spring; better to attack before they could gather their wits to coordinate themselves – four was the most dangerous number of opponents.

The inn shook then, as if swatted by a giant's hand.

'Conan! The devil-wind!' That from Kinna.

'Ow, I'm cut!' one of the men guarding the door screamed in pain, drawing the attention of the pair set to attack Conan.

The Cimmerian looked that way, to see little Eldia

hacking away at the man with her weapon. Her speed was dazzling, and the man bore only a long dagger, with which he was ineffectually trying to protect his legs. Even as Conan watched, the girl darted in and sliced the man's leg again.

'Brat!' the man yelled, but he backed away from the door, nearly bumping into his fellow.

Vitarius was trying to work some kind of spell, Conan saw, mumbling and waving his arms; there was no effect apparent to the brawny Cimmerian. He turned back to the two men facing him and moved on them, weaving a deadly pattern of razor-sharp edges.

The man with the eyepatch tried to circle outside Conan's reach, but the Cimmerian followed him, avoiding the second man, who was too fat to move quickly. The fat man was breathing hard as he tried to bring his sword into play against Conan's side.

The inn shook again, and the sound of the wind and fight was joined by that of voices yelling from up the stair. With a howl of joy Conan jumped for One-eye, blade whirling.

Loganaro watched the approach of destruction, feet frozen by his awe. Never in all his travels had he seen such a storm; that it was unnatural seemed all too obvious. Who had sent the terrible whirlwind, and why, also flitted across his mind, but that thought was quickly chased away by the fear of dying amid a hail of debris. His cutthroats could look to themselves for survival; the barbarian was not so important as living for a short time more. Loganaro turned and sprinted away from the oncoming disaster. He would worry about what to tell Lemparius later.

Djuvula was nearly home when she saw the magically created monster wind rip its way through the maze of Mornstadinos like a ferret seeking a particular rat. Her occult eye immediately noted the storm for what it was, and it was only the work of a second to realize by whom it had been sent, as well. Hurriedly, the witch turned and began to run back toward the inn, splashing through the gutters and driving rain. If Sovartus's tame whirlwind collected the girl,

Djuvula would lose a chance to increase her powers. More, there was the brave-hearted barbarian to consider. Of course, he was less important; Loganaro had another candidate for her, but of his opinion she was less than certain. Any man who could take the hand from a demon and survive had to be more than ordinary. But the girl was paramount in her interest.

Stalking in the wake of destruction walked a giant figure, unseen by the eyes of men. Red the figure was, and one-handed. It muttered to itself as it walked, the rumble of its voice merging with the thunder. 'You think wrongly, magician, if you think to cheat me of my revenge by employing other means to your evil ends. I *will* have this man!'

The walls of the Milk of Wolves Inn began to moan, as if in anticipation of their destruction. The exit door was blown open violently, tearing itself nearly from its crusty brass hinges; the sign marking the name of the place crashed to the ground and pinwheeled through the open doorway. The wolf *salient* had finally leaped; it came to rest against a table.

Conan had backed One-eye into a corner, and the man was fighting for his life. The pair of blackguards with daggers had been driven from the doorway by Eldia's small but deadly sword, assisted by the dagger of her sister; finally, Vitarius must have managed to get some kind of magic to work, for the fat assassin screamed as he began to glow redly, and to float half a span from the floor.

Vitarius yelled, to be heard over the heavy thunder created by the whirlwind which was nearly upon them.

'Conan! We must leave! Now!'

The Cimmerian made no answer, but lunged instead at One-eye. The man managed to block the sword, but in so doing, opened his head to attack. Conan curled the fingers of his right hand into a huge fist and slammed it against the man's jaw. The bone snapped and the man was flung half his length backward, to smack into the now-vibrating wall. He slid to the floor, unconscious. Conan turned. 'Go! Get out!'

Vitarius obeyed, leaving the fat man floating and screaming. Eldia and Kinna backed away from the two cutthroats with daggers, who showed no inclination to pursue them as Conan ran toward the door, waving his gore-smeared sword.

Outside, the wind struck the four with such force that for a moment they could make no headway. Conan alone could fight the blasts of the storm, but even his great strength would not be enough to tow an old man and two sisters against the wind.

Vitarius waved madly, his voice lost in the tempest. Conan understood what he wanted: they must move along the building, using it for support.

The four people seemed to be flies sticking to the wall, but they managed to creep along until they reached the corner of the building. There Conan led the way around the edge, his arm linked to Kinna's. She in turn held her sister, who clasped Vitarius's bony wrist. The wind shoved the human chain down the street like so many leaves. They ran so fast, Conan almost lost his footing. He remembered, however, what Vitarius had said earlier: they must run aslant to the oncoming twister and get behind it. After moving a short way down the street, Conan ducked into the lee of a temple, dragging the trio with him. He paused long enough to allow them to catch their breath.

A portion of some building blew by in the street, torn from a structure. Conan pointed and yelled, 'That way!'

They ran, gathering their energies when they had to leave the protection of houses or fences, leaning into the wind.

Behind them, the devil-wind changed direction, so that only its edge sliced into the Milk of Wolves Inn. Conan turned to stare at the rampaging black monster, still reflecting its own ghostly light. He saw the bodies of the cutthroats fly into the air, spinning into the maw of the tornado. There was one he had slain; there went the fat man. He did not see the man with the patch. He did see that the storm tried to pursue them, and so redoubled his efforts. Through it, Conan felt no real fear; rather, it was the challenge of beating the storm that drove him. By Crom, no storm was as agile as a Cimmerian!

The wind tried to turn, but the clouds from which it dragged its sucking tip could not adjust their path so easily. The storm angled toward them, but slowly. When Conan judged they were far enough, he turned again, heading more into the wind. Debris smacked into him, but he held fast to the woman behind him, digging his boots deeply into the churned mud of the street. At one point Vitarius slipped; such was the wind that for an instant he floated flaglike from the taut arm of Eldia. Fortunately for him, the girl's grip was strong, else he would have been blown away.

The tornado raged, ripping the houses and stables and temples asunder, shredding planks as if they were straw, driving the resulting straws like spears to impale all before them. A stick of wood penetrated a thick fence post in front of him as if the stick were steel and the post no more than butter. The whirlwind seemed to stretch, to try to reach its quarry, brushing aside obstacles as easily as a man brushes crumbs from a table. Such a force seemed unstoppable; indeed, nothing man-created could withstand it. After what seemed several lifetimes, the Cimmerian drew level with the wind-devil; several lifetimes later, he was past – and behind it.

The tornado seemed to stand still; it tried to move back along its path. Conan held his breath, watching. After a moment, one stretching very long, the funnel began to move again, away from the young Cimmerian and the others.

The storm had been defeated. In a moment the swirling clouds overhead lifted their dragging tail of destruction, and the whirlwind was reclaimed. Gone.

CHAPTER EIGHT

Conan saw the demon first. The wind died slowly after the clouds sucked their whirling maw skyward: gone the tornado might be, but not the rain and ordinary airs of the storm. Conan led Vitarius, Eldia, and Kinna across the path left by the wind-beast, a path much like a road cut through a forest. Following the whirlwind's trail was the red demon, who saw Conan near the same instant he himself was spotted by the man. Despite the lashing rain, the Cimmerian could observe the demon's face as it contorted in hatred. Conan drew his sword as the monster turned and began to sprint toward him.

'Vitarius!' This from Eldia, who pointed at the approaching devil.

The old magician turned and beheld the scene. Quickly, he laid one hand upon the head of the girl; the other hand he raised and pointed at the fast-arriving creature.

The demon skidded to a stop twenty paces away. 'No,' he said loudly. 'Score me not with your Fire's tongue again.'

Vitarius hesitated. He looked at Conan.

The Cimmerian shook his head. 'Nay,' he said. 'He would speak, I think. Allow him.'

The demon drew himself up to his full impressive height. 'I would have you know my name,' he said. 'You are of the White, and so cannot use it against me even were I not bound to another. I am Djavul.'

Conan never lowered his blade a hair. 'Why should we care, demon?' Rivulets ran down the sharp steel onto his hands.

'I am bound against you, wasp, but even were I not, *your* life is still forfeit under any circumstances. You owe me for this.' Djavul raised his arm and extended the stump toward Conan. 'Because you have done what no other man has ever done in injuring me so, I would have you know the name of the one who sends you to the gray lands. Ah, but very slowly you shall make the transition, wasp.'

Vitarius raised his hand and aimed it at the demon, but Conan shook his head. 'Nay, I say again, magician. I have my blade; I need not your protection. Let him come.' The young giant shifted his stance, spread his legs wider for balance, and gripped the wet leather handle of the broadsword tighter. 'You have been stung once, Djavul of Hell; come, I shall sting you again.' Conan shook rain from his eyes.

Djavul looked from Conan toward Vitarius and Eldia, then back at the Cimmerian. 'I think not, wasp.'

'The magician stays out of it,' Conan said, inching forward slightly. Mud squished under his boots.

Djavul laughed. 'Trusting the words of men has led more than one night-child into foolishness. This is not the time or place. But I will see you again, wasp.' Djuval flicked a red-eyed glance back at Vitarius. 'And you as well, White one.'

Abruptly, there came a clap of noise that rivaled the storm's thunder, and Djavul vanished.

With the rain still falling upon them, Conan turned to glare at Vitarius. 'It would seem that I have made an enemy for myself.'

'The fault is mine,' Vitarius said.

'It would seem you have made more than one enemy, Conan.' This from Kinna, who stood staring at the spot where Djavul had vanished.

The Cimmerian looked at her. 'How so?'

'Those men who attacked us as we left the inn. They came for you, not for us. Recall what the patch-eyed man said?'

Conan brought the memory forth: *There he be, boys. Come to save us a climb, I reckons.* Kinna was right. But – why had they come for him? He had no enemies in this place save the hellspawn, Djavul. The devil wanted him, to be sure, but it seemed unlikely he would have sent human cutthroats to do his bidding. Who had sent them, then? It was a puzzle, a mystery, and Conan liked such things not.

'Perhaps we would be better served to get out of the rain,'

Vitarius said. 'We might sort things out just as well dry as wet.'

'Aye,' Conan said, but his disquiet remained.

Djuvula watched her brother rage at the beautiful man with the sword, smiling as she did so. Ah, yes, this one was surely the one she sought. Her gaze covered the barbarian lovingly, despite the rainy darkness. Such thick, smooth muscle he had, and such a wonderful rage simmered in his flashing blue eyes as he faced Djavul with only a sword. His heart would drive her Prince as no other heart had been able to move him. Yes.

Djavul vanished to Gehanna. Djuvula slid back into the cover of soaked hay bales, stacked head-high. It would not do for them to see her just yet. For a moment Djuvula's mind warred with itself: so much to have! Here was the girl, the essence of Fire: the child glowed with it as a beacon lit to guide ships in fog – at least to one able to see such things, as a witch of power could. And the barbarian with the beautiful body, ah, how she wanted him!

Her smile increased. Perhaps she might allow this man that which she had given up on in other men, before she excised his mighty heart. Who knew? Such a barbarian might be possessed of vital energies beyond ordinary limits. She could ... utilize him for a time before animating her Prince. Certainly he looked capable ...

Djuvula shook her head, as if to clear away the fantasy within by her action. She should think of the girl first. Then she laughed softly to herself. Why not slay two birds with the same stone? If she exercised care, she could have the girl and the man together. It would not be easy; the White Mage had demonstrated his power to Djavul before, and the witch could see the fear in her brother's eyes as he faced the old man again. No, it would have to be carefully done, using guile instead of force. Even as she thought it, Djuvula began to think of a plan. Yes, a plan that would allow her to use her very special talents ...

Senator Lemparius shed his wet clothes and went directly to the hot bath kept ever so, awaiting his pleasure. As he sank into the water the warm vapors swirled around his head, bringing the scent of crushed mint to his nostrils. Ah . . .

One of the deputies scurried into the room, bowing as he came. 'My lord Senator,' the man began, 'a terrible windstorm has wreaked much damage to the city, killing dozens of citizens.'

Lemparius shrugged within the womb of blissful heat. 'So? What is done is done; why disturb my bath for such?'

The deputy appeared undisturbed by the senator's lack of concern. 'The man who brought this news awaits without, to speak to you of a matter related to this disaster.'

'Send him away.' Lemparius managed to raise one hand languidly to wave at the deputy; vapor rose from his skin into the cooler air of the bathchamber.

'As you command, my lord. The man would have you know his name, however. He calls himself Loganaro.'

Senator Lemparius smiled. 'Ah, there is a beast of a different strain. Admit him.'

As the deputy left, Lemparius sank yet deeper into the perfumed water, until his nose was barely clear of the liquid. A shame cats hated the water so.

Loganaro entered the chamber. The man was muddy and bedraggled, his face filled with a mix of ratlike cunning and fear.

The senator bobbed up slightly, clearing his mouth. 'Where have you deposited my barbarian? You have collected him by this time?'

'Honored Senator, there was a complication –'

'Complication? Speak not of such! Complications in my service most often lead to ultimate simplication, if you understand my meaning?'

The fat man swallowed. Water still dripped from his gray hair. 'It – it could not have been foreseen, lord! A windstorm arose even as my minions collected the barbarian. The inn containing them was demolished, smashed, and scattered; there was nothing to be done!'

Lemparius sat up in the bath and pointed one sharp fingernail at his agent. 'I hope you are not telling me my prey was sucked up by a storm.'

'N-nay, Honored Senator. My . . . collectors were; somehow, the Cimmerian and his friends escaped.'

'Where, then, are they?'

'My agent follows them currently; he will report back to me as soon as they alight.'

Lemparius relaxed a little, sinking into the massive tub. 'Then I see no complication. Merely a delay. As soon as this man settles, you shall simply . . . retrieve him, eh? Only take care that this Cimmerian stays within your grasp, Loganaro mine. Otherwise there is that simplification of which I spoke. A state of being ever so much more simple than one so complex as, say, living and breathing.'

Loganaro swallowed and nodded, his damp pale face going more ghostly.

When he had gone, Lemparius smiled. He took a deep breath and sank beneath the water, staying long enough for the warmth to caress his closed eyes and soak his hair. When he came up for air, he was still smiling.

Castle Slott rang with the shouts of its master. 'Set curse them all! By the Eternal Fires, I *will* have her!'

The three children iron-linked to the cold wall shrank back, as if they could sink into the stone away from Sovartus's wrath.

Sovartus flashed a grimace filled with hatred at the three, concentrating his gaze particularly upon Luft, the boy of Air. 'You resisted me somehow,' the magician said. 'Else that wind would have drawn my quarry up and delivered her to me. I shall remember this, never fear.'

With that, Sovartus stalked away from the three, his mind whirling with schemes for achievement of his goal. He muttered to himself as he moved. 'Where rests my demon? If he cannot win the girl, he can at least *find* her and watch her! And what have I done with my casting sphere? Ah, may the Black-Souled Ones take everyone!'

The place was a shed for storage of dried meat and fish, hardly fit accommodations for men; still, it was dry under the solid roof. Crowded into the small cleared space beneath

76

hanging racks of jerky and smoked fish, Conan stood glowering at Vitarius. The old man spoke.

'I cannot say who sent the assassins, if that was their intent. Because of the ropes they carried, I suspect the unfortunates intended to capture you.'

Conan shook his head, fanning his damp black hair away from his face. 'There is no sense to that,' he said. 'I am unknown in these parts; no one would have reason to hold me.'

'An old enemy, perhaps?' Kinna said this as she tried to light a stub of candle from a flint-and-steel she worked. Sparks flared in the shed, falling like shooting stars.

'Most of my enemies lie dead,' Conan said. 'None who live would bother to follow me this far from where I earned their enmity.'

One of Kinna's sparks touched the greasy wick of the candle, appeared to smolder for a moment, then went out. Conan thought she uttered a curse, but her voice was too quiet for even his ears to understand what she said.

Almost absently, Eldia raised her finger and pointed it at the candle. The stub of wax and string lit, seemingly of its own accord, casting shadows to the walls and ceiling of the shed.

'So,' Kinna said, looking away from the candle at Conan, 'what will you do now?'

He considered his choices. He still cared little for practitioners of sorcerous arts, White, Black, or any other color; a quick exit from this city would serve his purposes well enough. Numalia beckoned, and there was certainly no profit to be had in staying here to contest with demons and magicians, not to mention the unknown master of the cutthroats dispatched by wind and blade to their destinies.

On the other hand, Conan felt a perverse stubbornness rising in him, a feeling of rage at being threatened. No matter that the hellish demon had reason for anger, nor that the master of the cutthroats now had similar reasons – his minions were scattered meat, no more. Conan had been minding his own affairs and had been provoked; such provocation deserved no less than he had given. Likely a prudent man would interpret such attacks as a sign from his patron gods to travel elsewhere at a goodly pace. Cimmerians were not, however, always prudent. Conan's anger at those responsible for causing him such discomfort was great; those who held Crom as their deity could not be fainthearted. Crom was a hard god who offered little to his followers: he was savage, gloomy, and dealt in death; more. Crom hated weaklings and cowards above all. Crom dispensed courage and will, taken in with life's first breath from out the womb. A man did not honor Crom by running from danger, no matter how great.

Conan stared at the trio gathered around the light of the single candle. He was bound for Nemedia, to be certain, and he did not like magicians, but there were matters to be attended to here.

The others waited for Conan to speak. At last, he did.

'It seems as if we are allies for a time,' the Cimmerian said, his voice nearly a growl. He liked it little, but there it stood. He focused on Vitarius. 'I trust you have some plan for defeating our mutual enemy?'

The old mage smiled. 'Of a sort, Conan. Of a sort.'

CHAPTER NINE

Loganaro found himself beset by a large problem: where was the barbarian? That he had lied to Lemparius bothered Loganaro not a whit; he *had* seen Conan flee the destroyed inn, even as he had made good his own escape. Unfortunately, there had been no agents following the Cimmerian in the midst of that tempest.

Such a lie was simply an elementary precaution Loganaro had long since learned to take when dealing with powerful men. Conan had somehow escaped and still lived; therefore, he could be located, in time. If, however, Lemparius had suspected that Loganaro had lost the barbarian, events might have taken a decided turn in the direction of ... simplification, a term that left no doubt in Loganaro's mind as to its meaning.

The short figure hurried through the dampness of the early morning, only now beginning to be awash in the rays of the rising sun. The storm had done much to rearrange whole streets and alleys; Loganaro picked his way toward what had been the Milk of Wolves Inn.

Even though the full might of the whirlwind had not struck the inn, there was left little to proclaim it so. The wooden bones of the inn lay mostly scattered; only a single wall remained, standing guard over the pile of rubble. Loganaro felt drawn to this wall, even as he wondered why he had returned to this place. He had a network of informants second to no other free agent in Mornstadinos; he should be locating runners to put forth the word on the barbarian, alerting his eyes and ears to the search. For some reason, however, he was here.

A few stunned men and women wandered about in the wreckage, searching for survivors and, perhaps, lost possessions. Loganaro watched them for a short while, then decided his own time was being wasted here. He turned to leave.

The rubble issued a groan. Or, rather, someone under the rubble moaned. Mildly curious, Loganaro moved toward the source of the sound. As he neared an overturned table, the free agent saw a hand scrabble up and shove at the remains of what had been a wall.

While Loganaro seldom performed any act without considering the gain for himself, he did so now. He bent and pulled at the impedimenta covering the owner of the hand. After a moment the face of the man under the debris became visible: it was Patch, one of Loganaro's cutthroats. Loganaro helped the man dig free, noticing that the Zamorian seemed unscathed save for a swollen jaw.

'What happened?' Patch mumbled painfully.

'You do not know?'

'I remember nothing but the big man. He be a formidable foe, right enough. Where be the others?'

'There was a twisting storm which took them. It did this.' Loganaro waved one fat arm at the ruined inn.

'Got the barbarian, this twister?'

'Nay. He escaped with his friends.'

Patch nodded, gently rubbing his swollen jaw. 'Then you be still seeking the big man.' It was not a question.

'Aye. And the reward has been raised.' Loganaro had not thought of this before he said it, but he had no desire to leave life just yet. He had accumulated a great deal of ill-gotten monies, and the thought of profit on this venture no longer drove him as much as the fear of joining his ancestors prematurely. 'Thirty pieces of gold.'

Patch nodded, wincing. 'Aye, a goodly sum, but who claims it shall have to earn it. Two, maybe three of my men lay dead 'fore the big man felled me. The whirlstorm claimed more dead than living here. This one you be seeking owes me.'

'Alive,' Loganaro said. 'He must be taken alive.'

'Aye, alive it be, but maybe some damaged.'

Loganaro nodded. Patch was reputed to be one of the

best men in Mornstadinos at this kind of work; it would not hurt for him to have a personal stake in retrieving Conan.

'Collect him within the next two days and there will be a bonus of five solons for you personally,' Loganaro said.

Patch tried to grin, then apparently thought better of it as he clapped a hand to his swollen jaw. 'Aye, pursemaster, you'll have your barbarian. Alive.'

'Since it would seem that others seek us, in addition to Sovartus and his demon-thrall, it might be best if we stayed out of sight as much as possible until we can implement our plan,' Vitarius said.

Conan leaned against a rack of dried fish and chewed with less than enthusiasm on a chunk of jerky. The meat was salty and dry; he wished for some wine to wash the leathery beef down. Might as well wish for a palace in Shadizar while you are at it, Conan thought. Aloud, he said, 'I see flaws in your plan, old one.'

Kinna took a piece of dried fish from the point of her sister's blade and regarded it with mild distaste. She said, 'What flaws?'

'Our master magician purports that we leave the city soonest, mounted and well-supplied, for a journey to beard the lion in his den. A direct assault is to my liking, but I question how we are to become affluent enough to afford this journey. Have we gold or silver of which I am unaware?'

Conan looked at the three faces in turn, seeing negative shakes and raised eyebrows for his answer.

'I thought not. How, then, do you propose we obtain fine horses, saddles, and sundry supplies? Will you create such with your magic?'

'Ah,' Vitarius said, 'unfortunately, no. White spells generally allow the worker little for personal gain.'

'A pity. If one must deal with magic, it is too bad one cannot benefit.' Conan grinned and picked at his teeth with his dagger's point, clearing away bits of meat. 'Now it seems we come to something that falls into *my* area of expertise.'

Eldia speared a chunk of dried fish with her blade, flipped

it into the air, and caught it in her mouth. She chewed lustily, obviously enjoying the tidbit. 'How so, Conan?'

Conan paused long enough to open the door of the drying shed, to allow the morning's light into the dank room. The sun shone brightly from an ice-blue, cloudless sky. He looked back at the trio. 'Tell me, who are the richest two or three men in the city?'

Vitarius scratched his cheek, considering. 'Well, Tonore the rug merchant certainly would be one; then either Stephanos of Punt, the landlord, or Lemparius the Whip, I would think. Why?'

Conan ignored the question, asking yet another instead: 'How do these men keep their wealth? Gold? Jewels?'

'Tonore's money is tied up in his wares mostly. He has a collection of carpets from as far away as Iranistan and Zembabwei. Too, he collects works of art, statues and paintings mostly. Stephanos is a landowner, and I would say most of his wealth consists of inns, brothels, and other such properties. Likely somewhat reduced since last eve's devilish storm.'

'What of Lemparius the Whip? And what does that mean?'

'He is the Center Strand of the Senate Flail, the most powerful of all the senators. In the city-states of Corinthia there are a few kings, but in Mornstadinos the people are ruled by a Senate. Many of the senators are wealthy, Lemparius probably more so than most.'

'And how does he hold his money?'

'He has a palace, very opulent, so I understand. And he has a fondness for magical and mechanical toys, upon which he spends no small amount; by and large, though, I suspect Lemparius has more than a few sacks of gold and silver within his walls.'

Conan's grin increased. 'Ah, good.'

Kinna spat a fish bone onto the dirt floor. 'But – why are these things important, Conan?'

Conan faced the young woman, taken again by her beauty despite the dingy surroundings. 'Because, Kinna, we need horses and supplies and cannot afford the time or effort needed to earn such things honestly.'

Eldia understood more quickly than did her sister. She said, 'You mean we're going to –?'

'– steal from the senator?' Conan finished. 'Aye, Fire-child, that we are.'

One of the items in a witch's arsenal was a simple spell to create a magical, invisible thread of great length and strength. After she watched the beautiful barbarian and his friends enter the ramshackle shed, Djuvula created such a thread. Moving with all the stealth at her command, she stretched a section of this thread across the doorway, anchoring it lightly on either side of the entrance. When the inhabitants left the shed the thread would entangle one or more of them, stretching to follow them from the shed as far as they might travel. The caster of the spell need only follow the glowing line, a line unseen by all without magically enhanced vision. There was a chance the old wizard might discover it, but such a possibility seemed unlikely. The spell was so simple and unthreatening, it almost always passed unnoticed save by one searching specifically for it.

The spell thrown, Djuvula hurriedly returned to her manse. The magic she contemplated required more than the small ingredients she normally carried upon her person. When that cantrip was completed, Djuvula could return and await her chance to get the beautiful barbarian alone. *He* would then deliver the girl to Djuvula. She smiled, thinking of it.

There existed some risk in the spell – the woman would have to be removed from the barbarian's presence somehow – but such a risk was small compared to the possible gain.

In her spellroom Djuvula quickly stripped away her clothing, to stand naked in front of her focusing mirror. Nakedness was required for most of her major spells, but Djuvula had long since been undaunted by such a necessity. She had, in fact, come to enjoy the feel of air on her nude body, a sensual part of witchery that suited her much better than any clothing men could produce.

There was another inn, some distance away, of which

Vitarius knew; he led Conan and the sisters from the shed toward this place. As they exited the home of dried meat and fish, Conan thought he felt a strand of spider's silk brush his arm. He brushed at the line of web, but saw nothing, and so quickly forgot about it.

Even in the middle of disaster, people rallied and scurried to repair the damage. Already, teams of horses and oxen were at work, dragging rubble from pathways, clearing away downed timbers and adobe walls from alleys. As the four walked, they happened upon a further disaster in the making. Seven or eight men tugged on ropes attached to a fallen roof beam as thick as a fat man; the beam stood balanced precariously against a half-destroyed wall. The crew sought merely to topple the long timber in order, Conan thought, to bring down the fragment of wall that remained. That the men were inexpert was all too apparent to Conan; at least two of them stood directly under the heavy beam. If it should fall . . .

As he watched, the beam slipped from its support and came crashing down. One man jumped from under the falling weight with great agility, but the second man's speed was not sufficient. The beam pinned the unfortunate victim to the ground as a man's sandaled foot pins a snake. He screamed as the wood smashed both his legs to the dirt. The remaining men immediately began trying to lift the beam, cursing as they realized they had not the strength. It looked hopeless.

Conan sprang, unthinking. Such was the speed of his movement that the men gripping the timber jumped back, as if fearing attack.

The Cimmerian ignored them. He wrapped his great arms around the end of the fallen beam and squatted, so that he held the wood to his chest. He shifted his feet slightly wider and tried to stand. Individual muscles stood out on his thighs like a network of thick bands; the hard flesh of his bare arms writhed as though small animals roved under his skin. The beam did not move.

Conan adjusted his grip, took a deep breath, and screamed a wordless, guttural yell that caused the hair to stand on the necks of several watchers. With a contraction that caused his rock-hard thews to vibrate, the young giant stood, keeping his back stiff as his legs straightened. For a moment he stood there holding the giant beam, great veins standing out all over his exposed flesh like tiny snakes. Then the barbarian heaved the timber away from himself with a thrust of his hips. The heavy wood fell with a ground-shaking crash just past the end of the formerly trapped man's feet. Conan shook himself once and stretched his shoulders. 'Best you be more careful,' he said 'I might not walk this way again.' He turned and strode back to where his friends stood, staring.

Kinna spoke first. 'By Mitra! No man can be so strong!'

Conan grinned. 'What? For lifting that twig? Are there no men where you come from?'

Kinna's voice was soft and full of admiration. 'None such as you.'

Conan grinned wider, pleased with himself. This was the kind of chore for a man, one that needed quick reactions and strength – and one that impressed women and men alike.

The Cimmerian felt the slightest touch upon his leg then, just where his leathern breech gapped over his boots, but when he looked there was nothing to be seen.

The Smoking Cat Inn might have been constructed on the same pattern as had the Milk of Wolves. The same benches, the same tables, even the same servers. The place was not crowded, however, likely owing to all the work needed to be done outside. Conan and the others found a table easily, and ordered wine and breakfast. 'Might as well spend what we have,' the Cimmerian said, 'for we should have much more shortly.'

'Stealing from a rich man could be very dangerous,' Eldia said.

Conan smiled at the girl. 'Aye. But I have some . . . experience in such things.'

'There is a high wall surrounding Lemparius's estate,' Vitarius put in.

'They have yet to build a wall a Cimmerian cannot climb,' Conan said. He quaffed a cup of wine.

Kinna stared at him with curiosity in her eyes. Finally, she spoke. 'How is it that you are so strong and so adept, Conan?'

He shrugged. 'Cimmeria is a rocky land; ofttimes the rocks are in places where they impede a man's progress. Such rocks must be moved; some of them are heavy. As to my skills, well, a man learns what he must to survive.'

'How are we to accomplish this – ah – liberation of valuables?' Vitarius said.

'Not "we," magician, me. I work best alone. You shall arrange today for our supplies; on the morrow I shall return with funds sufficient to pay for these things. Simple.' Conan lifted another cup of wine to his lips and smiled again. This was more to his liking, and what he should have done in the first place – then he would have never become entangled with the nasty webs of magic he so disliked.

Djuvula the Witch smiled as she followed the glowing line of the thread that led to her prey. Soon he would be hers!

Patch, the cutthroat, grinned evilly as he watched the barbarian drink his third cup of wine. Good. If the man were drunk, so much the better. He had planned to assemble a host of assistants earlier, but upon seeing the barbarian, Patch felt such a rage that he dismissed his earlier thoughts. No. He would strike when the big man was not prepared; he would knock him senseless and then work on the unconscious form with his bare hands and shod feet until he felt some measure of revenge. Aye, that be the way of it, to do it singly, to balm his wound and pride. No man defeated Patch and escaped unscathed. No man!

CHAPTER TEN

Conan decided to sleep for a few hours so that he might be rested and fresh for his nocturnal business. While the others went to arrange for their travel supplies, the barbarian ascended the stairs to the rooms the group had rented. The pair of rooms could have been twins to the ones at the destroyed Milk of Wolves Inn. Conan picked one and entered, bolting the door behind him. He sprawled upon the ticking and soon fell fast asleep.

Djuvula followed the magic thread up the stairs of the inn. The glowing line ended at the door to one of the sleeping rooms. One or more of those she sought must be inside. It was important, however, that she find the beautiful barbarian alone. Her spell would do her little good if there were another woman within the man's reach. How could she find out?

After a moment the idea came to her. Quickly, Djuvula descended the stairway and found a clean-up boy clearing tables. 'Like to earn a few coppers, boy?'

'Aye, mistress. Whom shall I slay for you?'

'Not such a large task as that, boy. Just knock on the door of the room I point out and see how many people are within when you are answered. Say you have come to change the bedding.'

Djuvula handed the boy several coppers, and then followed him up the stairs. She pointed out the door, then moved back down the stairway, out of sight.

After a few moments the boy returned.

'Well?'

'There is but one in the room, mistress, and he seems an ill-tempered one at that. He said he would skewer me, were I to bother him again for such stupidity.'

'What did he look like, boy?'

'A giant of a man, mistress. A barbarian.'

Djuvula smiled and gave the boy a handful of coppers. 'Speak of this to no one, boy.'

'I should hope not,' the boy said. 'Fat-arse the owner would take my money faster than flies locate dung.'

When she was alone in the hallway again, Djuvula brought forth from her silken robe a vial stoppered with cork and wax; inside this clear-walled vessel was a liquid that glowed faintly, like phosphorus. She pried the cork from the bottle's mouth and bent to pour a line of the fluid along the base of the door. Vapor rose in a thick yellow cloud, and the sorceress hastily backed away from the smoke.

Conan awoke suddenly. Something was wrong. Some strange smell had invaded his dreams . . . He sat up suddenly and stared. In the light admitted by the poorly fitted shutters he saw a thin haze of yellow smoke filling the room. He sniffed deeply, then coughed as the irritating fumes filled his nostrils. Was the inn on fire? No, this was like no odor he had smelled before; no wood fed this noxious vapor –

He suddenly found himself suffused with an emotion altogether different from curiosity: his body seemed about to burst – with lust.

There came a knock at his door. A female voice called to him. 'Open the door, my beautiful barbarian.'

Conan felt confusion. The voice was seductive and carried the tones of warm honey, the promise of undreamed of fulfillment. His lust increased. He moved to the door, slid back the bolt, and jerked the door wide.

The woman who stood there was covered from head to toe in a deep blue robe of fine silk. As he watched, the figure raised pale hands to slip back the hood covering her face and head. By all the gods, she was beautiful! Her hair was flame, her skin unblemished white, her lips ruby and smiling.

'Am I to stand in the drafty hallway?' she said.

Conan took two hesitant steps backward, and the woman

followed, gliding smoothly across the floor. She eased the door shut behind her and smiled at him. She stood motionless for a moment, then slowly brought her hands to the front of the robe. With a quick flip of her fingers she opened the front of the robe and shrugged it away.

Beneath the blue silk she was naked.

Conan licked suddenly dry lips. By Mitra, what a woman! She was glorious! Her legs, her breasts – her whole body was perfect!

The mysterious woman reached out toward him with both hands.

Conan's desire knew no bounds. He stepped forward and wrapped his thick arms around the woman, hugging her to him, lifting her clear of the floor. He felt the stab of her fingernails, but such did not matter. Nothing mattered in all the world save taking his pleasure with this woman!

The boy pointed to the door of the sleeping room. 'That is the room you seek, sir.'

Patch flipped a coin at the boy, a silver piece, but he begrudged it not. In a short while Patch would be thirty-five gold solons richer – what mattered a single silver? He waited until the boy was gone and he was alone in the hall; then Patch stole softly to the door of the barbarian's room. Caution was called for despite his desire for revenge.

As Patch placed his ear against the door, the wooden plank moved a hair. Unbolted, by Set's black hand! He grinned. The barbarian be foolish not to lock his door; he'd sealed his doom! Still moving quietly, the one-eyed man drew his sword.

A soft moan came from within the room. Patch paused, cocking his head to one side. What be this? Why, that sounded like –

The cutthroat grinned more widely. Ah, this be a stroke of good fortune, indeed! Asura smiled upon him, for the barbarian likely would not notice his entrance in that he seemed occupied with . . . other matters. Patch took a deep breath, lifted his blade to strike, and shoved wide the door.

*

Conan could not understand the reason for his sudden lust or the appearance of the woman who seemed bent on slaking it; neither, it must be said, did he try particularly hard to fathom it. But when the door to his room crashed open and a man sprang through the entrance waving a sword, Conan understood that well enough. The spell holding him broke.

The woman in his arms pulled back at the look on Conan's face. 'What –?' She twisted, to ape Conan's stare, and beheld the assassin.

Conan thrust the naked woman away from him with a snarl. 'So, dog-sister, you sought to occupy me for your butcher!'

'No!' the woman yelled.

There was no time for such a discussion, Conan knew. He rolled across the floor as the attacker brought his blade down. The sword cleaved the bed and not Conan. The Cimmerian grabbed his own blade and sprang to his feet, facing the cutthroat. By Crom, it was the patch-eyed man he'd fought in the tavern before the windstorm!

Behind the two men, the woman cursed with a command of invective Conan had seldom heard, even from soldiers or seamen. The Cimmerian grinned wolfishly at Patch and moved half a pace toward him. 'Back for more of the same, One-eye?'

'The bells will toll your dirge, barbarian,' Patch snarled. 'Alive, you be wanted, but no man taunts me and lives! You be a dead man.'

Conan's grin remained in place. 'When last we met, I survived – we will see whose dirge plays, assassin.'

Patch lunged, feinted with his blade, then swept a fanlike stroke across his body, aimed at decapitating Conan. Conan gave no ground, however, but instead moved toward the other man, holding his blade in a grip of iron. The one-eyed brigand's sword clanged against Conan's and rebounded. Patch cursed.

The Cimmerian raised his sword overhead, to split his opponent from skull to crotch; before he could strike, however, Patch pulled a short dagger from his belt with his free hand and slashed at Conan. The bigger man leaped back, but the dagger drew a furrow across his thigh; blood welled and ran downward.

Conan reached down and touched the redness of his blood with the fingertips of his left hand. Lifting the salty fluid to his lips, he tasted it, and laughed at the sudden flash of fear on Patch's face. Suddenly, he flicked the blood left on his fingers at the cutthroat, aiming for his eyes.

Patch cursed and leaped back. Conan circled to his left, then sprang, his sword doing its steely dance. The one-eyed man stabbed at him with the dagger as he swung his own sharp blade, but the brigand's defenses served him poorly. Patch left an opening: Conan took the offer. With a yell the big Cimmerian drove his broadsword at Patch, as he would a spear. The point took the would-be assassin just under the breastbone, slicing through his heart and out his back, between two vertebrae.

'D-d-damn you!' Patch managed as he fell.

With a powerful contraction of his upper back and shoulder, Conan jerked his blade free of the dying man. Turning his attention away from Patch, he spun, looking for the woman who had bewitched him.

She was gone.

The innlord had removed the body and replaced the bloody bed upon which it had finally fallen, being careful to keep his eyes respectful when he chanced to gaze at the Cimmerian. Conan offered the man a silver coin for his effort – his last such coin – with instructions to keep the Senate's Deputation at bay for a few hours. After that he would be gone, and they could whistle for him.

As he cleaned his blade and honed the nicks in its edge, Conan considered the attack. It was unfortunate that he and the woman had been unable to complete their liaison before One-eye had interrupted. The man's appearance had certainly been a surprise; more, the woman had seemed surprised as well. If that were true, then perhaps the slain cutthroat had not been associated with her after all. Strange.

Of course, she *had* enspelled him somehow. That foul-stinking smoke, most likely. But if she were not part of the plot to slay him, then – who *was* she? Stranger and stranger. Some of the stink remained in his nostrils, and he felt the smell was less of the vapor and more associated with the reek of magic he so distrusted. This was no place for a man of honor, wrapped in some mystical web peopled with magicians, demons, and witches. The sooner he was shut of this business, the better. On the morrow, all things going as planned, he would ride from the west gate of Mornstadinos. Then all he would have to worry about would be an evil magician ensconced in a castle.

Conan shook his head, and continued to clean his blade.

Djuvula sat in her chamber full of black rage. Who had that one-eyed fool been? He had spoken of taking the barbarian alive, therefore he had been in the employ of someone else. Who? Who dared to interfere with her in this manner? The person responsible would be most unhappy when Djuvula found out. Most unhappy.

Loganaro shook his head as he stared at Patch's corpse. The fool had paid for his arrogance in thinking he could take the barbarian alone. Now what was he going to do?

Sovartus waved one hand at Djavul. 'Go and find the girl and this greater-than-ordinary man who guards her,' he said. 'I shall contact you when I am ready.'

'By your leave,' Djavul grated. And he disappeared.

In the dining room of his palace Lemparius declined other than dabbling with his food. He would, he reasoned with a smile eat something later in the evening.

Something – or someone . . .

CHAPTER ELEVEN

Mornstadinos lay deep in night's embrace when finally Conan approached the wall surrounding the estate of Lemparius, Center Strand of the Senate's Treble Whip. The Cimmerian moved easily despite the bound cut upon his thigh. The wound was shallow, and it caused him little concern; he had suffered much worse and survived. The man who had inflicted the injury no longer walked in the land of the living, and the slight pain Conan felt from his limb was small enough coin to pay for that privilege.

The wall was of smooth stones, set in an adobe mortar and covered with more of the claylike mud; in height, the wall was easily thrice Conan's own span. The tall youth grinned. Child's play, he thought, looking at the cracks in the adobe. To an ordinary man the wall might appear smooth; to a Cimmerian there might as well have been a ladder scaling the side. If Lemparius depended upon this wall for his primary protection, the man prepared himself ill for unsolicited night visitors.

It was but the work of a few moments for Conan to spider his way up the wall. At the top, shards of broken pottery had been set, along with splinters of rock. Were a climber fool enough to throw himself upon these jagged edges, certainly he could do himself injury. Conan laughed softly. Anyone adept enough to climb the wall was also likely to be adept enough to bypass the ragged points set in the top. He did so easily, undaunted by such small precautions on the part of the builder. He worked his way down the inner wall until he reached his own height from the ground, then dropped, landing lightly for such a big man. Easy enough.

The palace stood a hundred paces away. Perhaps *palace*

was too pretentious a word, Conan thought. Certainly, the manse was large, but it seemed less than imposing when compared to some of the structures he had seen in Shadizar. No comparison could be made with the destroyed Tower of the Elephant in Arenjun, to be certain; still, if the place held that which he sought, that would be enough.

The manse, too, was of adobe over stone, with gaps where the overlay had sloughed away to reveal the rock. Conan saw there was no moat; neither did there seem to be watch animals, dogs, or birds. He thought the last a bit strange; he had come prepared for either, with drugged meat and grain in a small sack tied to his belt.

Conan approached the house boldly, hoping to confuse any guards who might see him. If seen, he would try to get close enough to knock the guard senseless before alarm could be raised.

No guards materialized from dark recesses, however. Nor did Conan see any signs of guardhouses or posts. He shook his head, starlight gleaming from his blue eyes. This Lemparius was a gift from Bel to thieves, he thought. A wonder there stood no sign proclaiming invitation to steal.

Despite the ease of his entrance so far, he remained cautious. He was tempted to simply stride to the front entrance and enter the manse that way, but he decided against such audacity. Best not to press his luck; a window would do just as well.

From the ease of his work so far, Conan expected the window to be unlatched; he was not disappointed. The shutters swung wide easily, allowing him to clamber inside the building. Inside, he found himself in a storeroom laden with fowl hung to ripen for future meals, lit dimly by tapers in the hall beyond. He moved among the dangling carcasses gracefully, avoiding contact with the pungent flesh. He peered out into the hall.

Once again the young Cimmerian grinned widely. Empty. This was too easy. He began to relax. Such a man as owned this place deserved to be robbed; surely he must be swimming in arrogance?

He walked down the hallway, keeping to the edges of his

94

booted feet for silence. Such a precaution was automatic, and not one apt to be relaxed simply because of one easy bit of theft.

The hall led past a large room with a steaming bath centered on it, sunk into the floor. Wisps of vapor rose to condense on the walls, and drops of moisture ran down to form small pools upon the floor. But where were the inhabitants of this place? Could it be that everyone slept, without even a single guard? Such lunacy!

He moved past several rooms with doors ajar. He saw expensive furniture and rugs in some, paintings and statues in others; still others held mechanical devices, the purposes of which he could not immediately discern.

Finally, the Cimmerian came to a locked door. He grinned. About time. He bent to examine the lock, and his grin increased. Such a lock would not stymie a child bent on entering the room. And Conan was no child. He pulled his dagger and worked the point between the door's edge and the jamb. A simple twist of the blade freed the bolt from its recess; the door swung inward easily.

He took a taper from the hall and held it before him as he moved into the room. He stopped suddenly, and sucked in a quick breath. Crom!

The light from the flickering taper revealed a treasure room. There were gold statuettes, mostly of cats, set with precious stones; ivory tusks inlaid with spirals of gold and silver lay piled in a heap; plateware and soft leather bags — no doubt filled with coins — seemed scattered everywhere.

Here, then, was his goal. Conan shut the door behind him softly and held the taper high. Past thievery had taught him to take those things most easily converted to ready coin, and, since there seemed to be bags of coins among all the other richery of this room, best he should take advantage of such. Of course, were there jewels filling some of those leathern sacks, why, it would be foolish to bypass them. There was, however, no point in being greedy. A few hundred pieces of gold and a queen's ransom in precious stones should be sufficient for his needs. He suppressed a laugh. A pity he had not brought a cart; so poor was the security, he was certain he could have loaded a wagon and driven away unseen.

The Cimmerian bent to begin examining the potential loot. Here was a bag of gold solons, hefty and fat; there, a small sack of fine emeralds, cut in rectangular fashion. He put the precious green stones into his own purse. The next bag contained perhaps sixty pieces of silver; reluctantly, he discarded these. Too heavy and not enough value, silver, compared to all this other wealth.

Using a large leather pouch, he loaded enough gold coins so that the triple-stitched leather threatened to tear with the weight. It was all the Cimmerian could do to keep from laughing. Not only would he travel to Nemedia in style, he would arrive a rich man. Why, they could hire an army to besiege the magician who held Eldia's sister. Or buy wizards of their own.

As he started to leave, Conan paused. There was a device sitting upon a pedestal of carved ivory near the door; he had missed it upon his entrance. He paused to look at this object. It was of gold, or, perhaps, brass, and resembled nothing so much as a ball within a cube. There was, however, some kind of distortion in the construction; something he could not quite put his finger upon seemed wrong. Because of the position of the device upon the stand, he figured the construction must be quite valuable. He considered taking the object, then shrugged. No, he had enough. A good thief knew when to quit. He turned away.

'A wise choice,' came a male voice. 'Since you obviously do not know what the *storora* is or what it does. It would be wasted upon you.'

Before the voice finished, Conan was already moving. He spun to face the source of the sound, pulling his sword with his right hand, even as he clutched tightly the bag of gold with his left. The taper he had held fell and was extinguished. The room filled with darkness, a tenebrous shroud in which the young Cimmerian could see nothing. Good. If he were blind, then so would his opponent be.

The voice, when it came, was mocking. 'If you think to

lose me so easily, you are mistaken. I see you there, doomed thief.'

Such was unlikely, Conan thought as he marked the position of the voice. He edged towards the speaker, sword leading.

'No, you shall not find me so easily, outlander.' This came from a new position in the room, to Conan's left. He twisted to face it. His eyes had adjusted somewhat to the gloom; there seemed to be a slightly blacker blob against the darkness just ahead, though he could not be certain. The only light came from a crack beneath the closed doorway, and such was only a faint glimmer.

'You must certainly be an outlander,' the man said, 'for no resident of Mornstadinos would be so slackwitted as to try robbing the house of Lemparius.' He had moved again.

Conan considered his options. Here was a man who seemed to move much better in the dark than he had any right to; more, he had managed to sneak up on him without being heard. The young Cimmerian had his loot and had marked the door by the light-bearing gap beneath it. A successful thief is one who escapes with his booty, and that was his purpose. Time to leave.

Conan sprang for the door.

Even as he moved, Conan saw something pass in front of the light, forming two dark thick lines. A man's feet, he reckoned. And, if those feet bore the owner of the voice, they belonged to a man with supernatural speed, to have moved from his former position in that short time. Even as he thought this he swung his sword, to bisect the still-invisible figure. But the feet blocking the light vanished and his blade cut only air.

'You are quick, for a fool,' said the voice. 'Not that such shall save you.'

Conan did not waste his breath in answering. Instead, he waved his sword back and forth as he backed toward the door, whipping the steel so that it sang in the darkness. Let the hidden speaker try to pass that barrier!

Conan reached the door, felt the handle touch his back, and considered his next move. This might be tricky. He dared not turn and expose his back to the man in the blackness. Opening the door with the sack of gold weighing his hand would be difficult, but not impossible. And there was the matter of possible confederates lurking in the hallway, awaiting his exit.

He shook his head. Too much to think about. A man could die of old age worrying about possibilities! He caught the latch, jerked it up, and pulled the door open as he moved away. Then the Cimmerian turned and leaped into the hallway.

And found himself alone. Conan laughed, and began to sprint down the taper-lit hallway. He heard a noise behind him and he glanced back, but saw nothing. He had only to make another turning in the hall and he would be nearly to the storeroom where he had entered the house. Once outside, he would make for the gate; it would be faster than climbing the wall. He was all but free.

He rounded the corner of the hallway, saw what lay before him, and uttered a curse. He slid to a stop, his powerful chest working to pump more air to his lungs.

At the end of the hallway, blocking his exit, stood a dozen men armed with pikes and swords. He would not be leaving that way. He turned and ran back in the direction from which he had only just come. Better to meet the one man from the darkness than a dozen armed troops, he figured. Especially now that he had the lighted hallway on his side. As he rounded the corner again the young Cimmerian noted that the men did not follow him. For some reason this worried him more than if they had.

Standing alone, thirty paces ahead, stood a single figure. The man was tall and blond-haired, with fair skin. In his hand he held only a curved knife, no sword, and he looked too relaxed to be expecting battle.

Briefly, Conan considered running the man down, not slowing, using his sword to sweep the figure aside. Something in the man's demeanor, however, caused the Cimmerian to slow, first to a trot, then a walk. Finally, he stopped three paces away, and stared at the man blocking his escape. There was a danger here, something unnatural, and Conan felt the hairs on his neck prickle and rise as he beheld the man.

'So, you are less stupid than you appear,' the man said. 'Not much, perhaps, but some. Allow me to introduce myself: I am Lemparius, senator, and master of this house you thought to rob. What say you to that, thief?'

'Stand aside,' Conan said, his voice almost a growl. 'I have no particular desire to slay you.'

Lemparius laughed, a high giggle. 'Oh, the richness of this.' He twirled the fang-shaped knife he bore into the air and caught it neatly. He looked at the massive youth's sword disdainfully. 'Come and pass me, outland fool. If you can, you shall live; if not, your corpse will gather flies before the morning sun breaks.'

Conan moved. He leaped at Lemparius, slashing power-fully with his razor-edged broadsword. The sinews of his arms bunched as he swung the steel. Had it connected, the blade would have sheared the senator in half – had it con-nected. The senator moved, catlike, and Conan's strike missed cleanly. With a motion too fast for Conan to accept, Lemparius darted past and laid his curved knife across the bigger man's forearm. It was almost a gentle touch, but it drew blood, a thin line the length of Conan's middle finger. The senator laughed as he stroked Conan with his knife.

Conan swung the weighty sack of gold hard. The move was unexpected by the senator, for the heavy coins slammed into his ribs solidly, knocking him sideways. Lemparius grunted and almost stumbled, but managed to regain his balance. Once again he blocked Conan's exit.

'A good move,' Lemparius said. 'You are quicker than I thought.' With that, Lemparius took a deep breath and let out a piercing whistle.

The sound of sandals on the stone floor began, then in-creased, behind Conan, and the pikemen approached.

'If you have gods, best you make your peace with them,' Lemparius said. 'And quickly.'

The Cimmerian dropped the bag of gold and brought his left hand over to join his right upon the haft of the broadsword. Fast Lemparius might be, but whether he could block with his funny knife a two-handed swing with Conan's full might behind it remained to be seen. Conan lunged forward and chopped at the other man, his sword moving so fast, it was little more than a shiny blur.

Lemparius gave ground. He skittered back, and tried to counterattack once Conan's stroke missed. But Conan's own recovery was too fast, and Lemparius was driven back yet again. Conan began to think he would be able to drive the man before him quickly enough to escape the men rapidly approaching from behind. He moved as a man reaping grain, using short, rapid swings of his sword to push his opponent back.

While taking several of his scurrying steps backward, Lemparius slipped. The senator's feet shot out from under him and he sprawled suddenly, flat upon his back. The look of surprise upon his face at that moment was worth the sack of gold to Conan. He raised his blade.

At that instant his hope of escape was dealt a shattering blow. From the hallway behind Lemparius at least another dozen pike- and swordsmen appeared, running toward the Cimmerian. He was boxed!

Conan turned. The treasure room door was between him and the first group of troops. If he could get there, perhaps he could block the door from inside; perhaps there was another way out. Perhaps not, but he had little choice. If there were no other exit, then he would have more space in which to swing his blade at least. He would take as many of them with him as he could; Crom would appreciate his entry into the gray lands more were he preceded by a dozen or so of his enemies, dispatched there personally by his hand.

'Yield!' one of the pikemen yelled.

'I am Conan of Cimmeria. I yield to no man!'

In the periphery of his sight Conan saw Lemparius scramble back up to his feet. 'Conan?' the senator said. The question caused the big Cimmerian to pause but an instant in wonder. That instant was enough to allow the first of the first group of pikemen to come within jabbing range. As the four-edged pike sought his face he slapped the shaft of

100

the weapon aside with his sword and completed the circular motion in a downward slice. The pikeman screamed as the blade took him. His fellows paused enough to give Conan a chance to leap at the door. The Cimmerian gathered himself to spring.

'Conan! How wonderful!'

Puzzled, Conan half-turned to stare at Lemparius in wonder. His motion allowed him to see the senator swinging the bag of gold Conan had dropped just before that heavy bag crashed into his head.

Blackness reigned.

CHAPTER TWELVE

Conan swam up from the depths of a pulsing red mist; as the mists grew thinner, so his brain grew clearer. When he opened his eyes, the Cimmerian's awareness was full: he lay in utter blackness, surrounded by dank air and some foul stench. For a moment he could not imagine how he had come to such a place; memory returned, however, and the sight of Lemparius swinging the heavy bag of gold came to him.

He took stock. His head throbbed, but allowed him to sit up; his arm bore a small cut, nothing to worry about; his leg was still a bit sore. Carefully, he slid from the hard bench upon which he sat to stand barefooted upon a cold floor. His sword was gone, as was most of his clothing. He wore brief underbreeks, and above that his belt and purse, nothing more. Conan opened the flap of his purse and reached inside. Empty – no, wait, there was something . . . a stone it felt like, trapped in a fold of his pouch. He retrieved the stone and held it close to his face. There was no glimmer of light to sparkle from its contours, but from its shape Conan knew what it was: one of the emeralds must have fallen from the sack he had taken. Whoever had pent him in this Stygian pit had missed the hidden stone when he removed the contents of Conan's pouch.

He returned the emerald to its hiding place and closed the leathern flap again. If he escaped, the jewel would be useful; until then, a sword, dagger, or even a stick would be of more interest.

Exploration of the chamber in which he found himself took but a few moments. Roughly square, the room extended no more than three armspans in either direction. There stood on one end a massive wooden door, bound with strips of rusted iron, judging by touch, securely bolted from without. He found no hinges; therefore, the door opened outward. He set his bare feet as solidly as was possible upon the damp flagstones, and put his big hands against the rough wood. Using all his strength, the powerful Cimmerian shoved.

The door might as well have been the side of a mountain for all it yielded. He backed away so that only the fingertips of one hand remained in contact with the door. He gathered his energies and jumped, slamming into the wooden barrier with his tensed shoulder, itself seeming no softer than the door when he connected. The door remained firm.

Conan took a deep breath, and his fists knotted unbidden into hammers. He was truly captured. He wanted to rage and pound upon the door for release, but he held his temper. Such a display would be foolish, and a waste of strength.

Instead, the brawny Cimmerian walked back to the platform upon which he had but recently awakened. He moved easily now in the darkness, as the dimensions of the cell were graven upon his consciousness. He sat upon the platform and leaned back against the wall, to wait.

The time that passed while Conan waited was but small, no more than an hour. A cavalcade of footsteps echoed down a hallway outside the Cimmerian's cell; moments after he heard them, the door swung open. He held his pose, eyes slitted against the influx of torchlight that splashed into the small room. At least a dozen torches he saw, held by that many well-armed men. It would be foolish to think of attacking them barehanded.

Lemparius the Senator strode into the cell. 'So,' he said, 'you have finally awakened from your swoon. Good. I thought perhaps I might have struck too hard. Not that it matters, after all – it is not your *brain* which endears you to me, Conan of wherever.' Lemparius smiled. 'Is not life strange? I sought to collect you, but you avoided such, dancing away like a flirtatious demi-vierge; now, you have come to me on your own. Find you that not amusing?'

Conan said nothing.

'Oh, dear. I hope I have not struck away your voice with my golden club.'

Conan glared at him. 'So, it was you who sent that pack of cutthroats against me during the windstorm.' It was not a question.

'Indeed.' Lemparius's smile never faltered.

'You should look to your help – they were ill-chosen fools.'

'It matters not, for you are now here, and mine. It is the end which is important, barbar.'

Conan nodded. That was true enough. He still breathed, was still sound of wind and limb; this was not yet ended.

'Surely, you wish to know why I have gone to such lengths to obtain your company?' Lemparius raised an eyebrow.

'Not particularly.' He would not give his tormentor the satisfaction of seeing him curious.

The senator's smile dwindled slightly. 'No? You do not care to know your fate, Conan of Barbaria? To know how you will spend the final moments of your existence?'

Conan measured the distance between himself and the man with a practiced eye. Likely, he could reach him before he was speared by Lemparius's cohort. But the man was devilishly fast; if he could lure Lemparius a step closer, he would have a better chance.

Conan said, 'I care only that the stench of my pen increased tenfold by your entrance, dog. Perhaps it is your diet of dung which offends me.'

Lemparius's smile disappeared, replaced by a scowl. He made as if to step forward toward Conan. The Cimmerian shifted his weight slightly on the bench, preparing himself to move quickly.

Lemparius stopped, and smiled again. 'Ah, am I a half-wit that I would allow myself to be tricked by such a simple ruse? Think again, barbar. And observe.' Lemparius waved his hand. A man came forward, to stand near the senator. Conan had not seen him, previously hidden behind the glare of the torches. The man bore a cocked crossbow, and the barbed head of the quarrel was aimed directly at Conan's heart. Lemparius waved again, and a second man, armed like the first, came to stand on the opposite side. The cell was becoming crowded, Conan thought.

'Dalius here, to my left, is master of the arbalest, the finest marksman in all of Corinthia. He can pin a moving butterfly to a wall at ten paces. At this range I need merely call "left" or "right" and that would be the eye the bolt would skewer, pinning *your* head to the wall behind you.'

Lemparius waited for a moment for that to sink in, then nodded to the second crossbowman. 'Karlinos came to me from Brythunia, where he was the best with his weapon. While not quite the marksman Dalius is, he is second to none other – your remaining eye would be transfixed by his bolt before the first quarrel fully emerged.'

Conan relaxed against the wall. As he did so, he laughed loudly.

That Lemparius had gone to great lengths to capture him alive was apparent. While he knew not what plans the man had for him, he felt certain that death was not among them. Not just yet, anyway.

There came a female voice from behind the ranks of men. 'He is the one.'

With the voice came a scent of an exotic perfume. The smell and voice triggered the memory of where Conan had known them before – in his room at the inn! It was the woman who had bewitched him. By Crom, what was afoot here?

Lemparius turned slightly toward the sound of the woman's voice; Conan saw his chance. He gambled that the crossbowmen would not fire without a direct order. With hard contractions of his powerful frame Conan lunged. He had no real hope of killing Lemparius barehanded before he was clubbed down, but the satisfaction of landing one blow would be worth the effort. So Conan kicked, and the instep of his bare foot flew between Lemparius's legs and smacked solidly into his groin. The man grunted and went dead-white, all Conan had time to see before he was once again sent to the land of throbbing mists.

'– shall cut his heart out myself!'

'Nay, he is mine now; you have given him to me.'

Conan's sight had not yet returned, but his hearing was not lacking. He would have leaped up, save that he realized several things at once. He was no longer on the bench in the stinking cell, but rather on a soft cushion. He might possibly overhear something of use, did they still think him unconscious. And he was bound hand and foot with soft yet tight straps. So the Cimmerian feigned sleep and listened.

'– came you by him?' That was the voice of the woman; Djuvula, the senator had called her.

'Ah, I was . . . approached by a free agent, a scurrilous fellow named Loganaro. He offered to sell me the barbarian for a goodly sum.' That from Lemparius. And that name – where had he heard it? Loganaro . . . ah, yes, the fat man he had met in the nameless inn at the opposite foot of the Karpash Mountains.

Djuvula said, 'Why should he do this? Of what use could a barbar be to you?' Conan could not see the woman's face, but her voice fairly dripped with anger.

'Why, none, normally; however, Loganaro mentioned that you had some interest in such a man. I sought only to detain him for you. As a favor.'

'As a favor. I see. And what might you expect in return for this . . . favor?'

'Dear Djuvula, let us not speak to each other as merchants, of trading this for that. You owe me nothing for this barbarian lout, not a thing.'

There was a pause, in which Conan debated opening his eyes a mere slit. He decided to do so, but this only afforded him a view of some silken pink cushion, which blocked the speakers from his line of sight. He would have to move, and that might not be wise just yet. He strained against his bonds, but they held firm.

Lemparius continued speaking. 'I would have things as they were between us before, dear lady.'

'You know such is impossible. I no longer engage in . . . those kinds of relations with ordinary menfolk.'

'Ah, but I have changed, Djuvula. I am more than I was.'

The woman laughed. 'Surely you do not think my mantology so poor that I would not have noted the addition of your . . . change?'

'Certainly, I meant no such slur upon your powers of divination, dear one. I merely meant that with my enhanced energies, I have a certain . . . vitality I lacked previously.'

Djuvula laughed again. 'Not so much as my Prince, I would wager.'

'Perhaps. On the other hand, there is something to be said for technique over mere staying power, is there not?' Lemparius's voice grew quieter. 'I could keep you satisfied, lady. I know I could, given the chance.'

'I have known such men as you have become, Lemparius. I suspect you boast beyond your capabilities.'

'A chance, then. Surely, you have nothing to lose in granting me an opportunity to demonstrate my . . . capabilities? Should I fail, you would still have the clutter-muscled boy for your simulacrum. And if – nay, "if," but "when"– I succeed, why there will be no need of your Prince.'

Another pause, this time of greater length. Conan sought to shift his body ever so slightly, so that he might see, but the cushion must have been as thick as a horse; it still blocked his vision with its pinkness!

'There is some merit in what you say, Lemparius,' Djuvula said. 'Very well. Demonstrate your newfound prowess.'

'Here? Now?'

'Why not? Your men have battered the barbarian well enough so that he might sleep for a day; if he should wake, I would not be bothered by his watching. Unless you have scruples about such things?'

Lemparius laughed, but it sounded strained to Conan. 'Hardly,' he said. 'All right, then.'

There came a rustle of clothing to Conan's sharp ears; he took the opportunity to shift a bit more on the cushions. Now he could see a bit of high ceiling and a wooden post; likely this post was part of some fancy bed upon which Conan lay trussed. Well, at least his hands were bound in front of his body, where he could get his teeth at the straps. He brought his hands toward his face very carefully and slowly, until the silken bindings were at his lips. He began to gnaw at the material, which tasted of dye. It would take some time to chew through, he knew.

'Set take this cursed barbarian!' Lemparius said loudly.

'Some problem, Lemparius?' Djuvula's voice dripped with the sweetness of a beehive in spring.

'You can see very well there is! I am injured! That oaf kicked me! I – I feel a terrible pain when I try to –'

'A pity,' Djuvula cut in. 'So much for your vitality –'

'Hardly a fair test, Djuvula! You must give me time to recover from my injury!'

'Must I?' The woman laughed. 'Well, I suppose I can wait a few more days before animating my Prince of the Lance. I shall allow three evenings, Lemparius. Perhaps the barbarian can keep me entertained until then.'

'You mock me!'

'Nay, Lemparius. I would not trouble to do so; I merely please myself. The barbarian is a brave man, truly, and it is his heart I will have, living in the chest of my Prince. Meanwhile, I generously give you and him three days.'

Conan had heard enough. He was to be sacrificed in some foul rite of magic! Abruptly, he sat up, and found himself seated on a bed next to a dead or unconscious black-skinned man of heroic proportions.

Lemparius and Djuvula lay on cushions near the bed. Both were unclothed. They turned to stare at Conan.

Conan brought his hands up in front of his face. He took a deep breath and expended it in a deep guttural yell. At the same time the young giant strained against the partially severed bonds on his wrists. Muscles rippled in his shoulders and back; sinews crackled and raised on his arms as he concentrated his entire being upon the straps binding him. Suddenly, the material gave way. There came a muffled snap, and his hands were free.

Lemparius cursed, leaped up, and scrabbled among his clothes for his knife. He found the curved weapon, jerked it from its scabbard, and turned toward the Cimmerian.

Conan grabbed up the silken cushion nearest his hand and flung it at Lemparius. It was soft, the cushion, but solid and thick. The pillow flew past Lemparius's startled slash

108

with the knife and knocked him backward. He stumbled and fell, landing smack upon his bare backside.

Wasting no time, Conan bent and tore the lashing from his ankles. As he finished he looked up, to see Lemparius recovered from his fall, already up and moving.

Conan sprang to meet Lemparius's charge. Fast the man might be, but Conan was not slow; in an eyeblink the Cimmerian locked his powerful hands around the wrists of the senator. Conan turned his hip into the knee thrust at his groin, was met with the senator's hip when he sought to bring his own knee into contact with the man's already-tender scrotal parts. The two men fell, still locked together. Conan was the stronger, he knew, and it would be but a matter of a few moments for him to overcome the other man.

The thin hair of Lemparius's wrists began to writhe under Conan's palms. And some trick of the light made the straining senator seem suddenly plastic-featured; his face seemed somehow to be sinking . . .

Crom! The man was no longer a man, but becoming a great beast! Fangs sprouted from his mouth, claws grew from his hands, and what had been Senator Lemparius now growled and tried to bite off Conan's face!

He cursed and flung the half-man, half-cat away from him, using the thick muscles of his chest and arms to their fullest. The beast flew across the room to slam into the wall.

A werepanther! Conan knew there were men who wore such guises to become wolves, but he had never heard of one who became a cat. He did not like his chances against such an unnatural creature with only his bare hands. And it was said that human weapons could not harm a wereman. It would not have helped if he had a sword, which he did not.

The panther rebounded from the wall and landed upon its feet. It turned and snarled, a throaty roar that sounded all too loud in the closed room. Slowly, the beast began to pad toward Conan. He would swear the cat smiled as it moved.

A weapon, he needed a weapon! Conan looked around

quickly, but there was no – ah, wait! Lemparius's curved knife lay near Conan's bare foot. He bent and snatched up the knife. Armed, he felt better.

'You must not kill him!' Djuvula screamed.

Conan glanced at her, but she spoke to the panther, not to him. The cat ignored the woman's imprecation. But when the Cimmerian extended the wickedly curved knife toward him, the werepanther stopped his forward padding and snarled.

Conan spared a glance from the beast for the knife. Perhaps since this knife belonged to Lemparius, it mght be more than it seemed. He might damage the beast.

With Conan, the thought was oft as the deed; he leaped toward the werepanther, slashing. The beast gave ground even as it struck out with its own sharp claws, batting at him, but missing. The big Cimmerian saw he was within a few steps of the door to the bedchamber. Time to depart. He cut the curved knife through the air to keep the panther at bay as he backed toward the exit. The beast snarled, but would not come close enough to strike.

Conan gained the door, jerked it open, and started through the portal. The cat made a desperate rush then, slashing at the Cimmerian's leg with its right paw. Conan snapped the point of the sicklelike weapon down hard, and buried the tip in the panther's foreleg. The unnatural creature screamed and jerked its foreleg back, laying open the tawny hide in a crimson gash. The panther retreated, screaming continuously, and Conan slammed the brass-bound door upon the sight. He saw nothing to stay him in the hallway in which he found himself, and so he fled, running like a man pursued by demons.

He did not look back.

CHAPTER THIRTEEN

Lemparius had departed to rally his minions. Djuvula sat alone in her chamber, staring at the inert form of her Prince. That she was furious did not begin to describe her black rage. Lemparius was a fool to think his wereman cloak would enhance either his anatomy or performance to majuscule proportions; worse, he had allowed her beautiful barbarian to escape! He would pay for that.

Then there stood the matter of Loganaro, free agent and betrayer. His proffered barbarian and Conan were one and the same, and the fat toad had sold him to her would-be-consort. Now, there was a man who was going to pay for a moron's mistake, and do it twisting slowly as well. The man who had sliced the hand from her demon-brother was without her grasp, and Djuvula needed small excuse to seek a target upon which to spend her anger.

Purple haze smote the air of her chamber within a yellow flash of tainted light. Well, well. Look who chose that moment to arrive.

Djavul bent to avoid hitting his head upon the ceiling. 'Sister,' he grated, 'I sense that you have captured my quarry.'

Djuvula laughed. 'Oh, 'tis hardly better you come late than never, half-brother.'

'Speak clearly, woman!'

'He is escaped, your hand-chopping barbarian. Due to an inept senator who fancies himself a kind of master swordsman.'

'I shall have his skull for a soup bowl!'

'Nay, brother, he belongs to me. And I shall have little trouble in locating our mutual prey, for I have his clothes and sword at my beck. I will cast the proper spells for you to locate him exactly – provided you return him to me before you exact your vengeance.'

'You would bargain with me, sister?'

'Nay, I say again. You may do what you will with the man, so long as I can remove his heart from his still-living form.'

Djavul laughed. 'So, you still seek to make yourself a new toy?' The demon nodded toward the form on Djuvula's bed. 'I could easily summon better from the Depths for you, sister. Why, I would even undertake your pleasures myself – '

'Thank you, no,' Djuvula said. 'I'll not put myself into the thrall of a demon-lover, no matter how adept. The price would be more than I would care to pay.'

Djavul chuckled. 'Aye, were I you, I, too, would likely refuse such an offer; still, there is no harm in trying, is there?'

'I would expect no less of you, brother. But bide a moment; I have spells to produce . . .'

Vitarius looked up, startled, as Conan stormed into the room. 'Where have you been?' the old mage asked. 'We expected you this morning –'

'Never mind, I shall explain later. Are we supplied? Ready to travel?'

'Aye. Eldia and her sister are waiting at the provisioner's; I thought it best to wait here for you –'

'Then let us depart, Vitarius. Now.'

'You have acquired sufficient funds . . .?'

'We must be on our way, old man. No time to tarry. There was some . . . trouble during my venture. It would be best to clear the city gates quickly.'

There were four horses, saddles of fair quality for each animal, and a pack beast tethered at a post in one of the twisted alleys Conan was coming to hate. Eldia and Kinna stood nearby. The older sister had obtained a thick brass-bound staff, her own height in length. It was Kinna who spoke first when she saw the Cimmerian and the White magician approaching.

112

'Conan! Where are your clothes?'

'I was hot,' he replied.

The woman seemed as if she might inquire further, but apparently thought better of it, for she spoke no more. Conan strode past her and into the provisioner's shop.

The owner of the establishment was a swarthy man of small frame, with a gold tooth gleaming in the rays of the afternoon sun, allowed inside by a large window. He exposed the tooth hesitantly at the sight of the big man moving toward him.

'I need a sword,' Conan said, 'something with heft and length. And a cloak.'

'I have a stock of both,' Gold-tooth replied. 'And breeches, tunics, boots –'

'Aye, boots.'

The proprietor led Conan to a second room, filled with supplies. Conan tried on several pairs of boots, but found none large enough. He settled for some thick-soled sandals with leg lashings; they would do well enough, since he was riding and not walking. A well-spun cloak, dyed indigo, was draped over his shoulders, and he nodded. It would suffice. Finally, he chose a sword. He found a double-edged blade as long as the distance between his outstretched fingertips and the middle of his chest. The handle was more ornate than he liked, but the steel seemed sound, and the edges were of sufficient sharpness to shave hair from the back of one hand. He would rather have had his own broadsword, but this one would have to do.

'A wise choice,' Gold-tooth said. 'The steel is of the many-folds variety, brought all the way from Turan –'

'Do you know gems?' Conan asked.

'Why, certainly. I am passing familiar with –'

'Examine this, then.' Conan dug into his belt purse and produced the single emerald remaining from the booty he had attempted to remove from Lemparius's household. He flipped the stone at the man's face.

Gold-tooth deftly picked the jewel from the air. He held it up to the light and squinted at the emerald. From his jacket he produced an eyeglass, and used the instrument to peer at the stone. Conan saw the man's eyes widen at the sight of the emerald.

'Well?'

'It – ah – has some value,' Gold-tooth said. From the way he spoke, Conan thought the man's mouth had gone dry.

'Enough to pay for our supplies?'

The merchant started to smile, stopped, then turned the expression into a frown. 'It – ah – would go some way as payment, yes. Perhaps . . . half, I would think.'

Conan had dealt with men such as Gold-tooth; they would lie to their own mothers without a second thought, especially when matters of money were in question.

'In Zamora,' Conan began, 'such a precious stone would buy a dozen horses and five times the supplies you have furnished.'

Gold-tooth's eyes narrowed, but his voice remained bland. 'Perhaps it is so; however, this is not Zamora. Perhaps I might allow three-quarters of the debt for this – ah – bauble.'

Conan shook his head, and his blue eyes sent a penetrating gaze at the small man. 'I have not the time to play bargaining games with you. You shall have the stone for our supplies; speak no more about it.'

'Oh? It seems to me that I hold the upper hand here, outlander. I can choose not to trade.' Despite his words, he maintained his hold on the emerald, greed showing in his face.

Conan pulled his new sword from its stiff leathern sheath and aimed the point of the blade at Gold-tooth's throat. 'No more of your unctuous babble, merchant! Accept the trade and live. Refuse at your peril!'

'I – ah – have – ah – men I can call!' Gold-tooth's voice trembled. He licked his lips, flashing his tooth at Conan.

'Do,' Conan said. 'Such would make my day. A thick coat of blood upon your stock would no doubt improve its appearance. Call your men.'

Gold-tooth swallowed dryly, and licked his lips again. 'I find that – ah – I am willing to accept the loss on – ah – the trade as you suggest – in the interests of maintaining – ah – good market relations.'

Conan grinned. 'I thought you might see it so.' He turned and walked quickly from the room, his cape flaring behind him. He found Vitarius and the sisters awaiting him.

'Mount,' Conan commanded. 'It is time we departed this rabbit warren.'

Lemparius waved his left arm at his men and yelled loudly in his anger. 'Fifty solons to the man who brings me the barbar! Breathing. And slow torture to the man responsible if the barbarian dies before I see him again.'

A hundred men stared at the senator, nodding. None spoke.

'Go. I will not have him escape!'

The deputies left the courtyard at a double-time pace, accompanied by Lemparius's curses. His left fist clenched tightly, but not his right – that arm was securely bandaged and strapped to his body, protection for the wound which ran from elbow to wrist in length, and to the bone. Had such a wound been inflicted by an ordinary weapon, it would already have been healed; since the cut was made by his own saber-tooth knife, which bore a cat-enchantment, it would fare as any normal man's surgery.

Damn the barbarian! He would learn the meaning of pain once he was returned. Djuvula would have no need of his heart, of that Lemparius was certain – he could fill her needs. But Conan owed him for this injury.

Loganaro was close to panic. The barbarian and his party were leaving, an idiot could see that. How was he to stop them? The thought of facing Lemparius made the fat agent shudder. On the other hand, the idea of trying to stand against the truculent barbarian also had little appeal.

The four mounted their horses as Loganaro watched. By Yama, he could not simply allow them to *leave*! He must delay them somehow, must invent some story that would keep the barbarian in Mornstadinos until he could gather help.

With that thought Loganaro ran forward, mind working frantically. 'Sir,' he called, 'delay a moment! You remember me, don't you? I am Loganaro, we met in the village –' He stopped and gawked at Conan. Two things he noticed at once: the barbarian was pulling his sword – a new blade, from its look – and at his side he carried Lemparius's curved knife, sheathless, through his belt!

Conan stared at the fat man, intending to behead him. But there were people about; somebody might call the deputies, and he had enough to worry about as it was. Then a thought struck him, and Conan smiled. He sheathed his sword, recalling the conversation he had overheard while pretending to be unconscious in the witch's bedchamber. 'Nay, fat one,' he said, 'I shall not spit your carcass on my new steel. That would be too merciful.'

'Y-young sir, what can you mean? I have done you no harm –'

'Through no lack of trying, I'll wager. I see you recognize the knife I carry.'

'N-n-no, I've never seen it –'

'Its former owner is your master, cur. I speak of Lemparius, senator and werepanther.'

'Werepanther?'

'Ah, you did not know this? No matter. He is not your problem, doomed one. There is a woman, a witch –'

'Djuvula!'

Conan smiled. 'Aye, you know of her too. Well that you should, for she wishes to make tripe of your guts.'

'But – but – why?'

'Your former master gave you to her, dog. It seems the lady does not care for your manner of changing alliances. In trying to serve two, you have been abandoned by both.'

'No!'

Conan laughed again. 'Were I you, fat one, I would relocate my business to another city. Or another country. And quickly.'

Loganaro turned and sprinted away, uttering oaths as he

ran. It was one of the funniest things Conan had ever seen, and he laughed so hard, he nearly was unhorsed.

Vitarius said 'I was not aware you knew such a subdolous weasel as Loganaro, Conan.'

Conan's laugh dwindled to a chuckle. 'Only in passing,' he said.

Vitarius led the way through the alleys and back streets toward the west gate of Mornstadinos. Eldia and Kinna followed close behind, and Conan brought up the rear, watching carefully for signs of pursuit. He saw a group of five deputies once, but they were at cross-angles to his path, moving away. Good.

The west gate was unguarded, save by a single man. This one leaned on his pike, engaged in ribald conversation with a dark short-haired trull with a heavily painted face. As Conan rode past the sentry, the man, intent on arguing over the price the woman was asking for her favors, did not even look up.

The sun was past the mid-afternoon point when the four rode unhampered from Mornstadinos. Conan could hardly recall any place he was happier to leave. Weighed against the double-dealing and intrigue of the citizens he had encountered in Mornstadinos, an attack upon a wizard in a magically fortified castle seemed almost an insignificant task.

CHAPTER FOURTEEN

Several hours out of Mornstadinos the party of four stopped to allow their horses rest. Aside from themselves Conan had seen no other travelers: the Corinthian road was empty.

Vitarius drank from a goatskin, splashing wine into his mouth until it dribbled down his chin. He passed the skin to Conan, who filled his own mouth several times, swallowing noisily.

Eldia and Kinna moved toward a thick stand of bushes. Conan called to them. 'Careful.'

Kinna waved the staff she carried. 'Do not worry. I can attend to the rabbits and ground monks with this.'

Vitarius said, 'You had a story you were going to tell.'

'Aye.' Conan began to speak of his recent adventures. Shortly after he had started, the women returned.

When he finished, Kinna shook her head. 'It seems you live a life charmed of the gods, Conan.'

'Perhaps. I do not depend upon gods, however.' He patted his sword with one callused hand. 'Steel is much better. A good sword acts as a man demands, and is as good as the man who wields it. Gods act for their own reasons, and cannot be depended upon in times of danger.'

'Think you that the senator will send pursuit?' Eldia asked.

The Cimmerian shrugged. 'Possible. He has no love for me. If the whoremonger at the gate recalls our passage, Lemparius might well dispatch his minions our way. At the crest of the hill I looked back, but saw no dust along the road. If we are pursued, we have several hours on them.'

Kinna nodded.

'That will likely be the least of our worries,' Vitarius said. 'Sovartus has set certain . . . wards upon the roads leading away from Mornstadinos. We are five days ride from

Dodligia Plain, upon which his foul castle rests. Before then we must pass whatever guards he has posted – not to mention the Bloddolk Forest.'

'Bloddolk Forest?' the young Cimmerian repeated.

'Aye. A place of strange fauna and stranger flora. It lies away from the Corinthian road, to the north, along a side path. We must travel that way to reach Sovartus's domain. Not many men essay to ride that path; of those who do, few return.'

Conan shrugged. The forest was in the future, not something to worry about now. 'Best we resume riding,' he said. 'If men do follow, we are gained upon as we sit.'

The four mounted their horses and moved off.

Djuvula swayed, sweat drenching her naked form. She moaned once, and clenched more tightly the clothing she held. Conan's clothing.

Djavul watched with interest, but without any stirring of carnal passion for the unclothed woman. His interest lay in finding the savage who had wounded him.

Djuvula collapsed. After a moment she arose, breathing deeply. She walked to where she had hung her robe, donned the garment, then turned toward her demon half-brother. 'He rides the Corinthian road,' she said. 'With the girl and the others. They are half a day out.'

Djavul nodded. 'Good. I shall go and find them.'

'Carefully, brother. They are no less than they were the last time you confronted them.'

Djavul waved his injured arm. Already at the stump a new growth could be seen, the outline of tiny fingers. 'I have learned some caution in dealing with the Fire-child. I shall bide my time until an opportune moment presents itself.'

'See that you do. And remember, I want the barbarian's living heart – I care not for what shape the rest of him might be in.'

Djavul grinned; slime dripped from his fangs. 'You shall have it, sister dear. He will hardly have any use for it after I am done with him.'

Djavul vanished amid his booming bruise of color.

Three days after the barbarian's escape from her chamber, Djuvula had a visitor, or, rather, two visitors. One was Lemparius; the other, Loganaro.

The senator shoved the fat man into the room before him. Loganaro's hands were bound, and his pasty face was stained with sweat and fear.

'A present for you, dear one,' Lemparius said.

Djuvula smiled, showing even white teeth. 'Why, Lemparius, how delightful! He's just what I wanted.'

'Ah, good. I thought it might be so. And there is the matter of something I wanted as well, lady.'

Djuvula's smiled increased. 'I recall. What of your . . . injuries?'

'The . . . first is healed. The cut nearly so – I have had it stitched with saber-cat mane hair.'

'Come into my bedchamber, then. Loganaro will wait for us here, won't you?'

Loganaro was too frightened to speak; he merely nodded dumbly.

Djuvula took Lemparius by the arm and led him into her chamber.

A long time passed, it seemed to Loganaro. Small cries occasionally issued forth from the bedchamber, but Loganaro knew these sounds were not those of pain.

After what seemed like years – hours, certainly – the chamber door opened, and Lemparius stumbled out. He looked as if he had been embattled; his face was flushed, his naked form was covered with sweat, and he moved as might a man twice his age. After a moment Djuvula followed the senator into the antechamber. She, too, was nude.

'Come, Lemparius,' she said, 'we have only begun.'

Lemparius shook his head. 'Nay, woman. I am finished. I can do no more.'

'What of your enhancement?' Her voice was as sweet as that of a young virgin nun. Loganaro swallowed dryly. He had no desire to be party to this.

'Do not mock me, woman! No man could do better!'

'You deceive yourself. Many have done so,' Djuvula said. Her voice sharpened a little. She had one fist clenched tightly next to her bare leg.

Lemparius growled. The sound startled Loganaro with its animal overtones.

'In fact,' Djuvula continued, 'I suspect an average eunuch might do nearly as well.'

The senator snarled. 'Witch! You will be sorry!'

Loganaro watched in horror as the man he knew shifted shape, becoming a great tawny cat that lashed its tail rapidly back and forth. The beast faced the woman, roaring.

Loganaro edged toward the exit to the antechamber. His heart pounded as if a maddened drummer worked it.

'So,' Djuvula said, 'you would turn the beast loose upon me, would you?'

The panther advanced a step toward her.

Loganaro sidled closer to the portal. They did not seem to notice him. By Mitra, Yamma, and Set, if he escaped this, he would reform, he would become a priest, he would never do another dishonest thing as long as he lived!

Djuvula raised her clenched fist in front of her face. 'You are a poor loser, Senator. Turn and leave now, and I shall forgive you your ill grace.'

The cat took another step toward the woman and lashed its tail faster. It began to settle into a crouch, preparing to spring.

Loganaro reached the doorway. With his bound hands he caught the latch and lifted it.

Djuvula made a backhand toss at the panther with her fist, opening her fingers as she did so; a fine white powder sprayed from her palm into the face of the animal.

The cat sneezed: once, twice, a third time. It backed away a step and batted at its face with one paw.

'You have just been enspelled, cat-who-was-a-senator,' Djuvula said, laughing. 'I suspected you might try such as this. So now, there are three things you can no longer do: You cannot attack me, you cannot change your form back to that which you were, and you cannot enjoy the company of female panthers, should you manage to find any.' The

121

witch laughed again, the sound deep and throaty and totally amused.

The panther snarled and leaped toward the woman, but seemed to meet an invisible wall two paces from her. It rebounded, recoiled, leaped again, and again hit the same wall.

Djuvula put her hands upon her smooth hips and continued to laugh at the panther.

Loganaro waited no longer. He jerked open the door and ran. For one so portly, he moved faster than he would have believed possible. He did not stop running until he had covered half the distance to the west gate. Then he slowed only long enough to catch his breath before he started running again.

'We'll camp here for the night,' Conan said. Ahead, he could see the edges of the forest Vitarius seemed to dread so. Despite his apparent lack of concern, the Cimmerian himself had no particular desire to camp in there.

The evening gloom was deepening as Conan gathered wood for the fire. He had the feeling he was being watched, no matter that he could see no one regardless of how fast he turned. He had learned to trust his instincts, and so resolved to stay alert.

When he mentioned his feeling to Vitarius, the old man nodded. 'Aye,' he said, 'I feel the prickle of a stare from hidden eyes as you do. It may be nothing, or some animal, but we are close to the forest, and it would be wise to take precautions. I shall mount a small spell, a warning enchantment to surround our camp. If anything larger than a rat tries to approach, we shall know of it.'

Reluctantly, Conan nodded. He could do without any forms of thaumaturgy were it up to him; still, if someone or some*thing* – watched and he could not see it with his own sharp eyes, then it was apt to be more lamialike than natural. One witch was enough; let the magician cast his spell – Conan would sleep lightly with his blade at hand.

Once the fire was blazing he felt better. No animal would

venture close to fire, and the darkness was kept at bay by the dancing flames.

After a cold meal of dried pork and legumes, Vitarius crawled into his blankets and quickly fell asleep. Eldia soon followed, wrapped in her robes and covers close to the fire. She looked much younger as the flickering shadows waved over her face.

Kinna came to sit next to Conan. They stared at the fire quietly for a time, neither of them speaking. He felt the heat and presence of the girl next to him in a way different from the fire's warmth.

Finally, Kinna spoke. 'This is all so strange to me. You are a man of the world; you have seen many adventures. I, on the other hand, have spent nearly all my life as a farmer's daughter, never venturing far from home. Until now.'

Conan looked at the young woman, but said nothing.

'I have never met a man as brave and strong as you, Conan. You risk your life for something that hardly concerns you.'

'Sovartus owes me a horse,' he said. 'And he has bedeviled me and caused me to be attacked by witches and werebeasts. A man settles his debts.'

Kinna laid one hand gently on his hard-muscled shoulder. 'The night of the windstorm, at the inn – do you recall how we were going to inspect your window before we were interrupted?'

Conan smiled. 'Aye, I recall.'

She stroked his bare back under his cloak. 'Perhaps we can inspect it now?'

Conan extended his arm, wrapping Kinna within the folds of his cloak, turning toward her. 'Aye,' he said. 'I think you'll find it ready for your inspection.'

Twenty paces from the ring of orange firelight Djavul snarled softly to himself as he watched the barbarian and the woman. The outer edges of the White One's spell glistened almost invisibly an arm's length away from the demon. To touch the enchanted air would cause noise and light sufficient to arouse the local dead. Djavul gnashed his daggerlike fangs as he glared at the human couple. 'You shall watch me violate her before you die, barbarian human. And you shall beg for the release of death before I am done. Your time is coming.'

The midnight moon shone wanly upon the pair of sleepy guards posted at the sides of the west gate of Mornstadinos. The clear sky threw its starlight upon the scene, joined by the guttering flames of four torches set upon the wall nearby. Sufficient light existed for the two men to see clearly the tawny form of a panther racing up the street toward them. So fast was the animal that the men scarce had time to do more than utter short oaths before the cat shot between them and out through the archway into the darkness.

Later, both men swore they had neither been drinking nor smoking hemp when they saw the panther. Such a beast was a great rarity in these parts, but not altogether unheard of, and none could fault them for having failed to stop it, as unexpected as it was. What both men failed to report was the sight of a long cut along one of the beast's forelegs, a gash that seemed nearly healed – and bound shut with sutures. Upon sincere reflection, the sentries had decided that particular portion of their tale might be best left unsaid.

In the Corinthian night, under the stars and fading moon, the panther who had once been a man ran, moving in a manner that might be called dogged had he been canine instead of feline. He had a goal, this panther, and he moved through his element, the darkness, with only one thought in his more-than-cat mind: murderous revenge upon Conan of Cimmeria.

CHAPTER FIFTEEN

Conan awoke to see Vitarius grinning down at him. Or, rather, at *them*, for Kinna was still wrapped within the folds of the Cimmerian's cloak, asleep next to him.

'Morning,' the old mage said. 'Best we ride early, to clear the forest before nightfall. It is a hard day's journey under the best of conditions.'

Conan nudged Kinna, who smiled in her sleep. 'Later,' she mumbled. 'I'm tired.'

Eldia peered from around Vitarius and laughed.

Conan felt a sense of unease, seeing the girl staring at her sleeping sister. Not precisely embarrassment, but something kin to it. 'Wake, Kinna,' he said gruffly.

Kinna rubbed at her eyes, smiled at Conan, then saw the magician and her sister watching her. She blinked, and came totally from the land of dreams. 'What are you two staring at?' she said. 'You're old enough to have seen men and women asleep together, Vitarius. And as for you, sister, I have no need to explain anything to one raised on a farm, do I?'

'No, Kinna,' Eldia said, giggling. 'No need at all.'

'Then be away and allow me to dress!'

Eldia giggled again, but moved off to tend to her horse. Vitarius began packing his blankets.

Conan and Kinna looked at each other briefly, and each smiled.

There was a dankness within the embrace of the forest, a smell of mold and vegetation that seemed to have lain rotting for a thousand years. The fir trees which were the mainstay of the forest were tall and barked with rough brown slabs like roof shingles; thick mats of brown needles graced the bases of these monsters, keeping the underbrush at bay. Bramble thickets filled the sunnier spots, though few areas were directly touched by the sun. Instead of the freshness Conan usually associated with greenery, a heavy atmosphere of rankness lay about them. No birds sang; no insects buzzed; no small animals darted about. Conan could well see why Vitarius disliked the place, and said so.

'Ah, this is only the fringe,' Vitarius said. 'Deeper into the wood, things truly seem foul.'

Conan suppressed a shudder. It seemed his life was filled with unnatural things of late. He did not like it.

The only sounds were the horses' hooves upon the packed dirt road, and those seemed half-swallowed by the thickening vegetation. The light grew dimmer as the trees closed on the road.

Conan thought he saw a flash of red through the trees, as if something darted between them and then behind a massive trunk thirty paces away. He stared intently, but saw nothing else. His imagination? He was tempted to ride into the wood to look, but decided against it. He would rather clear the forest on the other end by nightfall.

They stopped at midday to rest the horses, eat, and stretch their saddle-weary bodies. The still air was dark, the sunlight prevented from reaching the forest floor by the canopy of thick branches. It was an eerie sensation to know the sun shone brightly at its zenith, but even so could scarcely penetrate the heavy foliage.

Conan's sense of being watched had not abated. 'Stay near,' he ordered the others.

'If my memory serves correctly,' Vitarius said, 'there is a stream not far ahead. We must ford it, as the water crosses our path. It should be no problem this time of year. Earlier, in the spring, it would be a torrent, impossible to cross.'

Conan did not speak. He had again caught a glimpse of red darting among the trees. Enough of this, he decided. He drew his sword.

'What are you about, Conan?' This from Kinna, scratching a spot behind her horse's ear.

'Someone flits along our path,' he said. 'Hidden now in the wood. I would know who he is, and why he follows us.'

Vitarius raised one gnarled hand. 'Put away your blade, Conan. You shall likely see many strange shapes dancing in these woods. For the most part, the inhabitants offer no harm, only curiosity. It would be better to avoid antagonizing them.'

Conan lowered the point of his blade. Perhaps the old man was right. It cost him nothing to allow the wood-dwellers to watch him, so long as they kept their distance. And they would reach the plain by nightfall.

They came to the stream Vitarius remembered within an hour. Fording the rill would be another matter, however. A huge tree had fallen across the path leading to the brook, very near the edge of the water's flux. A man could clamber over the thick-boled trunk easily enough, but a horse could not. They could go around the great length of the tree, of course, but that, too, presented problems.

'This is the only shallow spot for a mile in either direction,' Vitarius said. 'From deposits built up by the bank's curve. A dozen feet on either side, the bank drops sharply. We shall lose time by detouring.'

'Can't we cut through the tree?' Eldia said.

Conan laughed. 'Aye, little sister, we could – if we had axes or long saws. Even so, it would take two strong men the better part of a day to move enough wood for a horse's passage. With my sword I might manage it in a month.'

'I could burn it,' Eldia said.

Conan looked at the girl, then at the old wizard.

The old man shook his head. 'Nay. A natural fire would take days to burn this much wood. And were we to use enough of the Power to do it faster, we might draw unwanted attention to ourselves. There are things attracted to high energies, things I would rather not meet in these woods.'

'What shall we do, then?'

'Go around,' Conan said. 'Unless you are willing to trust the swimming abilities of these horses, which I am loath to do. If we are only a mile from another crossing, we can return to the path opposite the stream within an hour or two, even allowing for the slower going in the woods.'

'That means we must spend the night in the forest,' Vitarius said.

Conan shrugged. There was nothing to be done. But as they passed the root ball of the fallen tree, he noticed the freshness of the moist soil still clinging to the roots. The giant tree had fallen but recently. That seemed somewhat odd, since there had been no storms since they'd left Mornstadinos.

A thirty-minute ride brought the group to a spot where a sandbar could be seen stretching across the stream. The bed was wide, but the water flowed no faster than at the ford by the downed tree. 'Here,' Conan said. He directed his horse toward the water's edge.

'Conan, wait,' Vitarius said. He pointed across the river at a tree that grew near the bank.

Conan looked at the tree. It was oddly shaped, looking more like a thorn bush than a tree for all that it was ten times the height of a man. And the thorns were fair-sized as well. There was some kind of litter on the ground around its base. The Cimmerian squinted, and saw what the litter was: bones. The skeletons of at least half a score animals ranging in size from muskrats to something as large as a big dog. What –?

Vitarius dismounted and removed an empty wineskin from his gear. He waddled to the water's edge and immersed the skin in the flowing stream. Bubbles rose to the surface.

'What are you doing?' Conan asked.

Vitarius rose and capped the skin. He had trouble holding the heavy bag up. 'Can you throw this across the stream to the base of the tree?'

The Cimmerian dismounted and hefted the water-filled bag. 'I think so,' Conan said. 'Why?'

'Do it, and see.'

Conan looked at the old wizard. Had the man lost his senses? He shook his head, but waved Vitarius back to give himself room to swing the bag. What was the old man trying to do? Likely the bag would burst on impact, giving the thorn tree a free drink of water, nothing else.

It was, perhaps, fifteen paces from where Conan stood to the tree. He whirled the rough goatskin around his head, flexing the sinews of his arm and shoulder. With a final hard spin Conan heaved the water container.

The skin seemed to move slowly, almost like a falling leaf. It hit the ground a few feet from the tree, and skidded toward the trunk. The seamstress who had stitched the bag deserved credit, for the bag held firm.

The next thing to happen did not seem to be slow at all. Three branches snapped downward from the tree, as if they were whips plaited of bullock leather. A dozen finger-long thorns stabbed the goatskin like tiny spears, and water sprayed in sudden fountains. When the bag lay drained of its contents moments later, the tree branches snapped away as quickly as they had descended.

Conan turned to Vitarius. There were startled expressions on the faces of Eldia and Kinna; he hoped his own face was less revealing.

'I mentioned that the flora in these woods was strange. Behold the Kiss-of-the-Lance tree – hardly one you would wish to pass unsuspecting, eh?'

'I see how the bones come to be there,' Conan said.

'Movement over the root system triggers the branches to attack. The tree feeds on blood and other fluids from its victims, absorbed by the same roots. The bigger the prey, the more branches it uses to hold the victim.'

Kinna shuddered.

'How are we to pass it?' Conan asked.

Vitarius turned to face Eldia. 'Child?'

The girl nodded. She dug her heels into the side of her horse and started toward the sandbar.

Conan reached for her mount's reins as Kinna said, 'No!'

Vitarius said, 'She is in no danger! Let her go.'

Conan looked up at the mounted child. She nodded. 'He is right. I shall be safe.'

Conan released the animal's reins.

'Conan! No!' Kinna urged her own mount forward, but

Vitarius blocked her path. She had to pull up her horse or run the old man down. 'She is a child! You saw what that – that – thing did to the goatskin –!'

The trio turned to watch as Eldia reached the opposite shore. With the first touch of her animal's hooves upon the ground, the branches of the tree quivered –

– and burst into flame! The whiplike branches, encrusted with long thorns, waved frantically, but this only served to fan the flames higher. The burning wood crackled like fat dropped into a cooking fire.

Vitarius pulled himself up onto his horse. 'A small fire, not much power. I do not think it will notice us now.'

The detour cost them nearly two hours. When the trail became too dark to see, Conan halted the party. He turned to Vitarius, who shook his head. 'We are still better than an hour from the edge of the wood. Too dangerous at night.'

'Then we camp here,' Conan said.

Djavul crouched behind the bole of a tree, watching. He did not doubt that the White One would set his magical wards again. The way to avoid being detected by the spell was simple enough: he must be inside the perimeter when the mage cast the spell. On the road before, or in the plains after, that would be impossible without being seen. But here in the heavy woods it could be done if done carefully. That was why he had felled the tree. His quarry, the girl and the barbarian, were delayed long enough so that night caught them in the forest.

Moving with a stealth he was unused to, Djavul edged closer to the path. He was, he knew, nearly invisible in the darkness, but he still took care to move as quietly as possible. It was hard; demons had little reason to learn how to creep. This time, however, it was important that he avoid being detected. He was careful. No sticks snapped under his massive horny feet; no branches ruffled loudly as he passed. It took him nearly an hour to move but a few paces. When he was done, Djavul was within two leaps of the man he had sworn to kill.

*

'My spell is cast,' Vitarius said. 'We can rest easily now.'

Conan nodded, but he still distrusted any form of magic. He laid his bare blade next to where Kinna had placed their blankets. When the young woman came into his embrace under the wool shelter, however, Conan ceased to think about the dangers of the forest.

It was smell, not sight or sound, that awakened him. The stink of hellspawn filled his sensitive nostrils. Instantly, he knew that the demon he had faced before had somehow found them. Conan's eyes flicked open, and he reached for his sword.

'Looking for something?' The metallic grate of the demon's voice was close, almost on top of Conan. He rolled from the blankets and came up, to see the giant red demon standing not two paces away. And the demon held his sword.

Behind him Kinna stirred. 'Conan? What is it?'

Djavul grinned at the Cimmerian. He mocked the woman in his deep rasp: '"Conan? What is it?"' Djavul tossed Conan's sword into the night. The fire had burned down some, but there was still sufficient light for Conan to see his enemy well. 'I am death, Conan, come for you. Not immediately, of course. I have some little entertainments for you first.'

Kinna sat up. Conan gave her only the smallest bit of his attention. His sword was gone, but there was the curved knife of Lemparius back near his blankets. If he could get to it –

'Conan! Where is Eldia?'

Conan spared a glance at the girl's blankets. Empty.

Djavul's toothy grin increased. 'I have moved her. It would not do that she and the old White One should splash her Fire upon me before I have a chance to finish my business.'

Vitarius stirred. 'What is – oh!'

'Come, wasp,' Djavul said. 'Grapple with me so that I might tear an arm or leg from you for my breakfast!'

Conan dived for his blankets and seized the knife. He rolled up, clutching the steel fang, to face Djavul.

'Your stinger has shrunk, wasp.' Djavul laughed. 'Come and match it against my one hand.' Djavul's nails flicked back and forth in the firelight like small daggers.

Conan edged forward.

Djavul leaped. He grabbed Conan's knife hand with his own remaining hand and wrapped his other arm around the barbarian's back. Conan felt the stump of the demon's wrist batter his spine. He drove his knee at the demon's groin, but hit the rock-solid flesh of a mighty red thigh instead. The two tumbled to the ground, locked together like wrestlers.

As strong as he was, Conan felt like a child in Djavul's embrace. The knife was wrenched from his grip and flew into the darkness. A moment later Djavul tossed the big youth away as a man might toss a loaf of moldy bread. The Cimmerian hit the ground hard, his wind knocked from him.

Djavul leaped the intervening distance to tower over Conan. 'You make it too easy, wasp!' He bent over, reaching for Conan.

The Cimmerian saw Kinna then, swinging her staff. The heavy wood, as thick as her wrist, whistled in the night air. She smashed the rod across Djavul's back at kidney level. The brass-bound staff splintered and cracked, so hard did she wield it. The impact brought a grunt from Djavul, but only staggered him. He turned, swinging his open hand. He hit Kinna on the shoulder, knocking her flying.

Conan regained his feet. At the same instant he heard Vitarius yell. 'Conan! Catch!' The white-haired wizard tossed something at the younger man.

Conan twisted, expecting to see a knife glittering in the firelight. What he snatched from the air was no blade, however. It felt like grease over crackly parchment, both stretched over wood. It had several points on one end, like small daggers. In an instant Conan recognized what he held: Djavul's severed hand!

Then the demon spun to face Conan. Firelight reflected from his white fangs, and slime dripped from his open mouth as he reached to grab the man. He must have expected the man to back away, but the Cimmerian did the opposite. He lunged at the monster. He had one chance, and he used it. He gripped the severed hand like a sword, and, with all his strength, he jabbed the taloned fingers at the face of their former owner.

The partially mummified fingers were spread. The forefinger and middle finger stabbed into Djavul's eyes and sank in to the third joint.

The demon screamed, a sound that shattered the night air. Conan's ears rang, deafened, as Djavul staggered back, clutching his dead hand with his remaining live one. He tugged at the instrument of his torture, but it now seemed a part of his face, immovable. The demon dropped to his knees, still screaming. A strange crackling orange light surrounded his face. As Conan watched, the light expanded to cover Djavul's entire form. When the light had bathed the demon from head to toe, it stopped abruptly, winking out. Djavul fell over backward. His body ran like heated wax, losing form, then bubbled into a puddle of redness that spread over the fir needles, until, at last, nothing remained of him save a damp spot on the ground.

In Castle Slott a pentagram sketched exactingly upon the flagstones of a certain chamber suddenly flared into orange flame. When the flames vanished, so did the pentagram.

In Mornstadinos, in her bedchamber, Djuvula the Witch bolted upright from a dreamless sleep, her eyes wide. She screamed, but it was a wasted effort. Her brother was no more.

CHAPTER SIXTEEN

By the light of the rekindled fire Conan sat with Vitarıus, Kinna, and the returned Eldia. The girl had been moved only a short way from the place where she had lain – still within the warding spell set by the old magician.

'He must have been very close to us when I cast the enchantment,' Vitarius said. 'The magic has not been disturbed.'

More than Conan could say for himself. 'What happened to him?' He glanced toward the damp spot that had been Djavul.

'Because I am of the White, the demon knew I could not use his name against him. But flesh of his flesh was, as it turned out, a more potent weapon.'

Kinna said, 'How did you know what it would do?'

Vitarius shook his head. 'I did not know. The White Square does not teach such things. But I had heard rumors; one learns something of the opposition if one lives long enough. I came across an old parchment some years ago, a page from some larger work that had been mostly burned by some wise soul. On this page it was written that flesh taken from a demon will rejoin its owner, can it be brought into contact with him again. Had Conan fitted the dead hand back to its wrist, I suspect the demon would once again have become whole. Apparently, however, the flesh of demons is not very discriminating – the hand adhered to the first portion of the devil it touched.'

Kinna shuddered. 'You mean the hand took root in the fiend's very face?'

'So it would seem. And since the eyes were a most unnatural place for it to be, the old hand killed him.'

'A fitting death,' Conan said. 'I shall sleep better, knowing I am no longer dogged by hellspawn.'

Near the edge of the Corinthian road, Loganaro the free agent slept fitfully. Coldness wrapped him, chilling him to his depths despite his overlay of fat. He had no blanket; neither had he supplies, having left Mornstadinos in a great hurry. He had managed to gnaw the bonds from his wrists, but other than the clothing he wore, he carried nothing.

Something unseen woke the fat man. He listened carefully as he peered into the darkness, but the only sound was of some distant night bird calling to its mate. Night sounds, nothing more. This far from Mornstadinos, he should have nothing to worry about. He was safe.

He relaxed somewhat. Nothing to fear. True, he was used to better accommodations when he traveled, but this setback was merely temporary at worst. He had contacts in many of the Corinthian city-states, even in several of the small kingdoms to the south. In no time at all he would be able to connive someone into furnishing him with a mount and supplies. After that he could quickly reach one of his caches of wealth, of which there were a fair number, in various places.

Mornstadinos might be the Jewel of Corinthia, but it was not the only city. He might travel to Nemedia, or Ophir, perhaps even Koth. He was well-connected in all of those places.

Of his hasty promise to become honest and even priestlike, Loganaro thought not at all, save to smile at such foolishness. One called upon the gods only in moments of great need. Should the gods answer that need, why, that was their concern, not his. He had made bargains such as that a dozen times, and each had been broken quickly thereafter. The gods were either forgiving, or disinterested in oathbreakers, in Loganaro's experience. A man did what he had to at the time. After that, well, things changed as often as the wind. What mattered was that he was alive and free to return to his less-than-honest-and-honourable ways. To hell with the gods.

The small grin on Loganaro's face faded slowly as he slipped back into sleep, lulled by the distant birdcalls.

Upon the starlit road a tawny shape ran. Dawn neared, presaged by its false brother, so darkness lay thickly over the western road from Mornstadinos. Only the breathing of the panther could be heard, and that breathing was tired.

Too, the panther was hungry. He had been running since he'd left the city, stopping only to rest for short periods, and to take a rabbit once, and later, a small ground monk. Hardly enough fare for a wildcat, much less such a large panther as was this one. Revenge fueled him, but revenge was not such a nourishing dish as warm flesh and hot blood.

As if some benevolent god had heard his wish, the panther suddenly caught the scent of living meat. *There*, just ahead, leaning against *that* tree. The cat slowed, and began his stalk, dropping his belly closer to the ground, moving more purposefully.

The meat slept. Good. That would make things easier. He could go for the throat and suffocate the prey. If the man tried to resist, the panther could rake open his victim's belly with his hind claws, and disembowel him.

The cat moved with all the stealth he had, silently as a ghost, but something startled the meat. Some inner sense, perhaps, warned him of his impending doom. His eyes snapped open and he tried to scramble to his feet. He yelled. 'No! Not you! Gods, forgive me, I will keep my vow, I will keep it, I swear!'

The cat who had been a man grinned, revealing his long fangs. Well, well. How appropriate this was! That his dinner should be this fat and treacherous fool. Most appropriate, he thought as he gathered himself to spring.

In the night the bird that had called to its mate suddenly went silent.

Once again quiet ruled.

Quiet, save for the sound of a great hungry cat rending its prey.

*

With the trees of the Bloddolk Forest behind him, Conan felt much better. Here lay a vast plain, dotted here and there by buttes and rocky ridges, but mostly flat and bare. This was more to his liking; a man could see danger for a long way, could prepare himself to meet it properly. Nothing would skulk to within a few paces under the cover of god-cursed trees and underbrush.

Ahead of him Vitarius and Eldia rode side by side, talking quietly. Just behind them Kinna's horse walked. Occasionally, the young woman would look over her shoulder and smile at Conan. He minded this not at all, for she was a woman of beauty and no small lusty temperament. The tension that had ridden Conan since his first encounter with the witch no longer troubled him in any way. He grinned, and hurried his horse a bit so that he rode closer to the others.

'Ho, Vitarius,' Conan said, 'perhaps a stop for breakfast might be in order. Now that we are shut of that cursed wood.'

'We should consider ourselves covered with good fortune,' Vitarius said. 'That we survived our passage unscathed.'

'Good fortune? That we were nearly spitted by a perverse plant and gobbled up by a giant red demon?'

'Our trip was mild compared to some. At least we survived to tell the tale.'

Conan nodded. The old mage had a point.

The four reined their mounts to a stop and unpacked dried meats and leathery strips of fruit, upon which they broke their fast. Between bites Conan mentioned to Vitarius how much he preferred this kind of terrain to that which they had just left.

Vitarius nodded, chewing thoughtfully on a brownish glob of some water-leached fruit. 'Aye, under most circumstances I would agree. But this is Dodligia Plain, and not as safe as it appears at the moment. A half-day's ride will bring us within sight of Castle Slott – it is another full day from there. And on the plains surrounding such a wicked place, there will be obstacles. I suspect the only reason we have not encountered wardens such as those you met upon entering Corinthia is because we travel towards Sovartus. He would hardly expect the flies to proceed directly to his web.'

The old man took another bite of fruit. 'But rest assured, Sovartus is not one to leave his castle unguarded even if he does not expect us in particular. He has created a few enemies for himself: more than one man would see Sovartus swinging upon the gibbet. And the line to spit on his corpse would stretch to the horizon.'

'I would lead such a line,' Eldia said, looking grim for one so young.

'Aye,' Conan said, 'and I would be near the front so as to collect my horse before all the spoils were gone!' He laughed.

Vitarius frowned. 'Better you should save your jests until after we accomplish our mission. Sovartus does not amuse easily, from my recollections, and once we sight the castle, we must assume the very ground to have ears.'

Conan turned his head away from Vitarius and cupped his hands around his mouth. 'See that you have my horse ready for my arrival!' he yelled. He turned back toward the trio watching him and smiled, his eyes full of blue fire.

No one smiled back at him.

As the sun passed midway over the land on its journey to night, the four came within sight of a far peak. An odd mountain, Conan thought, for it stood alone like a cone upon a table, without foothills or buttes near it. And the peak of the mountain was even more oddly shaped, jutting out so that it was somewhat wider above a pinched neck, like some distorted hourglass.

'Castle Slott,' Vitarius said.

Conan blinked in disbelief. 'That mountain?'

'Much of it. The rock is shot through with caves, most of which interconnect. That flare you see at the top is not natural; it was made by men and by magic. From here it appears small; closer you can see that the tip of Castle Slott is ten times as large as the largest palace in Mornstadinos.

And the top levels are linked to the tunnels below. Properly provisioned, a man could wander for years within the castle-mountain and never retrace his steps.

'From here on,' Vitarius continued, 'we must be on our guard.'

Conan stared at the castle. His earlier enthusiasm quickly waned as he contemplated the awesome construction.

Djuvula supervised the loading of her Prince of the Lance onto her wagon. The wagon was constructed of a sturdy wooden frame, with a square tent of heavy canvas stretched over hoops of steamed and bent ironwood.

'Careful there, buffoon! If you drop that case, I shall shrivel your manhood!'

The workman's eyes widened, and he moved more gingerly.

Djuvula turned away and went to finish packing her trunk of potions and powders.

As she carefully padded certain fragile glass balls full of brightly colored chemicals, once again the sorceress shook her head. She desired not this journey, but no help existed to save her from it. Djavul was dead; and, while there could be many reasons why, Djuvula knew in her own mind that her demon-brother must have met his fate at the hands of the barbarian, the old wizard, and the girl of Fire. Thus, revenge was added to her motives for wanting the man and girl. Revenge itself stirred her but little, though. Her relationship with Djavul had been based more on mutual self-satisfaction than on any true feelings; still, he had been kin. A point against her quarry.

With the expected failure of Lemparius as master swordsman of the bedchamber, it became more important to retrieve Conan for her Prince. And, of course, there stood the matter of the girl, possession of whom would buy her favor from Sovartus. Now that Djavul was dead, she would need a patron more than before. For all these reasons Djuvula knew she must follow the barbarian and the girl he protected.

She smiled. Fortunately, she would not have to ride the

Corinthian road for long. She had in her possession a powerful spell, taught her by Djavul, which would allow the caster to travel the in-between lands. A few hours ride on that hellish road would be worth as many days travel on any highway in Corinthia.

True, such travel was not without risk even for a witch of considerable power; there were things that existed in the in-between lands that would bring terror to the eyes of a demon, much less a mortal woman. Unwary travelers under the gray sun could die a thousand deaths in a thousand horrible ways. Djuvula had made other journeys on that route, however. She was cautious; and, because of their head start, the risk must be taken if she were to catch her quarry.

She smiled at the thought and continued to pack her magical gear.

Near dusk Conan saw a new menace. One moment the plain to the Cimmerian's left stood empty for as far as the eye could behold. The next moment a creature stood not twenty paces away. The thing was taller than Conan by a foot, and it looked like nothing so much as a very large dog standing upon its hind legs. The hind feet differed in shape from a dog's or wolf's, being more manlike, and the forepaws seemed more apish than canine, but otherwise it was doglike. The ears were pointed, the snout long and the muzzle filled with sharp teeth, and the nose was black, with twin nostrils.

Conan had no more time than to turn toward Vitarius and utter a curse, when the beast vanished. It was there, then it was not   dematerialized into the dusky air.

Vitarius turned. Conan quickly described the apparition.

The old mage nodded. 'A demi-whelf,' he said. 'A beast of Earth, and thus controlled by Sovartus – through Eldia's sibling.'

'They are magic, to disappear so?'

'No. They live under the ground, in tunnels. The one you saw needed merely step into a concealed entrance to drop from sight.'

'Ah.' That made Conan feel better. Beasts, controlled by wizards or not, could be fought with steel.

'No doubt Sovartus shall shortly know we are here,' Vitarius said. 'Best we continue moving; as like as not, the ground here is honeycombed with the whelves' tunnels.'

The Cimmerian nodded. 'What are they likely to do?'

Vitarius shrugged, his thin shoulders denting his robe slightly from within. 'They must certainly contact their master somehow. A runner, perhaps, if not by some magical means. While demi-whelves have not the keenest eyesight, that one was close enough to observe us and give a description. I have no doubt that Sovartus is by this time aware of our presence.'

'What will he do, then?' Kinna asked.

The old man shook his head. 'I know not. We proceed toward his lair. He can attack us now, or, perhaps, only await our arrival.'

'Then our advantage of surprise is gone,' Conan said.

'I had not counted greatly upon it,' Vitarius replied.

'Perhaps you should reveal your plan, then, magician.' Conan had not cared for the sight of the demi-whelf.

'When we arrive in the vicinity of the castle, I shall create a magical diversion of sufficient power and agitation to warrant Sovartus's attention. While he is thus occupied, you need merely enter the castle, locate the children, and free them.'

'*That* is your plan?' Conan shook his head. 'I am to scale a giant mountain, enter a castle, search perhaps thousands of rooms until I find our quarry, defeat the forces that might be mounted by a powerful wizard inside as guards, and return with three children?'

'That is my plan, yes.'

'Ah. And here I had thought there might be some difficulty in this undertaking. How foolish of me! It will be simple!'

'Sarcasm does not become you, Conan. I am open to better suggestions.'

The Cimmerian shook his head again. 'Nay, your plan suits me well enough.' He touched the hilt of his sword. 'I would rather rely on my blade than on complicated posturings in any event.'

'I shall go with you,' Kinna said.

Conan chuckled. 'Nay. I said before I work better alone.'

Kinna bristled. 'You would take me were I a man!'

'I would not take you were you a tame dragon trained to belch fire at my command. I work best alone; I have always done so. And I am most glad that you are a woman, Kinna. I would have you be nothing else.'

Conan could see the anger on her face war with another emotion. After a moment she smiled. 'Yes. I, too, am glad to be a woman, Conan.'

The in-between lands were never peaceful, at least during those times when Djuvula had traveled them. In two directions, the south and east, storms raged, spewing forth lightning and thunder; where she was the atmosphere seemed charged with some elemental force, so that the air swam with countless small motes, all dancing madly. The in-between lands twisted straight lines into curves and waves, made corners less than square, and surrounded every object with a fuzz of its own light – a total, encompassing delusion.

As Djuvula urged onward the frightened horses pulling her wagon, something dark flew across her path, gibbering loudly. The horses started and would have turned had she not used her whip. Despite blinders and a calming spell laid upon them, the horses were always skittish. Perhaps they somehow felt the danger that had once claimed one of their number while pulling Djuvula's wagon. That time, only Djavul had saved her from the fate of the horse, the filling of some monstrous thing's bloated belly.

Djuvula shuddered. She wished very much that Djavul still lived and was seated next to her now.

By her estimate she would need travel this hellish road only another ten minutes to emerge into her own world again. And ahead of her quarry. She already had her plans for handling the wizard and barbarian. If nothing went agley.

Even as she thought this, Djuvula saw a ripple in the

landscape ahead of her. The ground flowed upward in a pulsing mound as a wave swells in a storm. The earth split with a wrenching sound, as if giant nails were being pulled from solid wood. A cave filled with pointed stone teeth suddenly yawned before the sorceress. That this earth-demon would devour her, horses, wagon, and all, she doubted not at all.

The animals pulling her wagon needed no urging to turn aside. Djuvula allowed them to tow the wagon away from the road monster, then quickly pulled them to a stop. To travel away from the safety of the road would be folly of the highest order. Despite her desire to arrive in the real world ahead of the party she sought, she decided to leave the in-between lands. That the road monster somehow traveled toward her, moving like a wave in water, hastened her decision. She intoned the words of the spell quickly but carefully. The swimming air seemed to dance faster, and an actinic flash lit the scene . . .

She found herself on a small road on the edge of a dank-looking wood. Quickly, she determined that she had arrived at the northern limit of the Bloddolk Forest; a further working of her location spell, using Conan's clothing, showed that the barbarian lay ahead of her, at least half a day's journey. Damn! She would have to enchant the horses so they could run all night to catch up to them. Unless she wanted to risk the in-between lands again. The memory of the cave-mouthed monster drove that thought away in a hurry.

The witch laid the lash alongside the ear of the lead horse with a *pop*! and the horses moved. One of them snorted and tossed his head, looking nervous. Djuvula looked in the direction of his attention.

Sleeping in the crook of a twisted hardwood tree lay a panther. Djuvula cursed the horse. 'Fool animal, after what you have just seen on the highway through hell, you fear a sleeping beast?' She stung the horse's rump with the whip, and the animal went back to his job. The wagon moved away from the twisted tree and the sleeping cat.

Of the panther, once out of sight, Djuvula thought no more.

CHAPTER SEVENTEEN

The camp was laid, the fire banked, and Vitarius set his magical wards once again. Conan had just dozed into a light sleep next to Kinna when he was jerked from slumber by a terrible cacophony around him.

It sounded to the Cimmerian as if the world were ending: a blast of noise smote his ears, louder even than the screams of the slain demon, Djavul. With the screeching came also a flashing of light, multicolored and blindingly bright. It took but a moment for him to realize what had happened: something had entangled itself in Vitarius's magic spell.

Conan rolled from his bed, snatched up his sword, and came to his feet in a single fluid motion. The night sky was cloudy, but the splashes of light from the spell were sufficient to see all too well: the demi-whelves had attacked.

Vitarius untangled himself from his bedding and moved for Eldia, who was scrambling up with her own short sword held ready. Kinna had Conan's curved knife and was on her feet as Conan ran to meet the first whelf to enter the campsite. Muscles rippled under dark fur as the beast lunged at Conan, fangs bared to tear out his throat.

Those same fangs clacked shut in a final horror as Conan cleaved the head holding them from the whelf's neck with a single stroke of his night-cooled steel. Without pausing, the Cimmerian turned lightly on the balls of his feet to face another leaping wolf. This one spitted itself on the point of Conan's sword, howling wolfishly as it fell.

Unfortunately, the dying demi-whelf took Conan's blade down with him, twisting so hard that the handle was pulled from the Cimmerian's powerful grasp. Conan cursed, and bent to retrieve the embedded sword; as he did, a third whelf, attacking from the rear, missed its intended grab-

and-bite aimed at Conan's neck. The whelf hit the man instead with its skinny legs, tripped, and flew over Conan in a lopsided flip, landing upon its back on the hard ground.

Conan pulled on his sword, but the weight of the dead whelf held the blood-warmed steel fast. The beast that had smacked into the ground began to rise.

The Cimmerian abandoned his task, turning instead to face the third attacker. He growled, to match the voice of the demi-whelf. As the beast set itself to spring, however, it was suddenly distracted. The whelf's attention upon Conan faltered for two reasons: Eldia's small sword stabbed into its rump as Kinna's knife slashed its opposite leg to the bone. The beast howled.

Conan leaped and drove a hammerlike fist between the whelf's eyes. The creature dropped as might a sack of grain, its consciousness knocked from it.

Conan did not pause, but leaped back to retrieve his sword. With one foot against the downed whelf he wrenched his blade free.

Vitarius, at this point, managed to reach Eldia. The old mage put one hand upon the girl's head as the words of some magical chant rose against the din of the warding spell.

Conan had no more time to watch, then, as a phalanx of whelves suddenly breached the camp's perimeter and charged toward the human occupants. He grinned, and ran to meet the new threat, slinging from his sword the gore of their downed comrades at the new arrivals as he moved.

The tight formation of whelves scattered at the sound and sight of Conan's whistling blade. The beasts were fast, but they stumbled over each other in their haste to reposition themselves, being too many in too small a space. One moved too slowly from the Cimmerian's reach, and so became a kind of limb-brother to the destroyed demon, Djavul.

A flash of supernal blue light came then in a tight beam that speared first one whelf, then a second and third. Thick smoke and steam erupted from the lupiform beasts as the light touched them, the beam moving like some supernatural spear. Eldia.

The remaining whelves scattered, baying in fear. Conan turned in time to see a shadowy form come up behind Vitarius and Eldia. The Cimmerian yelled and sprinted for them, but even he could not move fast enough. A clubbed and apelike fist smote the old man above one ear, and he crumpled. The contact between the wizard and the girl of Fire thus broken, the blue flame died abruptly, winking out like a snuffed candle. The afterglow filled Conan's eyes as he ran for the attacker, who bent to grab Eldia. The girl whipped her small blade up, and the whelf leaped back a step.

The short delay was enough; Conan thundered across the ground, not bothering to slow as he barreled into the whelf. The big man's shoulder smashed against the beast's chest, knocking it from its feet. The Cimmerian followed, lifted his sword, and brought it down hard. This one would trouble them no more.

Conan spun, to see Vitarius trying to stand. Quickly, he moved to help the old man to his feet.

The wizard was stunned. 'What – what happened?'

'You were struck from the rear. I killed it.'

Vitarius shook his head. 'The whelves . . .?'

'Dead, mostly, or gone. I see none moving.'

The older man nodded, then looked about in sudden fear. 'Eldia! And Kinna! Where are they?'

Conan looked around quickly. Of the two sisters there was no sign.

In the high reaches of Castle Slott, Sovartus of the Black Square laughed maniacally in triumph. She was his! His enthralled whelves had her! Only moments before, a raven had come, bearing the message from the ruler of the demi-whelves. Even now, the girl of Fire was en route, traveling through the underground network of tunnels built by a hundred generations of the earth-dwelling lupines.

Sovartus stood in a bare tower room, festooned with loops of dust-laden spider silk. The room had not been used for years, but the dark stains upon the slatted wood floor testified to its grisly former purpose. This was the topmost enclosed space in the castle, a circular room with windows facing each of the four directions. It would be here that Sovartus would compound the Elements and create the most potent magic seen since before the sinking of Atlantis.

He strolled slowly about the perimeter of the tower, pausing to look through each arched window. He grinned. Soon each window would hold framed a view of a single Element: to the east would dance great winds; to the west, the earth itself would roil; to the north, storms would pour forth a deluge; and to the south – ah – finally, to the south would burn a pillar of fire, warm enough to scorch the dwellers of Hell itself. When the Elements were in place, then would he, Sovartus of the Black Square, command them to join; then would be born the Thing of Power.

Ah, yes, then would the Four meld and blend to become more than they had ever been. The idea, the *forestallning*, would be the conception and birth, the *befruktning*. And the world would tremble before it – and the man who mastered it.

Sovartus laughed again and clapped his hands. Immediately, a pair of black-robed and cowled figures entered the room and bowed low. Their faces were invisible within the shadows of their hoods, and they spoke not, but bowed again to the wizard.

'Fetch the Three,' Sovartus commanded. 'And have my talisman table and accoutrements brought here. And my robe of virgin's hair.'

The figures in black bowed low again and scurried from the tower, leaving Sovartus alone. When they had gone, the magician stared at the stains upon the floor. Soon, he thought, soon the cities of men would resemble that dark spot, did they not offer up to him total obeisance. The name of Sovartus would inflict fear and respect upon every man and woman hearing it, soon. Soon.

Conan found the bloody knife lying near a hole in the ground. He picked it up and hefted it. The same knife he had taken from Lemparius the wereman, the same he had last seen Kinna wielding against the demi-whelves. He stared

147

at the hole, which angled into the earth wide enough so that a man could slide into it easily.

Vitarius came to stand next to him. 'One of the entrances to the whelves' tunnels. They have taken the sisters underground.'

Conan nodded, then made as if to enter the hole.

Vitarius touched the younger man's shoulder with one bony hand. 'Nay, Conan. Crom may live inside a mountain, but this land belongs to the whelves. You would not find them in the darkness under the earth. Besides, likely they are a far distance away by now, heading for the castle.'

Conan turned away from the entrance to the demi-whelves' domain. 'Then we must ride for the castle ourselves. They must cover the same distance, tunnel or no, and if we hurry, perhaps we can arrive before Sovartus takes them.'

'It is dark,' Vitarius said. 'In the morning –'

'I do not fear the dark,' the Cimmerian said. 'If the beasts below are moving, so must we. If you would rather remain behind, I will go alone –'

'Nay,' Vitarius said. 'I shall accompany you.'

The two men started for their horses.

The wagon of Djuvula the Witch lay under a shroud of magically induced blackness, invisible to normal eyes beyond a few feet. The fire-haired woman stood nearby, watching Conan and the mage of the White Square mount their horses. She cursed softly as the men rode away, angry with the fates for delaying her transit.

What had happened was all too apparent, from the corpses of the demi-whelves scattered about. There had been an attack, and the girl of Fire now belonged to the beasts of the ground, and therefore shortly to Sovartus. Ah, to have come so close, only to be thwarted!

Djuvula considered her options. She could still have the heart of the barbarian, no small comfort. And, possibly, she might still somehow bask in the glow of Sovartus's victory; he was, after all, a man, and prey to the same desires as all men not infirm or perverted. Sovartus was known to be many things, but a lover of boys was not among them, so

Djuvula had heard. And she doubted not her skills in that arena.

Yes. Best to continue onward. She returned to the wagon and climbed onto the driver's bench.

In the darkness, hidden by a dry and sparse bush soon to become a tumbleweed, the panther who had been a man watched the woman who was a witch mount her shrouded wagon and depart. A normal cat's eyes were sharp in the night, and this particular cat had vision far better than normal in addition to a mind belonging to a man. True, the brain was going savage, so that in time the panther would be no more than a beast; still, there remained a strong gleam of manlike intelligence ruling the animal. And that intelligence had just seen its two greatest enemies depart.

There seemed hardly any choice but to follow. The witch he could not attack directly, but there might be some way to cause her downfall. The barbarian was but a man, and even with a magical knife he could be surprised and taken.

For the first time since he had become a panther for life, Lemparius felt a surge of pure happiness.

The cold dish of vengeance grew warmer.

In the highest tower of Castle Slott preparations were being made. Black-robed and cowled figures moved around the room, attending to the desires of Sovartus. Under three of the room's four windows, two sons and a daughter of Hogistum had been chained. Three of the Four Elements were present, the last due soon.

Sovartus moved away from the fourth window, where he had been watching the quiet plain of Dodligia. The formerly agitated Elements now stood quiet, almost as if in anticipation of Sovartus's final victory. No breeze stirred; no ground trembled; no rain fell.

The talisman table stood in the center of the room, a square shape covered with carven symbols and resting on four gargoyle feet. Each quad-clawed foot clenched a square gem; these were black onyx, black pearl, black jade, and sunset opal. In the middle of the magical table was set a leather-covered book, also the color of a raven's breast, and square in shape. Midnight was the room's tone, darker yet its purpose. This suited Sovartus well, and his smile remained constant. Soon, now, his striving would come to an end; when it did, there would be a new beginning to shake the world.

CHAPTER EIGHTEEN

Conan and Vitarius had not ridden far toward Castle Slott, when the older man reined his horse to a stop and motioned for Conan to do the same.

'Why do you halt? The journey is just begun –'

'Silence!' Vitarius's voice held a tone of command that Conan had not heard before. The power of that single word startled the Cimmerian.

The old magician dismounted and took several steps in the direction of their travel. He reached out and seemed to be feeling for something in the night air. Conan saw nothing there. After a moment Vitarius nodded. He stepped back a pace. 'Sovartus has set a warding spell; we are at its boundary.'

Conan stared into the darkness. 'We are still some way from his castle.'

Vitarius nodded. He mumbled something Conan did not quite hear, and waved his hands in a strange pattern. A faint reddish glow appeared in the air just ahead of the two men, and quickly expanded away from them. 'As you can see, he covers a large area. Once we enter the spell he will become aware of us. And I, with my magical abilities, will draw his attention more than an ordinary traveler would. Before we enter his realm, I must prepare myself. There will be guards for men – he is no fool – but likely, too, will there be guards for those bearing magics that would oppose the Black Square. I must be ready.'

Conan dismounted and walked about, stretching his sinews as Vitarius sat cross-legged on the ground and chanted quietly to himself. The Cimmerian was impatient, eager to put his blade to work. Enough of this magical foolery. If Sovartus found himself transfixed upon cold and sharp steel, he would deflate readily enough, Conan would wager. All of these night-glowings and mummeries sat ill with the big youth. He would be shut of this kind of work as soon as possible; he was more than willing to hack his way out of it.

Time passed, and Conan grew yet more impatient. What was the old man doing? Crom, they would be here for the next season's change!

'I am ready,' Vitarius said.

Once again Conan was startled by the magician's voice. There was the new note of power he'd heard before, but something additional also rode there. It seemed as if a young man had spoken. And though Conan saw nothing so changed he could name it, Vitarius seemed to move differently from the way he had before. Somehow more assured, his manner was.

They remounted their horses and approached the glowing air.

Conan noticed no difference when they entered the warding spell; no lights flashed, no screeches filled the night air. Vitarius, however, said, 'He knows we have come. Be on guard. He cannot turn his full attention to us, for he is preparing himself for his abominable experiment. Still, he controls much power – and much danger lies ahead.'

The Cimmerian pulled his sword free of its leathern home and held it angled across the front of his saddle. 'Good,' he said.

A wind began to blow, driving sand into Conan's face. His horse whinnied and tried to sidestep away from the dust, but the Cimmerian held the beast to its course.

'Sovartus,' Vitarius said. 'He seeks to test our mettle.'

Conan nodded. 'A breeze shall not stay us.'

The wind increased suddenly, a gust rocking Conan in the saddle. He slitted his eyes and leaned into the dusty wind. With his free hand he tried to shield the eyes of his horse.

The old mage intoned the words of some spell then. Abruptly, the wind died.

'Air,' Vitarius said. 'But not much of it. He thinks us little threat, it would seem.'

'I look forward to correcting his mistake,' Conan said.

'I hope your optimism is well-founded.'

Djuvula wrapped her scarf more tightly around her face to keep the dust from her eyes. She would not oppose Sovartus with her magic, of the Black, as was his own; therefore, it was unlikely he would deign to attack her directly. She had no fear of mortal guards who might be posted along the Dodligian road to Castle Slott.

She felt the force of the old wizard ahead of her flash out, and the wind died. That one had more power then she had thought. She had been surprised at how strong he truly was when he had paused to focus the White energies a short time earlier. He had just brushed aside Sovartus's nightwind as a man might brush away a pesky insect. Interesting.

Of course, her major concern lay in how the wizard might utilize those energies against her, did he know she followed so intently. She must wait, it seemed, until Conan and he of the White Square were separated enough so that she could strike against the barbarian. The castle grew closer, and her dealings with Sovartus would have to be considered as well; still, enough time lay ahead yet to complete all her business. All the time in the world.

The panther moved in the lee of the wagon, partially protected from the wind in this manner, but not altogether so; some of the road grit found his face, and he blinked against it. The panther trod carefully, to avoid coming within range of the magic shroud that cloaked the witch's conveyance. He did not think she knew of him, trailing her this way; neither would he have her know – yet. She had humbled him once with her foul magic, and he would not have such happen again.

As Lemparius padded along behind the wagon he considered for the hundredth time how he might effect Djuvula's destruction. She had rendered him impotent against her directly, but there must be another manner in which he could attack. Something indirect. But – what?

For a moment the beast took over. Lemparius had to resist the urge to snarl; he had to hold himself in check to keep from sprinting to the front of the wagon, to slash at the horses, to drink from their blood before leaping upon Djuvula to rend her lifeless.

The moment passed, and the mind of the man once again rode in full control of the animal's form. It would have been a foolish move to be prompted by such feline passions, a wasted effort, doomed from the start.

The catman shook his head. He would have to do something soon; he must do something ere he lost his human sanity to become a panther in thought as well as in form. He had but one hope in that regard: if Djuvula were to die, perhaps her bewitchment of him might also die. He might then regain his human form. A fragile hope, he knew, but all that he had.

Of course, there was the matter of Conan, who must die in any event. But whether the barbarian was killed by the panther or by the man he had been mattered little. He would die; more, he must die in such a way that Djuvula – if she still lived – could not obtain the man's heart for her simulacrum. She must be denied that pleasure even if she survived it by only a moment.

Revenge was a dish to be savored slowly, Lemparius was finding, in all of its flavoring, before settling into partaking of it in full earnest.

The wind and dust settled then, but a sniff of the night air brought to the cat's sensitive nostrils the smell of something he liked less: rain, and coming soon.

Lemparius held the cat's voice, but the snarl and low growl existed in thought if not sound.

The rain came across the plain at a driving slant, presaged by lightning and booming thunder. In the light of the crackling discharges Conan saw the first fat, heavy drops splatter against the dry ground, raising dust as they thunked into the earth. In a moment the wall of water neared, a blanket of gray reaching to enshroud the two riders.

Despite the moisture in the air, the hair on Conan's arms and neck stirred, as it sometimes did on removing a heavy woolen cloak on a winter's day. His horse made as if to bolt, and Conan held him steady only with difficulty.

Vitarius suddenly reached skyward, arms extended fully, fingers spread. He yelled a short phrase.

A jagged bolt speared from the heavens, straight at the pair of men and horses. Conan saw the bolt deflected somehow, several spans over his head. The thunder that followed the thwarted charge was also muted, so that it was felt more than heard.

Vitarius now glowed with a pale light not unlike that produced by the flashes of lightning. The rain that should have fallen upon them fell before and behind and to either side, as though an invisible tent had been erected over the men and mounts. The storm raged at the shield; lightning crackled at it, thunder drummed upon it, hail the size of Conan's fist shattered against the clear air. The dry ground around them, outside of Vitarius's protection, became like a swamp, yet Conan could smell the dust disturbed by his frightened horse's hooves as the animal pawed the ground.

The storm standing over him must be supernatural, Conan knew. Unprotected from the tempest, he would have surely paid a dear price, maybe even his life. Despite his distrust and dislike of any form of magic, Conan found himself most glad to be next to Vitarius at the moment. Most glad.

Spray from the driving rain found its way through the canvas that formed the roof of Djuvula's wagon, thick as the material was. She dared not use any more of her magic to augment the material's natural protection, for fear of attracting either Vitarius's or Sovartus's attention. She had risked erecting a shelter for the horses, speeding up the process with a spell so that the hail, at least, would not bash them senseless. That same hail battered at her own roof, denting it deeply in places and making a terrible racket when the ice struck a supporting wooden hoop.

Djuvula lay on the bed next to the box containing her Prince. She stroked the smooth wood idly, and spoke to the form inside as if it were alive. 'Fear not, my love. We may be dampened, but not for long. Do not allow the din to disturb your slumber . . .'

Crouched under the witch's wagon, the panther held very still, even to breathing shallowly and with great care. He did not think that Djuvula would hear him with the storm howling about them, but he knew he must not be careless.

He would have found other shelter had there been any; upon this portion of the plain, however, there existed no protection from even a normal rain, much less one driven by wizardry. Despite his ability to withstand ordinary dangers, the panther was no proof against such magic as Sovartus controlled. Hail so heavy that it dug holes in the ground would smash a skull easily enough, even his.

A runnel began near one edge of the dry spot underlying the wagon and sought to cross to the opposite side. Lemparius would have moved, but the hail chose that moment to cease falling, and the relative quiet might have allowed the witch to hear such a movement. So the panther held his place as the cold finger of water reached his belly and began to puddle there, running along his length.

His nostrils flared, and the panther laid his ears back in rage. Yet another indignity for which Djuvula owed him. He cursed inwardly, but remained as a stone statue as the cold and muddy water soaked his fur.

As quickly as it had begun, the rain stopped. The stars appeared behind the scudding clouds along with a sliver of settling moon. As the storm faded so did the glow surrounding Vitarius. For a moment the wizard looked tired. Then he took a deep breath and straightened slightly, shaking off the weariness as a dog shakes off water.

'It has been too long since I played these games,' Vitarius said. 'I am out of practice.'

Grudgingly, for all his dislike of sorcery, Conan said, 'You did well enough.'

'Aye, but these are but small tests. When Sovartus tries with real force, I shall have to do better.'

The Cimmerian nodded.

'Then the sooner we get to yon castle, the sooner we can depart this cursed plain.'

'Aye, Conan. Ride on.'

They urged their horses onward.

High in his castle, Sovartus became aware of an irritation, something amiss in the mystical web of forces with which he surrounded himself. On Dodligia Plain a faint glimmer of antithetical forces existed where none should, as a boil upon otherwise healthy skin. Well, he had no time for such things. He sent a wind to blow it away.

Sovartus returned to his preparations for the arrival of the girl of Fire. He donned his virgins'-hair robe, feeling the power it carried. He called for a bottle of his oldest and finest wine and sipped of the liquid as he contemplated his new place in the cosmic scheme of things. Ah, what power he would command!

He felt an itch in his side then, but it was metaphysical and not manifested in his own flesh. He expanded his consciousness, searching for the source of the bothersome itch –

Damnation! That glimmer upon the plain remained despite his broom of nightwind. Well, he could take another moment from his anticipation of glory to deal with it. Within his own sphere of influence Sovartus need not call for everything upon any of the Three he had pent. He was not without powers of his own, especially so close to his lair. He called for a storm, sending hellish force upward into the skies to shape the resulting tempest to his will. Then, like a boy casting a ball, Sovartus sent the tropical zephyr toward the troublesome speck. Defy this, insect!

Presently, the itch grew worse. After his astonishment that it persisted, Sovartus knew it for what it was: Vitarius, of the White, moved against him!

Truly astounding. Surely the old man knew better? He had not even kept himself young with his magic – those of the White seldom used their powers for personal gain or enhancement – and even if he were senile, he must know how foolish it would be to proceed against one of the Black in his own Square of power.

When the girl of fire had been taken, Sovartus had given Vitarius no further thought; unless the man were mad, he would simply go away, for he could not hope to compare his feeble powers with those of Sovartus's own. To contend would be suicide – the man had to know that – even if Sovartus did not control the Thing of Power, which he shortly would. There was very little for the White Square to draw upon here, not with the near-omnipotence of the Black focused as it was upon this plain. Hogistum had taught them both that White and Black had their places; and this place belonged to the Black as surely as night followed day. Vitarius had been the better student, he *must* know that.

Unless – unless Vitarius had some hidden focus? Some trick he concealed to spring upon an unwary opponent?

Sovartus rubbed at his face with one hand. Yes. That must be it. The old man has some hidden card; he had to have such. Best I find out what it is before I do anything that might turn back upon me, Sovartus thought. A probe, to see how Vitarius reacts.

Sovartus smiled, pleased with his sharpness of wit. And he had just the thing to try upon his old training mate. Just the thing . . .

Dawn approached, but darkness still reigned when Vitarius once again motioned for Conan to halt. The two men had only a short distance left before reaching the base of Sovartus's mountain-castle, and Conan had hoped they might do so without further incident. He was wrong.

Vitarius said, 'Our enemy is about to task us. And it will be no small thing this time. I think it better that we should part, Conan. You must ride for the castle; I shall try to occupy Sovartus while you search for the children. And Kinna. May the White protect you, Conan of Cimmeria.'

Conan slapped at the hilt of his sword. 'I will put my

faith elsewhere, old one. But I wish you good luck. I will return with the children and Kinna as soon as I can.'

The old mage nodded, and waved one aged hand. He alighted from his horse and sat cross-legged upon the ground.

Conan spared him a final glance before turning his attention – and his horse – back toward Castle Slott.

Djuvula felt a prickling on her skin as she drew near the old magician. The air was full of anticipatory flux, presaging some magical production. Even within her concealing shroud of darkness she felt a chill touch her.

She was nearly past the old man, who sat upon the bare ground with his eyes closed when he called out. Djuvula started at his words.

'Ho, witch; best if you depart this area quickly. There is apt to be some spillage from my coming confrontation with Sovartus.'

Djuvula almost spoke, then thought better of it. Could he really see her?

Vitarius answered her unspoken thought. 'Aye, I have known you followed us for some time, witch. And I know, too, of that which shadows you. Whatever your purpose, you would be better served to turn around and flee. My sense of future is very dim for the most part; but in this instance I see ruin for many near to this venture.'

Djuvula stared at the White magician. What did he mean, that which shadows me? And what of his ill prophecy? Djuvula's chill intensified, and she glanced around the edge of her wagon, searching for any pursuer. She saw none.

No point in maintaining the cloaking spell, she knew. She allowed the shroud to dissipate. For a moment she considered what the old man had said. She decided to ignore him. He was about to receive the brunt of Sovartus's magical ire; he was no threat to her. And, more important, the barbarian no longer had the White to look after him.

The witch grinned. Conan would have gone on ahead to the castle. Djuvula still knew not why, but that was where she would find him. She popped her whip at the horses.

The White mage never opened his eyes, but he spoke three words as Djuvula drove past, three words that touched her as might a fiery brand upon her flesh:

'You were warned.'

CHAPTER NINETEEN

The first gleamings of morning light found Conan staring at the entrance to a large cave in Castle Slott's mountain base. The hole in the rock was easily large enough for a mounted man to enter, a perfect, open invitation at the end of the trail leading to the wizard's home.

Conan grinned. The cave mouth was, if anything, too perfect and too open. His experience as a thief had taught him many things, not the least of which was to beware of things that looked too good to be true. His memories of the easy stroll into the home of Senator Lemparius were all too fresh in his mind; only a fool refused to learn from his mistakes. Conan of Cimmeria would not march into what must be a trap.

How else to enter the mountain, then? He smiled and looked up at the wall of craggy rock. He was, after all, a Cimmerian; mountains had yet to be made that could not be climbed, especially by those hardy northern people from whom Conan had been bred. He would go up, and he would find a way.

Before he did, however, Conan was curious about something his sharp senses detected in a stand of trees not far from where he now sat on his horse. There came the sounds of pent animals, and the odor of beasts tainted the morning air.

He slid from his mount and used a large rock to peg the animal's bridle to the ground. Moving with catlike grace, the big man went to see what lay within the cover of the trees.

Horses: a corral full of them milled about, guarded by a single man wearing a hooded black robe and holding a long staff. To one end of the enclosure sat a wattle-and-daub stable, with piles of hay and grain within.

From the cover of a thick-leaved bush Conan's grin stretched as wide as it got. Well, well, well.

The Cimmerian backed away from the corral. He would certainly return here when he had done his business with Sovartus; for now, however, he must finish that business.

Conan removed the bridle and unsaddled his mount, allowing the animal to graze among the sedge. No telling how long his errand might take, and there was no point in the horse suffering while his master was gone. He hid the mount's gear carefully, taking only a skin of wine and some dried meat for supplies. He made certain his sword and Lemparius's knife were securely in place, then approached the outcrops of the mountain. Pausing only to remove his sandals, he began his climb.

Sovartus was seated near his talisman table, working the intricate spell of the Rain of Cosmic Fire, from the unholy book called the *Zilbermankarikatur*, the use of which nearly always brought ruination to its object. That powerful and cursed energy now focused upon Vitarius of the White Square, a shower of annihilation that rarely failed.

Let's see you escape this time, old classmate!

One of his black hoods arrived then, and interrupted Sovartus's gloatings. The shrouded form bowed low and pointed speechlessly. Sovartus turned to see what the hooded servant wished him to see.

A brace of demi-whelves stood there, looking nervous at being inside Castle Slott. More important, however, was the child held between them: it was her! The Child of Fire, his, at last!

So taken by this vision was Sovartus, that at first he did not notice the young woman standing near to the girl. When he did, Sovartus asked, 'And who are you?'

The woman drew herself up stiffly. 'I am Kinna, half-sister to those children you have stolen!'

Sovartus smiled, to reveal teeth as white as bleached bone. 'Ah,' he said, 'then you are sister to me as well.'

'Nay, black-souled warlock, I am not! Stepsister, perhaps, and that reluctantly.'

Sovartus swept his gaze over the girl's comely form.

'No matter,' he said. 'I am certain I can find some good use for you, dear. But later we can discuss our mutual pleasure; for now I have other matters to which I must attend.' The wizard clapped his hand, and more hooded figures appeared. Sovartus pointed to the girl. 'You two, take Eldia to join her brothers and sister.' To Eldia he said, 'I have been waiting for you since you were born, girl. You will no doubt enjoy meeting your long-lost kin – for a few moments anyway.'

Kinna said, 'What are you going to do with them?'

Sovartus shrugged. 'After they are drained of the essences I need, I shall have no further use for them. Magically, that is. I suppose I can devise some entertainment utilizing such tender things.'

He waved at the remaining hoods. 'Take her to a lock-room; see that she is well fed and made comfortable against my future use.' To the two demi-whelves Sovartus said, 'You may depart. And see that you advise the whelves that it would be wise to descend to your lowest tunnels for a time; the surface of Dodligia Plain will not be a healthy place to be in a few hours.'

Sovartus spun, his robe flaring widely as he started for the tower. At last! At last!

The morning sun shone brightly, but not so brightly as the conflagration spraying from the skies onto Dodligia Plain. The panther had to swing wide to avoid the fires. Had he worn a man's body, the cat would have cursed; this would delay him, and he had already done one stupid thing by falling asleep at the wrong time. This act had allowed the witch to pull away from him. There had been no help for it; even his supernormal panther abilities had limits, and he had been stretching them for days, resting and eating little. He now thought to hurry and catch Djuvula, only this magical assault upon the empty plain slowed him again –

Wait. The plain was not empty. Squinting against the splashes of brilliant red and orange, the panther saw a seated figure, protected from the incandescent air by a shimmering

163

white glow. The old magician? It must be, though the eyes of the feline watcher were not efficient enough to discern such details amid the surrounding brightness.

But, as the panther-who-had-been-a-man looked, the seated figure managed to stand. It raised one arm, and the hand seemed to ignite with a cooler flame, more blue than red. The flame grew into a ball half the size of the figure, then an indigo beam shot out, undimmed and unhampered by the fiery rain. The line of glowing energy arced away from its generator and splashed against the mountain with the castle atop it, creating a fountain of blue sparks where it hit.

The panther turned and loped away. He wanted no part of this, whatever it was. He had his own problems that must be attended to, and they did not include being fried by an angry wizard.

Djuvula stood by the cave, staring into the darkness. That it would be guarded she was certain; that she would try to pass those guards unaided she was certain she would not. The way inside meant risk, for Sovartus would have his privacy even from those who walked the Black Path, as did he. Her strength was hardly a match for one so steeped in thaumaturgy as was Sovartus. Womanly wiles would avail her little over the hooded ones who served the master of the Black Square, since these were not born of woman and were not equipped as men who might desire woman. But there was a way: the hooded ones had weak minds and could be commanded by only a medium-complex spell. This she could do, though Sovartus would hardly approve. Still, the fastest and safest way into Castle Slott would be with an escort of those who guarded it. And one of those creatures stood near a corral of horses only a short distance away.

Djuvula went to her wagon to prepare the proper spell.

Conan clung to a sheer rock face, his fingers and bare feet clutching at the narrowest of cracks like a human fly. Just above, another body length, gaped a narrow entrance to what seemed a small cave. Likely just what he searched for, he thought.

The Cimmerian had climbed to a fair height – he was at least the spans of thirty large men from the ground, and a fall from here would certainly be fatal. He was not afraid, since falling from a climb had never worried him greatly. He had first climbed only shortly after learning to walk, and grown Cimmerians seldom fell from their cold mountains.

As Conan reached for a new fingerhold, however, a sudden jolt shook the mountain, as if it were struck by a giant's first. The Cimmerian caught only a short peripheral glimpse of blue fire splashing against the rocks a dozen arm spans above him; then he was too busy trying to maintain his precarious grip upon the mountain's face. One hand slipped, and the vibration from the rock cast his feet away. For a moment Conan hung by the tips of four fingers, and only his great strength saved him from a deadly drop. He spent no energy in cursing, but snaked his feet against the rock, scrabbling for purchase with his toes. In a moment he managed to dig his toes into a fault; his left hand found an outcrop of rock and clamped onto it. Safe again, for the moment, at least.

Conan began to climb quickly, his earlier tiredness gone. He knew not what the blue light had been, nor did he care; he wished only to be in a more secure place soon. What happened once could happen again, and the next time the blue fire might be closer or stronger.

With that thought as a spur, Conan reached the lip of the ledge bounding the cave. He pulled himself onto the wide ledge and paused to take several deep breaths. Then he untied his sandals from his belt and pulled them on.

Now, to see where this cave led. He drew his sword and stepped into the darkness.

Sovartus started as the floor beneath his feet shook suddenly. He looked at the four children, each chained under a window of the tower room. There flowed no real power from them toward him, though the new girl strived to turn him into ash with her thoughts. His skill was proof against that; besides, the force assailing his castle came from without –

Vitarius! He had forgotten the mage of the White Square in his joy at collecting the child. Sovartus cast his perception forth, feeling for the old man.

Yes, it had been Vitarius who had sent a tongue of White magic at Slott. He was indeed much stronger than Sovartus had thought. The Cosmic Fire fell upon him, and still he had sufficient force to attack. Amazing.

Briefly, Sovartus considered his response. It galled him that his castle should be attacked. On the other hand, the castle could withstand much worse without major damage; and, of course, he had more important things to do. Yes, to be certain, he had not the time to waste upon Vitarius.

Let Vitarius rail against him; it would not matter shortly. Once the Thing of Power came into being, all of the White Square combined could not stand against it. He would ignore the old mage. When he was done with his business, he would crush Vitarius with less effort than a man would expend to swat a mosquito.

Sovartus strode to his talisman table and laid his hands upon it. He uttered the first part of the phrase he had memorized a decade past. The table began to glow redly.

When he spoke the second part of the phrase, the four children moaned softly, surrounded by that same infernal glow. Sovartus smiled, and it was all he could do to keep from laughing.

Conan felt the mountain shake again, but the force seemed weaker this time. Perhaps it was because he was inside.

After walking in darkness down a narrow tunnel, feeling his way along, he came to a lighted hallway cut from the rock. Torches guttered from their holders every dozen paces; the new passage stretched for a long distance in either direction, with no clue as to which way he should turn. He decided to take the left path, for it seemed to climb slightly, and his direction must eventually lead him upward, were he to attain his destination.

He passed several smaller corridors branching to either

side. These confirmed his feeling that he traveled the correct track, for the corridor seemed a major artery, much larger than the others.

Now and again the floor would vibrate, as if shaken by a mild earth tremor, but the effect was small, and Conan had no difficulty maintaining his footing.

After a time he came to a widening of the tunnel. The corridor opened into a vast room carved from the solid rock, a room with a ceiling so distant, the flickering torches could not cast their light far enough to touch it, a room with walls so wide, the torches set upon them looked no more than slender tapers.

He decided against traversing such a vast cavern in virtual darkness. He retreated a few paces and reached for one of the torches set upon the wall. But as the Cimmerian touched the smooth wood of the light, he saw another such flickering torch moving toward him up the corridor along his previous path. He snatched his hand away and re-entered the cavern until he was hidden in deep shadow. He held his sword ready.

A black-robed figure, face hooded and hidden, moved slowly up the corridor, pausing now and then. Conan saw that the man – if a man, in fact – was replacing burned-out flambeaus with fresh brands, removing these unlighted sticks from a large pack upon his back. He – it? – would pause only long enough to flame the new torch into life, then trudged onward.

Conan's first reaction was a strong desire to behead this robed figure, for he now felt certain that whatever inhabited the black cloth was not a true man. Something in the way the figure moved cried out of foul wrongness to the sharp-eyed Cimmerian. Aye, likely the black mage's minions were evil constructs.

The young Cimmerian slid farther back into the embrace of the cavern's dark arms. He could slay the robed figure. On the other hand, he could allow it to live and follow it; certainly, it must eventually run out of torches and return to some central supply area for more, if it were not already headed for such a place. Aye, that was a better plan, to have a guide.

In the darkness the robed figure passed, moving slowly across the giant room. Silently as a shadow, Conan followed.

Led by her enthralled guide, Djuvula moved easily along the gently sloping corridor deeper into the bowels of Castle Slott. Aside from the spell that ensnared the hooded one leading her, she dared not use her magic, for fear of being detected by Sovartus. The hooded creature had been taken outside the mountain, the actual working of the diablerie done there, and done quickly, so that Sovartus might miss it. Much as she would have liked to use the sword and clothing that the creature now bore, strapped to its back, for a locating spell, she feared to do so. The barbarian walked within the bounds of Castle Slott, she knew that much. She would find him somehow.

The stink of the things dressed in black robes offended the nostrils of the panther as he slunk along the rocky ground, hidden by his coloration and the shadows. Not-men, and foul, they were, and also not very alert. A dozen of the robed things stood guard within the entrance of the cave mouth, each armed with a double-edged pike with a blade as long as a man's arm. And those pikes were no doubt drenched in some spellery or another that would make them effective against the panther's were. Still, they could not hurt that which they did not observe. A beast with the skills of a great cat and the cunning of a man had the advantage of these. Lemparius, once-senator, moved past the guards unseen, unheard, and unknown by them.

Past the stench of the hooded things the panther could detect the scent of his prey, the perfumed witch. And since she sought the barbarian, he, too, must be within. Soon, the panther thought, his time would be soon.

CHAPTER TWENTY

The hooded thing moved methodically, and Conan soon realized there was little chance of the creature noticing him: It never looked back.

For his part, Conan was impressed with whoever – or whatever – had constructed the vast array of tunnels and rooms that seemed to stretch endlessly around him. It must have taken hundreds of years; either that, or some very powerful magic. Conan did not wish to think too much about the latter possiblity.

Following the winding path of the torchlighter, Conan could tell they were in fact ascending. The particular tunnel in which they now walked had a definite upward slant to the stone floor. Good. He only hoped he could find Kinna and Eldia along with the half-siblings before it was too late.

A brighter light loomed ahead, and Conan dropped back somewhat from his pursuit of the hooded one. He preferred not to lose his guide, but neither was he ready to be seen, not just yet.

Another large chamber had been hewn from the granite, and this one was well-lighted with torches on the walls and fat black tapers set in man-high bronze candelabra about the chamber.

The torchlighter stood near the center of this room. With it there stood two others like it, save that instead of unlit faggots, they carried long-bladed pikes. The three appeared to be conversing, but even Conan's keen hearing could make out no voices.

Here was a problem: to follow his lead dog, he would have to pass the armed guards. At the very least, there would be some commotion in so doing, and his guide was certain to notice it.

Conan looked around the chamber, peering from behind the edge of the entrance to the room. To his left there stood a row of iron-barred doors along one wall; across from that wall a lighted tunnel exited. Ahead, a large vitruvian-edged tapestry of darkly colored material showed some hellish scene, with demons pursuing terrified naked men and women.

He hefted his blade, taking a tighter grip upon the leather-covered handle. He was a man of action, of deeds; so far in his association with the old wizard and the sisters there had been too much magic and too little honest fighting. Demons, wizards, and hooded things were not to his liking. He liked problems that could be solved with blade and sinew, not dark sorcery.

A flash of something pale caught the Cimmerian's attention. A face? At one of the barred doors? Why, this must be some sort of dungeon, another thing he had no love for, to be sure. And while the enemy of his enemy might not be Conan's friend, such a man might prove helpful –

Kinna! Conan recognized the girl at the same time she caught sight of his own visage. He motioned for silence, but too late to still an astonished gasp from the woman.

The three hooded things turned as one to behold the captured woman. Then, again as one, they twisted to look at the object of her surprise. Conan thought to duck back from sight, then decided against it. Enough of this cat-footed mincing! He sprang into the chamber, his sword gripped tightly.

The three facing him spread out instantly, as though controlled by a single mind. To either side the pikemen scurried, lowering their sword-tipped weapons to point at the intruder. Directly ahead, the torchlighter pulled two of the brands from his back pack and held them over an already-blazing torch. The new faggots flamed into life. For the first time Conan saw the thing's hands and wrists clearly: the flesh glowed with color in the firelight; green it was, and scaled like the belly of a snake.

The Cimmerian shook his head. What manner of man had such creatures for servants? Sovartus was beneath contempt. The pikeman to Conan's right edged a hair closer than his partner on the opposite side.

Conan took three quick steps forward and swung his sword with a force that would have cleaved an ordinary man in half. The hooded figure met his strike with its own blade. Sparks flew from the impact of steel upon steel, and the shock of the connection traveled up Conan's hands and arms to his shoulders. His cut was blocked, and from the angle of the pike it would have taken a very strong man to do that. Whatever these things were, they were not weaklings –!

'Conan! Behind you!'

The Cimmerian recovered from his surprise just in time. He leaped to one side as a second pike whistled through the air where he had just been. He spun and brought his sword downward, as a man would swing an ax to split firewood. His blade hit the outstretched pike, and despite the un-natural strength of the lizard-man, knocked the weapon from its owner's grasp. An angry hiss came from under the hood as the thing sprang backward to avoid Conan's follow-up slash.

The lizard-man with the flaming torches also edged back a step, out of the Cimmerian's reach.

Conan smiled. Well. They had taken his measure and decided to accord him a modicum of respect.

The first lizard-man drew back his pike, as if to stab Conan through the back. The Cimmerian caught the motion from the corner of one eye and realized his position allowed only one safe move. He bent his knees and leaped – straight up.

The pike passed just under Conan's feet, and as the beast-man fell helplessly forward, the Cimmerian came down upon his attacker's shoulders. Before the lizard-thing could rise, Conan chopped at his neck with the sword. It was like striking a tree. The thing squalled, and green liquid sprayed from the wound to ooze onto the bare stone floor.

There was no time for Conan to tarry and admire his handiwork. He jumped away from the downed lizard toward the second one, which was still trying to recover its weapon.

It must have realized that to continue to reach for the pike was worth death, for the thing jumped at Conan instead, catching the man's wrists in its scaled hands.

Conan felt the roughness of that powerful grip as he tried to bring the sword into play. He could not swing the weapon; his hand was trapped too tightly. The Cimmerian released the sword, and it fell, slicing a line across the bare green arm that now protruded from the black robe. The lizard-thing hissed, exhaling a charnel stench into Conan's face. Sensing movement behind him, he twisted, flexing his brawny legs and back, turning the lizard-man around. Just in time, for the torchlighter smashed both his lit brands onto its comrade's back instead of Conan's.

The Cimmerian brought his knee up then, and slammed it into the thing's groin. Only smoothness met the hard muscle of his leg when it connected with the juncture of the lizard-thing's crotch. He'd not stop it that way.

Conan danced with the lizard, trying to avoid the swinging torches being flailed at him by the other creature. This could not go on much longer, he knew. This abomination was at least as strong as he was, and it had help.

Enough! The Cimmerian's rage boiled up, and he screamed his anger into the face of the lizard. Reaching deep inside for new strength, he hurled the thing away from him into one of the massive bronze candelabra. The post cracked, and the metal taper holder toppled, landing on the lizard-thing; its robe took fire quickly, and in an instant the monster became a living torch. It leaped up and ran, smashed into the wall opposite the cells, and fell, a fiery corpse.

The torchlighter dropped its weapons then, and turned to flee. It ran for the exit Conan had noticed earlier. Without thinking, the Cimmerian leaped for one of the fallen pikes. He snatched the weapon up and hurled it, all of a single move. The sword tip struck the running lizard high between the shoulder blades. For a moment the thing stood transfixed, then fell forward. The pike was embedded so deeply, it remained standing upright from the impaled form like a leafless tree.

Conan retrieved his sword and went to the door of Kinna's cell. A simple bolt fastened the enclosure's entrance shut, high enough to be out of reach of an inmate. Conan threw the bolt back, and Kinna rushed out and into his arms.

'Oh, Conan, I thought never to see you again!'

He patted the girl with his free hand.

'He has Eldia and the others, Conan, in some kind of tower, I think. What of Vitarius?'

Conan said, 'He remains on the plain. I felt some of his handiwork earlier, when the mountain shook.'

'We must get to Sovartus before he unleashes his awful creation,' Kinna said. 'But I am not sure I can recall the way.'

Conan pointed with his blade. 'That way. The lizard-thing ran there before I stopped him. If he thought help lay in that direction, there we must go. Unless you would rather remain here while I continue?'

In answer, Kinna untangled herself from Conan's embrace and fetched the remaining pike. Her eyes flashed. 'I shall accompany you. I'll accompany you, or I'll go alone!'

Conan uttered a short laugh. 'I cannot fault your spirit, Kinna. Very well. Let us go and find this wizard and send him to join his ancestors!'

Djuvula's escort had moved silently and steadily, never hesitating, until they came to the lockroom chamber. There, the enthralled being stopped suddenly. The witch, startled, peered around the form of her reptilian guide to see what had given it pause.

Three of the hooded lizards lay dead in the chamber, one barely recognizable from being burned – it still smoldered against one wall.

Djuvula nodded to herself. This must be the work of the barbarian. From the looks of the congealing green blood on the floor, he could not be far ahead either.

Smiling, Djuvula prodded her escort with one sharp-nailed finger. The creature moved on, and the witch followed.

*

The panther would have stopped to eat had the flesh of the fresh-killed not-men been edible. The finely honed senses of the cat allowed it to know better, however. That meat was poison to any natural creature, and even to one wrapped in were it would not serve as sustenance. But no matter; the scent of the witch permeated the air; she was only a few paces ahead, down that corridor.

He could eat later, if not her flesh, then that of the barbarian – if Lemparius still had to wear the form of a panther.

The cat padded across the stone quietly and entered the corridor behind his prey.

From the highest tower of Castle Slott, Sovartus could see the beginning of life for the Thing of Power. The essences of the children were now wrapped within the spell he controlled; the plain itself seemed to live as great winds howled across the roiling ground, joined by rainstorms and bolts that arced from the earth to the skies and back. A crack split the ground asunder, and flames belched from the bowels of the earth to join the other Elements.

The four children seemed to be asleep, unseeing and unhearing of the energies erupting over the plain outside, but Sovartus felt those magical forces tugging at his own essence. Only his skill kept him from being torn apart by the elemental madness out there.

The hooded ones standing by his door cowered within their robes, but Sovartus only laughed to see this. Now, after all the years, after all the study and waiting, now, *now*, NOW!

Twin whirlwinds began to spin upon the convulsing plain, giant tornadoes of black air twirling at speeds never seen in such winds before. As Sovartus watched, these funnels detached themselves from the storms that created them, moving freely against the prevailing winds driving the clouds. The tornadoes moved to a point where they stood side by side, then like giant drills began to dig up the earth, twisting it upward.

Yes, yes! Sovartus shook with the power of it.

The ground rose in chunks the size of houses, of castles, and it came together over the tornadoes to form a body, a torso like none ever seen.

Sovartus laughed again and extended his arms toward the skies. Another pair of spinning winds, somewhat smaller than the first pair, howled forth from their mother storms and became as arms on the figure building itself upon the plain.

The castle shook then, struck by a line of blue light that arced from farther out on the plain. Sovartus nodded at the source of the light. Too late, old classmate.

The master of the Black Square waved his arms yet again and pointed his stiffened fingers at the rainstorms. A single cloud broke away from the main body of the storm. Spitting lightning, the cloud moved to hover over the gigantic earthen body, then settled upon it. Three holes opened in the cloud, looking like eyes and a mouth; lightning formed jagged and flickering teeth in the gaping maw.

Sovartus howled in his glee, a sound to mimic the roar outside.

The black wizard ran to the window and leaned out into the rain to stare at the ground. The sundered earth still spat fire below, turning the base of the mountain white with steam as the fire met the rain. Sovartus turned his hands palms up and raised them. The flames roared higher, and a pair of fireballs broke free of the pit and surged upward. Like demonic fireflies these globs of matter flew, soaring until they stood in front of the cloudhead that rode the massive body of earth, which in turn rode on legs of devil-wind. The fireballs moved into the empty sockets with a hiss . . .

Yes! Yes! YES! Sovartus took a deep breath and yelled out the final word, the last word in the most powerful spell he or any other mage had ever created.

The storm died. The earth sealed over, stopping the fire. The plain grew almost quiet save for those sounds coming from the construct that now towered as tall as the mountain which was Castle Slott. The thing made of the Four Elements turned, so that it faced Sovartus. It blinked, hiding its

175

eyes of living fire with lids of cloud unaffected by the heat. When it opened its lids again, Sovartus knew that it truly saw him, that he had succeeded. Slowly and ponderously, the giant bowed toward Sovartus.

The Thing of Power lived.

And Sovartus was its master.

CHAPTER TWENTY-ONE

Kinna led, for she recalled more of the route to the heart of the wizard's lair than at first she'd thought. In only a short time she and Conan ascended past the rock base and into the castle proper. The stones of the constructed portion of Slott seemed as old as the mountain itself. Here the walls bore the stains of many years of taper and torch soot; here, too, a maze of twisting tunnels honeycombed the construction, as they had in the rock beneath. The gloom was broken, however, by infrequent windows, allowing light from outside to war with the inner darkness. Passing one of these artificed cracks in the outer wall, Conan drew up suddenly to stare at the thing he saw taking form upon the bare plain.

'What is it?' Kinna called.

Conan pointed wordlessly.

The young woman returned two paces to look along the line of Conan's pointing finger. She gasped.

'Aye,' Conan said, 'of all the evil in this venture, that is the worst.' He continued to stare at the tornadoes and churning earth, at the formation of a head from the thunderstorm, and the eyes of fireballs. The thing blinked then, and seemed to stare directly at Conan; then it bowed.

Conan turned away. 'We must hurry,' he said. 'Whatever it is, Sovartus owns it – it bowed not to us!'

They ran. So quickly did they climb the slanting floor that they almost blundered into disaster. Conan's keen nose caught the scent of the robed lizards first, and he grabbed Kinna's arm and covered her mouth to still her surprised outcry. 'Shhh. There are more of the hooded things just around the corner.'

Kinna tugged at Conan's hand, and he removed his palm from her lips. 'How do you know?' she whispered.

'By their stench. Wait here.'

Conan left Kinna standing in the shadows while he edged along the corridor to the turning. He squatted low, then carefully peeped around the corner, keeping his face close to the dank stone.

The hallway opened into yet another room, this one not much larger than a rich man's bedchamber. There stood next to the walls nine of the hooded reptiles, each armed with a pike like the one Kinna now bore. From their positions it seemed as if these beings were guarding the arched doorway on the opposite wall. Deep in his gut Conan felt a surge of knowledge: through that doorway must be Sovartus, and, with him, Eldia.

Conan slid back before any could see him. Here was where they must go; but passing nine of the hellishly fast and strong lizard-things would be dangerous. He arose from his crouch and moved silently toward Kinna to tell her what he had seen.

Djuvula had a premonition, and so stopped before allowing her guide to lead her around the next angle in the castle's corridor. She bade the enspelled reptile to stand fast, and she moved to steal a glimpse of what lay ahead.

Beneath the light of tapers sending spirals of black smoke toward the ceiling of the corridor stood the barbarian, talking to a young woman! At last! She would take him now, by Set!

From the pack that she had caused the reptile to bear, Djuvula withdrew two items: the first was a curiously shaped vessel of magical design by which she could keep alive for a time any organ placed within. The second item was a thin-walled porcelain bulb. This latter Djuvula unpacked carefully from a thick, soft padding of lamb's wool. Within was a powder made from the dried petals of the black lotus. She had traded a magical spell to one of the priests of Yun for the deadly dust, against the time when she might need to deal instant death to anything that breathed. To inhale even the smallest portion was fatal, so the yellow-skulled priest had said; his demonstration upon a dog had proven it to Djuvula's satisfaction. The witch hefted the porcelain ball in her left hand and drew a small, sharp dagger from her girdle. She had some surgical skill at removal of hearts from recently dead or dying men – all the failures – in the service of her Prince. But the barbarian must not flee before the black lotus blossom could do its work.

Djuvula jabbed the hooded creature with her dagger. 'Go,' she said, 'and catch me that man you see just ahead.'

The hooded figure moved, and Djuvula grinned at its back. It would not matter if Conan slew it, for the thing need only delay him a moment until she could toss her deadly gift within range of the barbarian. Then all in the corridor would die, and quickly . . .

The mind of the panther slipped back and forth now, from man to beast. It was only with the greatest concentration that Lemparius could maintain a hold on his humanity within the form of the werecreature he had become. His fear drove him faster in pursuit of the witch. If he did not catch her soon, he was certainly lost, doomed to live out his days as a cat; worse, he would not even be aware of his state, for his mind would be gone, submerged under that of the beast. He would be less than the flicker of a single spark in an endless Stygian night.

With this fright riding his supple form, the panther ran. And so, rounding a turning in the dank, rat-infested castle, he found himself staring at the back of Djuvula.

The man in him knew he wore a prohibition against attacking the flame-haired woman, but the beast surged forth and held sway over the cat's body. Lemparius, former senator, former man, roared his rage with the voice of a maddened panther.

The sound startled the woman; she jumped and uttered an oath before she knew she had nothing to fear from this particular cat.

Lemparius's mind fought for control even as the panther gathered itself to spring. He almost won control. Almost, but not quite.

The werepanther leaped for the witch.

*

Conan spun at the sound of feet scrabbling upon the flagstones. Several things happened then, with that particular kind of slowness that sometimes wrapped itself around moments of great danger. It was as if the air became cold-congealed syrup, arresting the motions of the players in this sudden drama.

One of the hooded lizards appeared out of the darkness, running toward him. Almost immediately, the thing was followed by a woman – the witch, Djuvula – Conan recognized. Then a sand-colored form seemed to float through the air – that was a panther, going for the witch's throat. Conan thought he knew this beast.

He saw the line of a cut on the beast's leg, and knew he was correct. Lemparius. But why was he attacking the witch? Just then the panther was deflected by an invisible wall from his would-be prey. More sorcery!

No time to wonder how they had come to be here. Conan raised his sword as the black-garbed lizard-man leaped for him. The roar of the cat would draw others, Conan felt sure, and he had no plan, and no time to formulate one. The time for thinking was past; only action would serve him now!

Conan sidestepped and brought his blade down as the hooded thing lunged. The creature could not stay his charge, and the sharp steel met the scaly back and became part of it. The thing fell, loglike, bearing Conan's sword. The barbarian swore, and bent to yank the blade free.

The sound of many shuffling feet reached Conan. He turned toward the noise, and saw the first of the guards round the corner. That was a mistake, for Kinna leaped at the thing with her pike outstretched and skewered him like a pig for roasting.

The panther roared again, and again rebounded from the shield that protected the witch from his attacks. Growling and screaming in incoherent rage, the beast whirled, and espied Conan. It moved for him.

Four or five of the lizard-men cleared the corner, pikes held at the ready. Kinna's own pike was useless, still clutched by the entrails of the one she had slain.

'Kinna! To me!'

Conan caught another movement: the witch was fumbling with something. She dropped whatever it was, but managed to catch it before it hit the floor. She cursed.

Conan swung around to face the panther, realizing too late that his sword offered no proof against the wereman's attack.

The cat leaped for Conan's throat, and the big Cimmerian swung without thinking. The blade sank into the beast's side, shearing ribs and knocking the panther to one side. But even as it landed, Conan saw the welling blood cease its flow, and the wound knit itself together.

The Cimmerian turned quickly toward Kinna and tossed her his sword. 'Here!' he yelled.

With that, he snatched Lemparius's curved knife from his belt just as the cat sprang again. Conan ducked and stabbed upward with the steel tooth. The tip speared the panther under the throat; the force of the cat's leap carried it over Conan's squatting form, and the magical blade laid it open from neck to hindquarters. Steaming entrails gushed forth, and the panther who had been a man hit the ground, rolled once, and died.

'Conan!' That was Kinna, who swung Conan's heavy blade wildly and with little effect against the cluster of hooded lizard-men, who all jockeyed to get at her.

Conan caught the sword from her and lunged forward. One of the lizards took the point under his chin. It fell back, mortally wounded.

'Now I have you!' came a voice behind him. Conan backed away from the clutch of pike bearers and risked a quick glance down the hall.

Djuvula the Witch stood straight and still, holding a small globe high over her head. 'It is your time, Conan, and the time of all with you!'

The castle shook, the walls glowing briefly with a bluish light. Vitarius! He still carried the fight against Sovartus! Good, Conan thought, for certainly he and Kinna were doomed –

Djuvula screamed as she lost her balance on the vibrating floor. The globe she held spun away from her clutching fingertips, and she screamed again. 'No!'

The globe smashed upon the floor as the blue light died. A thick cloud of dust burst from the shattered ball, a greenish-yellow mist that billowed out to fill the corridor.

Instantly, Conan knew the cloud for what it was: he had seen it used before by a Nemedian thief when they had scaled the Tower of the Elephant in Arenjun. The thief was long dead, but what he had said lived in Conan's memory. Black lotus dust, and breathing it meant death!

Conan's instincts took over. He grabbed Kinna by the hand. 'Hold your breath, girl – do not breathe! – and run for your life!' With that, he led Kinna *into* the cloud of death.

Even without breathing, Conan caught the taint of a sickeningly sweet and cloying odor as the thick cloud closed over him. He tripped on the fallen form of the witch, nearly fell, but recovered, towing Kinna along with him.

Behind him, Conan heard the sound he had hoped to hear: the footsteps of the hooded lizard-men, chasing them.

The man and woman passed out of the cloud, but Conan kept going, to shake the traces of dust that clung to them. When he stopped, he still did not breathe as he brushed more of the vaporous substance from his and Kinna's clothes and bodies. He moved away from this spot before he finally allowed his inhaled air to escape. He drew in another lungful of air carefully, but no hint of the powdery death remained. He nodded at Kinna. 'Breathe,' he said.

Kinna panted noisily, and followed her inhalation with a question: 'What of the hooded ones?'

'Listen,' Conan commanded.

The sound of heavy forms dropping onto the flagstones reached his ears.

'I hear nothing –' Kinna began.

'Wait.'

After a time the cloud of dust began to settle and dissipate; as it did, the silent forms of the hooded lizards took shape upon the floor. Among them, too, lay the bodies of Djuvula the Witch, who had wanted Conan's heart for some foul spell, and near her a naked man was sprawled on his back, gutted.

'What –?'

'A poison,' Conan explained. 'I have seen it work before. Vitarius shook the mountain and the witch dropped the vial, destroying herself.'

'Who was the man?'

'Lemparius. And he was also a panther. Now he is neither. Come, we have your sister to rescue, and her siblings. And Sovartus must be stopped, or that thing on the plain will rule us all.'

CHAPTER TWENTY-TWO

The blue streak broke against the castle, and Sovartus nearly pitched out through the window as the building shook from the impact. He clutched at the facing and managed to thrust himself back into the tower. The magician glared at the unseen figure on Dodligia Plain, and his face lit with hatred. He might have died in the fall had he not been quick. To control such as the Thing of Power and then to die from some base stupidity would be a cruel irony indeed.

Sovartus drew himself up to his full height and smiled. Time to end this farce with his old classmate. The master of the Black Square regarded his creation, which in turn stared back with unblinking eyes of fire.

'Go,' Sovartus commanded, 'and swat me that bothersome insect!' The magician waved his hand in a casting motion.

The Thing of Power, built of the Four Elements, turned away from Castle Slott, moving more quickly than it seemed possible. Walking on legs made from tornadoes, it took gigantic strides across the plain.

A line of blue shot from the seemingly empty plain toward the Thing of Power, and a small spot on its earthy body blackened and smoked, but the creature slowed not.

Sovartus grinned, looking to see if any of the children noticed. None had, for each of the captives seemed to be in a stupor, eyes closed, breath coming slowly.

No matter, the mage thought. It is enough that *I* see it!

Another line of blue fire scored the Thing of Power, but this time the flash was dimmer, and the beam passed harmlessly through one of the arms of spinning wind.

In a few moments the Thing of Power had dwindled, so that it seemed no larger than a man seen across a wide street. A third blue flame arrowed up from the ground and struck the creature, who was almost upon the source.

As Sovartus watched, the awesome Thing of Power bent and raised one of its arms. The arm came down hard, and the force of the blow shook the ground, even into the castle, so that Sovartus felt the strike through the soles of his boots.

That blow meant much to Sovartus, ah, yes. He knew then that Vitarius, pupil to Hogistum, and his enemy, was no more. He had been snuffed out with no more effort needed than to command it.

Nothing could stand in his way now, Sovartus knew, for there was no power capable of withstanding the creature he had created and was master of, no power on Earth. Not since the sinking of Atlantis had such forces been under the direction of men; his triumph was as awesome as the Thing of Power itself. It would live as long as he lived, and he could live forever!

Sovartus continued to stare at the Thing of Power as it marched back toward him. Soon the nations of the world would bow to him and offer him all manner of tribute. Soon he would destroy cities, lay waste to whole countrysides, slaughter armies, did not the people offer him his due. Soon he would rule the world, and it would function to his whim – or it would function not at all!

The thought of it filled Sovartus with black joy.

The passageway opened into an antechamber. Conan saw the backs of two more of the hooded lizard-men as he stepped into the antechamber. The lizard-men's attention lay elsewhere, and when Conan looked beyond them, he saw what held their gazes: a thin man with black hair and a pointed beard, dressed in a woven-hair robe, looking through a window.

'Sovartus,' Kinna whispered next to Conan.

'At last,' Conan said. He raised his sword.

Something must have alerted the two lizard-men, for they turned, as one, to stare at Conan and Kinna. They raised their pikes.

'I'll take the one on the left!' Kinna said.

Conan hesitated not at all, but leaped to do battle with the hooded figures. Sovartus glanced in his direction, then turned back to his contemplation of whatever lay outside the window, as if he had not the smallest of worries.

Knowing the lizard-men's speed and power gave Conan an advantage; he did not try to fence, but rather went around the jabbing pike. A single two-handed cut with his sword, braced for the shock, and Conan batted his foe down. He spun just as Kinna jabbed her pike into her opponent's hood, bringing forth a militant hiss from the reptilian creature. Conan whipped his blade around and chopped into the thing's head; it went down in silence. The big Cimmerian leaped into the tower room.

Eldia lay chained under a window; indeed, there were three others pent in the same manner, and all looked to be either in deep sleep or in the arms of death. Conan snarled his anger and took two steps toward Sovartus.

The magician turned away from the window and waved one hand at Conan, twirling his fingers as he did so.

Conan's sword handle suddenly grew hot, too hot to hold, even through the thick leather wrapping the haft. He switched the sword to his opposite hand, but the heat increased; the leather began to smoke, then burst into flame. Conan dropped the sword. The blade flashed into redness, then blue-white so bright that the Cimmerian had to look away. There came a clap of noise, and when he looked back, the sword was gone, leaving only a black mark upon the floor.

Behind him, Kinna yelled, then followed the *clunk*! of her pike hitting the floor. There came another flash and thunderclap, and he knew her weapon had been destroyed.

Undaunted, Conan sprang again, drawing the curved knife that had killed Lemparius. It wore a spell, perhaps such was proof against Sovartus –

The knife pulled itself from Conan's grasp and spun away, to stick up in a table nearby. Deviltry!

Conan growled in fury. He still had his hands, by Crom! The big Cimmerian lunged, seeking to smash the thin man with his hammerlike fists.

186

An invisible boot slammed into Conan's belly. His corded stomach absorbed the blow, but it knocked him backward and off his feet.

Sovartus smiled and raised his hand. Another blow struck Conan, this one from the side. He swept his hands about, looking for an opponent with whom to grapple; there existed none, and yet a third blow crashed into his head, dazing him.

Kinna tried to reach Conan, but some magic beset her as well, for she fell back, gasping for breath. Conan came to his hands and knees, then to his feet.

Sovartus laughed and raised his hand again. 'Fool! You cannot contend with me! I am your new god! Bow to me, and I shall spare you, as my first worshipper!'

'Never!' Conan said.

The invisible boot caught Conan under the chin, knocking him onto his back. He groaned involuntarily, sat up, and shook his head, struggling to rise.

Sovartus looked on, still apparently amused.

Behind Sovartus, chained to the wall, Eldia awoke. Her eyes flickered open. She blinked and looked at Conan, then at Sovartus.

Conan shook his head, this time in warning to Eldia to remain still. The Cimmerian managed to get to one knee and one foot.

Eldia stared at Sovartus. She raised one hand and reached toward the magician's strange robe. Sovartus must have heard something, for he started to turn toward the girl.

Conan drew a deep breath and spat at the wizard. The man jerked his attention back toward Conan. 'For that, you will die, fool!' He started to bring his hand down –

Suddenly, the back of Sovartus's robe erupted into flame. The wizard spun. 'What –?' But the robe only flared out, fanning the blaze higher. Sovartus cursed and tore the robe from his body. His attention left the massive youth.

Conan managed to regain his feet. He gathered his strength into his legs and jumped. This time he reached his object: he locked his hands like clamps upon Sovartus's throat. The two men fell, rolling through the fiery robe upon

187

the floor. Sovartus brought his own hands into a grip upon Conan's neck. Though thin, the wizard had great strength, and he was driven by desperation. Conan felt fingers like steel bars dig into his flesh. He tightened his neck muscles and his grip, and screamed in savage rage.

Sovartus's grip slackened. The wizard's face went dark red, shading to purple; his eyes bulged from their sockets and blood ran from his nose; his lips drew back from his too-white teeth.

After what seemed the lifetime of a god, Sovartus's hands left Conan's neck, and he went limp.

A terrible sound broke over the castle, a wordless cry of rage and agony that vibrated Conan to his depth. He stood and looked out through the window.

The massive monster on the plain shook violently, waving its arms. It screamed again, and a landslide rumbled along its body, dropping a shower of dirt away from the torso. Its eyes flashed with living fire, and lightning broke from its mouth as it screamed a third time. The monster started toward the castle.

Conan found a pike. He thrust the weapon between the metal links holding Eldia to the wall. He took a deep breath, and tore the chains from their mounting. He turned toward Kinna. 'Help her, and wake the others if you can! The monster on the plain comes!'

Conan moved quickly around the chamber, breaking the chains that bound the children, shaking the sleeping forms, trying to awaken them. The three came to, but were still groggy.

The floor began to shake as the monster drew nearer. Conan risked a glance at the plain again. The creature trembled and gyrated, and seemed on the verge of collapse; great chunks of its body broke off and tumbled away; the eyes of fire roared forth along with the lightnings, and the winds of its limbs waxed and waned.

'Up!' Conan yelled. He snatched up a still-bleary-eyed girl and pointed at the room's exit. 'Out, fast! We do not want to be here when that thing arrives!'

Kinna led, half-towing one of the boys. Eldia followed,

being the most alert, and Conan carried and dragged two of the children. They ran as if a hellish beast followed, as indeed it did.

When they neared the place where the witch and were-panther had died, Conan called a halt. 'Slowly,' he commanded, 'lest we stir up the killing-dust.'

Conan led the way. As he stepped over the body of one of the lizard-men, he paused. A large pack was strapped upon its back, and from one corner protruded the point of a sword. Conan bent and carefully opened the pack. Inside, he found clothing – *his* clothing! – and his broadsword. He managed a small smile. This one had been the witch's thrall, he guessed. He removed the sword and clothing, being careful to keep the poison dust from stirring.

'Move,' Conan said when his belongings were reclaimed.

The group followed the winding aisles downward, occasionally passing the inert forms of lizard-men. These bodies bore no wounds, but Conan guessed that the death of their master must have doomed them as well.

The Cimmerian led Kinna and the children from the constructed portion of the castle and into the bowels of the mountain. A violent shudder hit the rock, so strong that the fleeing band found itself shaken from their feet to the floor.

'The monster has come home,' Conan said. 'I think it means to take the castle with it when it goes.'

The six stood and ran.

The journey seemed to take forever. Several times, the floor shifted so much that footing was impossible. Once, a huge section of stone ceiling broke loose and fell, crashing down with a roar, barely missing the runners.

Finally, they reached the base of the mountain and the tunnel exit. 'This way,' Conan yelled over the rumbling of the earth. 'There are horses, if they still live.'

While the monster battering at the castle stood partway around the mountain, the winds created by the tornadoes it bore as limbs raised dust and leaves all around Conan as he ran. Past the grove of trees he found the horses panicky, but still pent. With the thunder of the thing tearing at the mountain all around them, Conan managed to get the children and Kinna mounted before climbing onto a horse himself.

'Now, ride!' Conan commanded.

They rode, and fast.

Conan called a halt. The group turned to stare at the mountain-castle they had recently left. The elemental monster tore at the mountain, though the top of the castle itself was no more. Great chunks of granite flew high into the air, some smaller bits flying even past where Conan and the others sat upon their horses.

'Look!' Kinna said.

The thing reared and came down with both arms. It smashed into the solid rock. The main part of the mountain shattered. With it went the monster, dissolving into a massive cloud of rock dust and stone wind.

For a time no one said anything. Finally, Conan broke the silence: 'It is done. Over.'

Riding back along the Dodligian road, Conan spotted a figure in the distance, waving. He drew his sword. But as they moved closer he grinned and sheathed his blade. No threat here, in this familiar figure.

Eldia recognized the man then, and called out: 'Vitarius!'

'Aye, Vitarius,' the old man said as the riders drew nearer. 'No one thought to bring a horse for me, eh? Well, no matter, I can ride double with Eldia, I suppose.'

'We thought you might be . . .' Kinna began.

'Dead? Aye, Sovartus would have had it so. He sent the Thing of Power to squash me. I lanced it a few times, but I was as a gnat to a bullock. When it got too close, I chose to be elsewhere.'

Conan looked around the bare plain. 'That must have been some trick.'

'I would take credit for it,' Vitarius said, 'but it was hardly anything to brag about. I slipped into the entrance to one of the whelves' tunnels and scuttled as deep as I could get. What the thing smashed was merely a simple illusion. Those are what I do best.'

'So I recall you saying,' Conan said dryly.

CHAPTER TWENTY-THREE

'Well,' Vitarius demanded, 'are you going to tell me the tale or not?'

Conan grinned and related their adventures since last they had seen the old mage. Vitarius nodded and made appropriate noises as he listened. Occasionally, he interrupted with questions.

'But – what caused Sovartus's robe to take fire?'

Conan pointed at Eldia.

'Odd. I had thought that the children would have been drained of all force by the creation of the Thing of Power.'

Eldia nodded. 'So it was. I no longer felt the fire within me when Sovartus enspelled me. My fires were transported to the Thing. But when I awoke and saw Conan injured, I somehow knew I still had a single spark. So I sent my final flicker of heat into Sovartus's robe.'

'And glad I am that she did,' Conan said. As he spoke he unwrapped the bundle of clothing he had retrieved from the dead lizard-man's pack. While so doing, a shower of glittering green suddenly erupted from the breeks he unrolled.

'What is this?' Kinna said.

Conan laughed. 'The emeralds! Lemparius must have put them there, thinking to retrieve them later! I purchased our supplies with but one of these beauties, and there must be fifty of them!'

'You are rich,' Kinna said.

Conan shook his head. 'Nay, rather say *we* are rich. We shall share them equally, for we all certainly earned them.'

He apportioned the stones, and when he finished, each person had seven, with two to spare. These he gave to Kinna. 'You'll likely have more use for them than I,' he said. 'You now have three new mouths to feed.'

'Yes,' she said, 'I shall return to our land and build us a fine house; we won't be poor. Will you go with us, Vitarius?'

The old man nodded. 'Aye. A fire to warm my old bones and such good company will suit me well enough. And I might teach the children a few conjures, just for amusement, of course.'

Kinna turned to Conan. 'And what of you, Conan? You would be most welcome in our house. And in my bed.'

Conan shook his head. 'My path lies elsewhere, Kinna. I traveled the road to Nemedia when we met, and I would continue upon it.'

'I understand. You would not be a farmer or a landlord, I cannot see such for you. I shall remember you always.'

'As I shall you,' he said.

Conan watched the group ride away before he turned his own mount westward, toward Numalia. He had a new horse, courtesy of Sovartus of the Black Square, and emeralds worth twice the gold he had lost crossing into Corinthia. All in all, not a bad bargain, considering he was alive and whole to enjoy both.

He smiled, and rode off toward the setting sun.

CONAN
THE INDESTRUCTIBLE
by L. Sprague de Camp

The greatest hero of the magic-rife Hyborian Age was a northern barbarian, Conan the Cimmerian, about whose deeds a cycle of legend revolves. While these legends are largely based on the attested facts of Conan's life, some tales are inconsistent with others. So we must reconcile the contradictions in the saga as best we can.

In Conan's veins flowed the blood of the people of Atlantis, the brilliant city-state swallowed by the sea 8,000 years before his time. He was born into a clan that claimed a homeland in the northwest corner of Cimmeria, along the shadowy borders of Vanaheim and the Pictish wilderness. His grandfather had fled his own people because of a blood feud and sought refuge with the people of the North. Conan himself first saw daylight on a battlefield during a raid by the Vanir.

Before he had weathered fifteen snows, the young Cimmerian's fighting skills were acclaimed around the council fires. In that year the Cimmerians, usually at one another's throats, joined forces to repel the warlike Gundermen who, intent on colonizing southern Cimmeria, had pushed across the Aquilonian border and established the frontier post of Venarium. Conan joined the howling, blood-mad horde that swept out of the northern hills, stormed over the stockade walls, and drove the Aquilonians back across their frontier.

At the sack of Venarium, Conan, still short of his full growth, stood six feet tall and weighed 180 pounds. He had the vigilance and stealth of the born woodsman, the iron-hardness of the mountain man, and the Herculean physique of his blacksmith father. After the plunder of the Aquilonian outpost, Conan returned for a time to his tribe.

Restless under the conflicting passions of his adolescence, Conan spent several months with a band of Æsir as they raided the Vanir and the Hyperboreans. He soon learned that some Hyperborean citadels were ruled by a caste of widely-feared magicians, called Witchmen. Undaunted, he took part in a foray against Haloga Castle, when he found that Hyperborean slavers had captured Rann, the daughter of Njal, chief of the Æsir band.

Conan gained entrance to the castle and spirited out Rann Njalsdatter; but on the flight out of Hyperborea, Njal's band was overtaken by an army of living dead. Conan and the other Æsir survivors were led away to slavery ('Legions of the Dead').

Conan did not long remain a captive. Working at night, he ground away at one link of his chain until it was weak enough to break. Then one stormy night, whirling a four-foot length of heavy chain, he fought his way out of the slave pen and vanished into the downpour.

Another account of Conan's early years tells a different tale. This narrative, on a badly broken clay prism from Nippur, states that Conan was enslaved as a boy of ten or twelve by Vanir raiders and set to work turning a grist mill. When he reached his full growth, he was bought by a Hyrkanian pitmaster who traveled with a band of professional fighters staging contests for the amusement of the Vanir and Æsir. At this time Conan received his training with weapons. Later he escaped and made his way south to Zamora (*Conan the Barbarian*).

Of the two versions, the records of Conan's enslavement by the Hyrkanians at sixteen, found in a papyrus in the British Museum, appear much more legible and self-consistent. But this question may never be settled.

Although free, the youth found himself half a hostile kingdom away from home. Instinctively he fled into the mountains at the southern extremity of Hyperborea. Pursued by a pack of wolves, he took refuge in a cave. Here he discovered the seated mummy of a gigantic chieftain of ancient times, with a heavy bronze sword across its knees. When Conan seized the sword, the corpse arose and attacked him ('The Thing in the Crypt').

Continuing southward into Zamora, Conan came to Arenjun, the notorious 'City of Thieves.' Green to civilization and, save for some rudimentary barbaric ideas of honor and chivalry, wholly lawless by nature, he carved a niche for himself as a professional thief.

Being young and more daring than adroit, Conan's progress in his new profession was slow until he joined forces with Taurus of Nemedia in a quest for the fabulous jewel called the 'Heart of the Elephant.' The gem lay in the almost impregnable tower of the infamous mage Yara, captor of the extraterrestrial being Yag-Kosha ('The Tower of the Elephant').

Seeking greater opportunities to ply his trade, Conan wandered westward to the capital of Zamora, Shadizar the Wicked. For a time his thievery prospered, although the whores of Shadizar soon relieved him of his gains. During one larceny, he was captured by the men of Queen Taramis of Shadizar, who sent him on a mission to recover a magical horn wherewith to resurrect an ancient, evil god. Taramis's plot led to her own destruction (*Conan the Destroyer*).

The barbarian's next exploit involved a fellow thief, a girl named Tamira. The Lady Jondra, an arrogant aristocrat of Shadizar, owned a pair of priceless rubies. Baskaran Imalla, a religious fanatic raising a cult among the Kezankian hillmen, coveted the jewels to gain control over a fire-breathing dragon he had raised from an egg. Conan and Tamira both yearned for the rubies; Tamira took a post as lady's maid to Jondra for a chance to steal them.

An ardent huntress, Jondra set forth with her maid and her men-at-arms to slay Baskaran's dragon. Baskaran captured the two women and was about to offer them to his pet as a snack when Conan intervened (*Conan the Magnificent*).

Soon Conan was embroiled in another adventure. A stranger hired the youth to steal a casket of gems sent by the King of Zamora to the King of Turan. The stranger, a priest of the serpent-god Set, wanted the jewels for magic against this enemy, the renegade priest Amanar.

Amanar's emissaries, who were hominoid reptiles, had stolen the gems. Although wary of magic, Conan set out to recover the loot. He became involved with a bandette, Karela, called the Red Hawk, who proved the ultimate bitch; when Conan saved her from rape, she tried to kill him. Amanar's party had also carried off to the renegade's stronghold a dancing girl whom Conan had promised to help (*Conan the Invincible*).

Soon rumors of treasure sent Conan to the nearby ruins of ancient Larsha, just ahead of the soldiers dispatched to arrest him. After all but their leader, Captain Nestor, had perished in an accident arranged by Conan, Nestor and Conan joined forces to plunder the treasure; but ill luck deprived them of their gains ('The Hall of the Dead').

Conan's recent adventures had left him with an aversion to warlocks and Eastern sorceries. He fled northwestward through Corinthia into Nemedia, the second most powerful Hyborian kingdom. In Nemedia he resumed his profession successfully enough to bring his larcenies to the notice of Aztrias Pentanius, ne'er-do-well nephew of the governor. Oppressed by gambling debts, this young gentleman hired the outlander to purloin a Zamorian goblet, carved from a single diamond, that stood in the temple-museum of a wealthy collector.

Conan's appearance in the temple-museum coincided with its master's sudden demise and brought the young thief to the unwelcome attention of Demetrio, of the city's Inquisitorial Council. This caper also gave Conan his second experience with the dark magic of the serpent-brood of Set, conjured up by the Stygian sorcerer Thoth-Amon ('The God in the Bowl').

Having made Nemedia too hot to hold him, Conan drifted south into Corinthia, where he continued to occupy himself with the acquistion of other persons' property. By diligent application, the Cimmerian earned the repute of one of the boldest thieves in Corinthia. Poor judgment of women, however, cast him into chains until a turn in local politics brought freedom and a new career. An ambitious nobleman, Murilo, turned him loose to slit the throat of the Red Priest, Nabonidus, the scheming power behind the local throne. This venture gathered a prize collection of rogues in Nabonidus's mansion and ended in a mire of blood and treachery ('Rogues in the House').

Conan wandered back to Arenjun and began to earn a semi-honest living by stealing back for their owners valuable objects that others had filched from them. He undertook to recover a magical gem, the Eye of Erlik, from the wizard Hissar Zul and return it to its owner, the Kahn of Zamboula.

There is some question about the chronology of Conan's life at this point. A recently-translated tablet from Asshurbanipal's library states that Conan was about seventeen at the time. This would place the episode right after that of 'The Tower of the Elephant,' which indeed is mentioned in the cuneiform. But from internal evidence, this event seems to have taken place several years later. For one thing, Conan appears too clever, mature and sophisticated; for another, the fragmentary medieval Arabic manuscript *Kitab al-Qunn* implies that Conan was well into his twenties by then.

The first translator of the Asshurbanipal tablet, Prof. Dr. Andreas von Fuss of the Münchner Staatsmuseum, read Conan's age as '17.' In Babylonian cuneiform, '17' is expressed by two circles followed by three vertical wedges, with a horizontal wedge above the three for 'minus' – hence 'twenty minus three.' But Academician Leonid Skram of the Moscow Archaeological Institute asserts that the depression over the vertical wedges is merely a dent made by the pick of a careless excavator, and the numeral properly reads '23.'

Anyhow, Conan learned of the Eye of Erlik when he heard a discussion between an adventuress, Isparana, and her confederate. He invaded the wizard's mansion, but the wizard caught Conan and deprived him of his soul. Conan's soul was imprisoned in a mirror, there to remain until a crowned ruler broke the glass. Hissar Zul thus compelled

197

Conan to follow Isparana and recover the talisman; but when the Cimmerian returned the Eye to Hissar Zul, the ungrateful mage tried to slay him (*Conan and the Sorcerer*).

Conan, his soul still englassed, accepted legitimate employment as bodyguard to a Khaurani noblewoman, Khashtris. This lady set out for Khauran with Conan, another guard, Shubal, and several retainers. When the other servants plotted to rob and murder their employer, Conan and Shubal saved her and escorted her to Khauran. There Conan found the widowed Queen Ialamis being courted by a young nobleman who was not at all what he seemed (*Conan the Mercenary*).

With his soul restored, Conan learned from an Iranistani, Khassek, that the Khan of Zamboula still wanted the Eye of Erlik. In Zamboula, the Turanian governor, Akter Khan, had hired the wizard Zafra, who ensorcelled swords so that they would slay on command. En route, Conan encountered Isparana, with whom he developed a lust-hate relationship. Unaware of the magical swords, Conan continued to Zamboula and delivered the amulet. But the nefarious Zafra convinced the Khan that Conan was dangerous and should be killed on general principles (*Conan: the Sword of Skelos*).

Conan had enjoyed his taste of Hyborian-Age intrigue. It became clear that there was no basic difference between the opportunities in the palace and those in the Rats' Den, whereas the pickings were far better in high places. Besides, he wearied of the furtive, squalid life of a thief.

He was not, however, yet committed to a strictly law-abiding life. When unemployed, he took time out for a venture in smuggling. An attempt to poison him sent him to Vendhya, a land of wealth and squalor, philosophy and fanaticism, idealism and treachery (*Conan the Victorious*).

Soon after, Conan turned up in the Turanian seaport of Aghrapur. A new cult had established headquarters there under the warlock Jhandar, who needed victims to be drained of blood and reanimated as servants. Conan refused the offer of a former fellow thief, Emilio, to take part in a raid on Jhandar's stronghold to steal a fabulous ruby necklace. A Turanian sergeant, Akeba, did however persuade Conan to go with him to rescue Akeba's daughter, who had vanished into the cult (*Conan the Unconquered*).

After Jhandar's fall, Akeba urged Conan to take service in the Turanian army. The Cimmerian did not at first find military life congenial, being too self-willed and hot-tempered to easily submit to discipline. Moreover, as he was at this time an indifferent horseman and archer, Conan was relegated to a low-paid irregular unit.

Still, a chance soon arose to show his mettle. King Yildiz launched an expedition against a rebellious satrap. By sorcery, the satrap wiped out the force sent against him. Young Conan alone survived to enter the magic-maddened satrap's city of Yaralet ('The Hand of Nergal').

Returning in triumph to the glittering capital of Aghrapur, Conan gained a place in King Yildiz's guard of honor. At first he endured the gibes of fellow troopers at his clumsy horsemanship and inaccurate archery. But the gibes died away as the other guardsmen discovered Conan's sledgehammer fists and as his skills improved.

Conan was chosen, along with a Kushite mercenary named Juma, to escort King Yildiz's daughter Zosara to her wedding with Khan Kujula, chief of the Kuigar nomads. In the foothills of the Talakma Mountains, the party was attacked by a strange force of squat, brown, lacquer-armored horsemen. Only Conan, Juma, and the princess survived. They were taken to the subtropical valley of Meru and to the capital, Shamballah, where Conan and Juma were chained to an oar of the Meruvian state galley, about to set forth on a cruise.

On the galley's return to Shamballah, Conan and Juma escaped and made their way into the city. They reached the temple of Yama as the deformed little god-king of Meru was celebrating his marriage to Zosara ('The City of Skulls').

Back at Aghrapur, Conan was promoted to captain. His growing repute as a good man in a tight spot, however, led King Yildiz's generals to pick the barbarian for especially hazardous missions. Once they sent Conan to escort an emissary to the predatory tribesmen of the Khozgari Hills, hoping to dissuade them by bribes and threats from plundering the Turanians of the lowlands. The Khozgarians, respecting only immediate, overwhelming force, attacked the detachment, killing the emissary and all but two of the soldiers, Conan and Jamal.

To assure their safe passage back to civilization, Conan and Jamal captured Shanya, the daughter of the Khozgari chief. Their route led them to a misty highland. Jamal and the horses were slain, and Conan had to battle a horde of hairless apes and invade the stronghold of an ancient, dying race ('The People of the Summit').

Another time, Conan was dispatched thousands of miles eastward, to fabled Khitai, to convey to King Shu of Kusan a letter from King Yildiz proposing a treaty of friendship and trade. The wise old Khitan king sent his visitors back with a letter of acceptance. As a guide, however, the king appointed a foppish little nobleman, Duke Feng, who had entirely different objectives ('The Curse of the Monolith,' first published as 'Conan and the Cenotaph').

Conan continued in his service in Turan for about two years, traveling widely and learning the elements of organized, civilized warfare. As usual, trouble was his bedfellow. After one of his more unruly adventures, involving the mistress of his superior officer, Conan deserted and headed for Zamora. In Shadizar he heard that the Temple of Zath, the spider god, in the Zamorian city of Yezud, was recruiting soldiers. Hastening to Yezud, Conan found that a Brythunian free company had taken all the available mercenary posts. He became the town's blacksmith because as a boy he had been apprenticed in this trade.

Conan learned from an emissary of King Yildiz, Lord Parvez, that High Priest Feridun was holding Yildiz's favorite wife, Jamilah, in captivity. Parvez hired Conan to abduct Jamilah. Meanwhile Conan had set his heart on the eight huge gems that formed the eyes of an enormous statue of the spider god. As he was loosening the jewels, the approach of priests forced him to flee to a crypt below the naos. The temple dancing girl Rudabeh, with whom Conan was truly in love for the first time in his life, descended into the crypt to warn him of the doom awaiting him there (*Conan and the Spider God*).

Conan next rode off to Shadizar to track down a rumor of treasure. He obtained a map showing the location of a ruby-studded golden idol in the Kezankian Mountains; but thieves stole his map. Conan, pursuing them, had a brush with Kezankian hillmen and had to join forces with the very rogues he was tracking. He found the treasure, only to lose it under strange circumstances ('The Bloodstained God').

Fed up with magic, Conan headed for the Cimmerian hills. After a time in the simple, routine life of his native village, however, he grew restless enough to join his old friends, the Æsir, in a raid into Vanaheim. In a bitter struggle on the snow-covered plain, both forces were wiped out – all but Conan, who wandered off to a strange encounter with the legendary Atali, daughter of the frost giant Ymir ('The Frost Giant's Daughter').

Haunted by Atali's icy beauty, Conan headed back toward the south, where, despite his often-voiced scorn of civilization, the golden spires of teeming cities beckoned. In the Eiglophian Mountains, Conan rescued a young woman from cannibals, but through overconfidence lost her to the dreaded monster that haunted glaciers ('The Lair of the Ice Worm').

Conan then returned to the Hyborian lands, which include Aquilonia, Argos, Brythunia, Corinthia, Koth, Nemedia, Ophir, and Zingara. These countries were named for the Hyborian peoples who, as barbarians, had 3,000 years earlier conquered the empire of Acheron and built civilized realms on its ruins.

In Belverus, the capital of Nemedia, the ambitious Lord Albanus dabbled in sorcery to usurp the throne of King Garian. To Belverus came Conan, seeking a patron with money to enable him to hire his own free company. Albanus gave a magical sword to a confederate, Lord Melius, who went mad and attacked people in the street until killed. As he picked up the ensorcelled sword, Conan was accosted by

201

Hordo, a one-eyed thief and smuggler whom he had known as Karela's lieutenant.

Conan sold the magical sword, hired his own free company, and taught his men mounted archery. Then he persuaded King Garian to hire him. But Albanus had made a man of clay and by his sorcery given it the exact appearance of the king. Then he imprisoned the king, substituted his golem, and framed Conan for murder (*Conan the Defender*).

Conan next brought his free company to Ianthe, capital of Ophir. There the Lady Synelle, a platinum-blond sorceress, wished to bring to life the demon-god Al'Kirr. Conan bought a statuette of this demon-god and soon found that various parties were trying to steal it from him. He and his company took service under Synelle, not knowing her plans.

Then the bandette Karela reappeared and, as usual, tried to murder Conan. Synelle hired her to steal the statuette, which the witch needed for her sorcery. She also planned to sacrifice Karela (*Conan the Triumphant*).

Conan went on to Argos; but since that kingdom was at peace, there were no jobs for mercenaries. A misunderstanding with the law compelled Conan to leap to the deck of a ship as it left the pier. This was the merchant galley *Argus*, bound for the coasts of Kush.

A major epoch in Conan's life was about to begin. The *Argus* was taken by Bêlit, the Shemite captain of the pirate ship *Tigress*, whose ruthless black corsairs had made her mistress of the Kushite littoral. Conan won both Bêlit and a partnership in her bloody trade ('Queen of the Black Coast,' Chapter 1).

Years before, Bêlit, daughter of a Shermite trader, had been abducted with her brother Jehanan by Stygian slavers. Now she asked her lover Conan to try to rescue the youth. The barbarian slipped into Khemi, the Stygian seaport, was captured, but escaped to the eastern end of Stygia, the province of Taia, where a revolt against Stygian oppression was brewing (*Conan the Rebel*).

Conan and Bêlit resumed their piratical careers, preying mainly on Stygian vessels. Then an ill fate took them up the black Zarkheba River to the lost city of an ancient winged race ('Queen of the Black Coast,' Chapters 2-5).

As Bêlit's burning funeral ship wafted out to sea, a down-hearted Conan turned his back on the sea, which he would not follow again for years. He plunged inland and joined the warlike Bamulas, a black tribe whose power swiftly grew under his leadership.

The chief of a neighboring tribe, the Bakalahs, planned a treacherous attack on another neighbor and invited Conan and his Bamulas to take part in the sack and massacre. Conan accepted but, learning that an Ophirean girl, Livia, was held captive in Bakalah, he out-betrayed the Bakalahs. Livia ran off during the slaughter and wandered into a mysterious valley, where only Conan's timely arrival saved her from being sacrificed to an extraterrestrial being ('The Vale of Lost Women').

Before Conan could build his own black empire, he was thwarted by a succession of natural catastrophes as well as by the intrigues of hostile Bamulas. Forced to flee, he headed north. After a narrow escape from pursuing lions on the veldt, Conan took shelter in a mysterious ruined castle of prehuman origin. He had a brush with Stygian slavers and a malign supernatural entity ('The Castle of Terror').

Continuing on, Conan reached the semicivilized kingdom of Kush. This was the land to which the name 'Kush' properly applied; although Conan, like other northerners, tended to use the term loosely to mean any of the black countries south of Stygia. In Meroê, the capital, Conan rescued from a hostile mob the young Queen of Kush, the arrogant, impulsive, fierce, cruel, and voluptuous Tananda.

Conan became embroiled in a labyrinthine intrigue between Tananda and an ambitious nobleman who commanded a piglike demon. The problem was aggravated by the presence of Diana, a Nemedian slave girl to whom Conan, despite the jealous fury of Tananda, took a fancy. Events culminated in a night of insurrection and slaughter ('The Snout in the Dark').

Dissatisfied with his achievements in the black countries,

Conan wandered to the meadowlands of Shem and became a soldier of Akkharia, a Shemite city-state. He joined a band of volunteers to liberate a neighboring city-state; but through the treachery of Othbaal, cousin of the mad King Akhîrom of Pelishtia, the volunteers were destroyed – all but Conan, who survived to track the plotter to Asgalun, the Pelishti capital. There Conan became involved in a polygonal power war among the mad Akhîrom, the treacherous Othbaal, a Stygian witch, and a company of black mercenaries. In the final hurly-burly of sorcery, steel, and blood, Conan grabbed Othbaal's red-haired mistress, Rufia, and galloped north ('Hawks Over Shem').

Conan's movements at this time are uncertain. One tale, sometimes assigned to this period, tells of Conan's service as a mercenary in Zingara. A Ptolemaic papyrus in the British Museum alleges that in Kordava, the capital, a captain in the regular army forced a quarrel on Conan. When Conan killed his assailant, he was condemned to hang. A fellow condemnee, Santiddio, belonged to an underground conspiracy, the White Rose, that hoped to topple King Rimanendo. As other conspirators created a disturbance in the crowd that gathered for the hanging, Conan and Santiddio escaped.

Mordermi, head of an outlaw band allied with the White Rose, enlisted Conan in his movement. The conspiracy was carried on in the Pit, a warren of tunnels beneath the city. When the King sent an army to clean out the Pit, the insurrectionists were saved by Callidos, a Stygian sorcerer. King Rimanendo was slain and Mordermi became king. When he proved as tyrannical as his predecessor, Conan raised another revolt; then, refusing the crown for himself, he departed (*Conan: The Road of Kings*).

This tale involves many questions. If authentic, it may belong in Conan's earlier mercenary period, around the time of *Conan the Defender*. But there is no corroboration in other narratives of the idea that Conan ever visited Zingara before his late thirties, the time of *Conan the Buccaneer*. Moreover, none of the rulers of Zingara mentioned in the papyrus appear on the list of kings of Zingara in the Byzantine manuscript *Hoi Anaktes tês Tzingêras*. Hence some students deem the papyrus either spurious or a case of confusion between Conan and some other hero. Everything else known about Conan indicates that, if he had indeed been offered the Zingaran crown, he would have grabbed it with both hands.

We next hear of Conan after he took service under Amalric of Nemedia, the general of Queen-Regent Yasmela of the little border kingdom of Khoraja. While Yasmela's brother, King Khossus, was a prisoner in Ophir, Yasmela's borders were assailed by the forces of the veiled sorcerer Natohk – actually the 3,000-years-dead Thugra Khotan of the ruined city of Kuthchemes.

Obeying an oracle of Mitra, the supreme Hyborian god, Yasmela made Conan captain-general of Khoraja's army. In this rôle he gave battle to Natohk's hosts and rescued the Queen-Regent from the malignant magic of the undead warlock. Conan won the day – and the Queen ('Black Colossus').

Conan, now in his late twenties, settled down as Khorajan commander-in-chief. But the Queen, whose lover he had expected to be, was too preoccupied with affairs of state to have time for frolics. He even proposed marriage, but she explained that such a union would not be sanctioned by Khorajan law and custom. Yet, if Conan could somehow rescue her brother from imprisonment, she might persuade Khossus to change the law.

Conan set forth with Rhazes, an astrologer, and Fronto, a thief who knew a secret passage into the dungeon where Khossus languished. They rescued the King but found themselves trapped by Kothian troops, since Strabonus of Koth had his own reasons for wanting Khossus.

Having surmounted these perils, Conan found that Khossus, a pompous young ass, would not hear of a foreign barbarian's marrying his sister. Instead, he would marry Yasmela off to a nobleman and find a middle-class bride for Conan. Conan said nothing; but in Argos, as their ship cast off, Conan sprang ashore with most of the gold that Khossus had raised and waved the King an ironic farewell ('Shadows in the Dark').

Now nearly thirty, Conan slipped away to revisit his Cimmerian homeland and avenge himself on the Hyperboreans. His blood brothers among the Cimmerians and the Æsir had won wives and sired sons, some as old and almost as big as Conan had been at the sack of Venarium. But his years of blood and battle had stirred his predatory spirit too strongly for him to follow their example. When traders brought word of new wars, Conan galloped off to the Hyborian lands.

A rebel prince of Koth was fighting to overthrow Strabonus, the penurious ruler of that far-stretched nation; and Conan found himself among old companions in the princeling's array, until the rebel made peace with his king. Unemployed again, Conan formed an outlaw band, the Free Companions. This troop gravitated to the steppes west of the Sea of Vilayet, where they joined the ruffianly horde known as the *kozaki*.

Conan soon became the leader of this lawless crew and ravaged the western borders of the Turanian Empire until his old employer, King Yildiz, sent a force under Shah Amurath, who lured the *kozaki* deep into Turan and cut them down.

Slaying Amurath and acquiring the Turanian's captive, Princess Olivia of Ophir, Conan rowed out into the Vilayet Sea in a small boat. He and Olivia took refuge on an island, where they found a ruined greenstone city, in which stood strange iron statues. The shadows cast by the moonlight proved as dangerous as the giant carnivorous ape that ranged the isle, or the pirate crew that landed for rest and recreation ('Shadows in the Moonlight').

Conan seized command of the pirates that ravaged the Sea of Vilayet. As chieftain of this mongrel Red Brotherhood, Conan was more than ever a thorn in King Yildiz's flesh. That mild monarch, instead of strangling his brother Teyaspa in the normal Turanian manner, had cooped him up in a castle in the Colchian Mountains. Yildiz now sent his General Artaban to destroy the pirate stronghold at the mouth of the Zaporoska River; but the general became the harried instead of the harrier. Retreating inland, Artaban stumbled upon Teyaspa's whereabouts; and the final conflict involved Conan's outlaws, Artaban's Turanians, and a brood of vampires ('The Road of the Eagles').

Deserted by his sea rovers, Conan appropriated a stallion and headed back to the steppes. Yezdigerd, now on the thorne of Turan, proved a far more astute and energetic ruler than his sire. He embarked on a program of imperial conquest.

Conan went to the small border kingdom of Khauran, where he won command of the royal guard of Queen Taramis. This queen had a twin sister, Salome, born a witch and reared by the yellow sorcerers of Khitai. She allied herself with the adventurer Constantius of Koth and planned by imprisoning the Queen to rule in her stead. Conan, who perceived the deception, was trapped and crucified. Cut down by the chieftain Olgerd Vladislav, the Cimmerian was carried off to a Zuagir camp in the desert. Conan waited for his wounds to heal, then applied his daring and ruthlessness to win his place as Olgerd's lieutenant.

When Salome and Constantius began a reign of terror in Khauran, Conan led his Zuagirs against the Khauranian capital. Soon Constantius hung from the cross to which he had nailed Conan, and Conan rode off smiling, to lead his Zuagirs on raids against the Turanians ('A Witch Shall Be Born').

Conan, about thirty and at the height of his physical powers, spent nearly two years with the desert Shemites, first as Olgerd's lieutenant and then, having ousted Olgerd, as sole chief. The circumstances of his leaving the Zuagirs were recently disclosed by a silken scroll in Old Tibetan, spirited out of Tibet by a refugee. This document is now with the Oriental Institute in Chicago.

The energetic King Yezdigerd sent soldiers to trap Conan and his troop. Because of a Zamorian traitor in Conan's ranks, the ambush nearly succeeded. To avenge the betrayal, Conan led his band in pursuit of the Zamorian. When his men deserted, Conan pressed on alone until, near death, he was rescued by Enosh, a chieftain of the isolated desert town of Akhlat.

Akhlat suffered under the rule of a demon in the form of a woman, who fed on the life force of living things. Conan, Enosh informed him, was their prophesied liberator. After it was over, Conan was invited to settle in Akhlat; but, knowing himself ill-suited to a life of humdrum respectability, he instead headed southwest to Zamboula with the horse and money of Vardanes the Zamorian ('Black Tears').

In one colossal debauch, Conan dissipated the fortune he had brought to Zamboula, a Turanian outpost. There lurked the sinister priest of Hanuman, Totrasmek, who sought a famous jewel, the Star of Khorala, for which the Queen of Ophir was said to have offered a roomful of gold. In the ensuing imbroglio, Conan acquired the Star of Khorala and rode westward ('Shadows of Zamboula').

The medieval monkish manuscript *De sidere choralae*, rescued from the bombed ruins of Monte Cassino, continues the tale. Conan reached the capital of Ophir to find that the effeminate Moranthes II, himself under the thumb of the sinister Count Rigello, kept his queen, Marala, under lock and key. Conan scaled the wall of Moranthes's castle and fetched Marala out. Rigello pursued the fugitives nearly to the Aquilonian border, where the Star of Khorala showed its power in an unexpected way ('The Star of Khorala').

Hearing that the *kozaki* had regained their vigor, Conan returned with horse and sword to the harrying of Turan. Although the now-famous northlander arrived all but empty-handed, contingents of the *kozaki* and the Vilayet pirates soon began operating under his command.

Yezdigerd sent Jehungir Agha to entrap the barbarian on the island of Xapur. Coming early to the ambush, Conan found the island's ancient fortress-palace of Dagon restored by magic, and in it the city's malevolent god, in the form of a giant of living iron ('The Devil in Iron').

After escaping from Xapur, Conan built his *kozaki* and pirate raiders into such a formidable threat that King Yezdigerd devoted all his forces to their destruction. After a devastating defeat, the *kozaki* scattered, and Conan retreated southward to take service in the light cavalry of Kobad Shah, King of Iranistan.

Conan got himself into Kobad Shah's bad graces and had to ride for the hills. He found a conspiracy brewing in Yanaidar, the fortress-city of the Hidden Ones. The Sons of Yezm were trying to revive an ancient cult and unite the surviving devotees of the old gods in order to rule the world. The adventure ended with the rout of the contending forces by the gray ghouls of Yanaidar, and Conan rode eastward ('The Flame Knife').

Conan reappeared in the Himelian Mountains, on the northwest frontier of Vendhya, as a war chief of the savage Afghuli tribesmen. Now in his early thirties, the warlike barbarian was known and feared throughout the world of the Hyborian Age.

No man to be bothered with niceties, Yezdigerd employed the magic of the wizard Khemsa, an adept of the dreaded Black Circle, to remove the Vendhyan king from his path. The dead king's sister, the Devi Yasmina, set out to avenge him but was captured by Conan. Conan and his captive pursued the sorcerous Khemsa, only to see him slain by the magic of the Seers of Yimsha, who also abducted Yasmina ('The People of the Black Circle').

When Conan's plans for welding the hill tribes into a single power failed, Conan, hearing of wars in the West, rode thither. Almuric, a prince of Koth, had rebelled against the hated Strabonus. While Conan joined Almuric's bristling host, Strabonus's fellow kings came to that monarch's aid. Almuric's motley horde was driven south, to be annihilated at last by combined Stygian and Kushite forces.

Escaping into the desert, Conan and the camp follower Natala came to age-old Xuthal, a phantom city of living dead men and their creeping shadow-god, Thog. The Stygian woman Thalis, the effective ruler of Xuthal, double-crossed Conan once too often ('The Slithering Shadow').

Conan beat his way back to the Hyborian lands. Seeking further employment, he joined the mercenary army that a

Zingaran, Prince Zapayo da Kova, was raising for Argos. It was planned that Koth should invade Stygia from the north, while the Argosseans approached the realm from the south by sea. Koth, however, made a separate peace with Stygia, leaving Conan's army of mercenaries trapped in the Stygian deserts.

Conan fled with Amalric, a young Aquilonian soldier. Soon Conan was captured by nomads, while Amalric escaped. When Amalric caught up again with Conan, Amalric had with him the girl Lissa, whom he had saved from the cannibal god of her native city. Conan had meanwhile become commander of the cavalry of the city of Tombalku. Two kings ruled Tombalku: the Negro Sakumbe and the mixed-blood Zehbeh. When Zehbeh and his faction were driven out, Sakumbe made Conan his co-king. But then the wizard Askia slew Sakumbe by magic. Conan, having avenged his black friend, escaped with Amalric and Lissa ('Drums of Tombalku').

Conan beat his way to the coast, where he joined the Barachan pirates. He was now about thirty-five. As second mate of the *Hawk*, he landed on the island of the Stygian sorcerer Siptah, said to have a magical jewel of fabulous properties.

Siptah dwelt in a cylindrical tower without doors or windows, attended by a winged demon. Conan smoked the unearthly being out but was carried off in its talons to the top of the tower. Inside the tower Conan found the wizard long dead; but the magical gem proved of unexpected help in coping with the demon ('The Gem in the Tower').

Conan remained about two years with the Barachans, according to a set of clay tablets in pre-Sumerian cuneiform. Used to the tightly organized armies of the Hyborian kingdoms, Conan found the organization of the Barachan bands too loose and anarchic to afford an opportunity to rise to leadership. Slipping out of a tight spot at the pirate rendezvous at Tortage, he found that the only alternative to a cut throat was braving the Western Ocean in a leaky skiff. When the *Wastrel*, the ship of the buccaneer Zaporavo, came in sight, Conan climbed aboard.

The Cimmerian soon won the respect of the crew and the enmity of its captain, whose Kordavan mistress, the sleek Sancha, cast too friendly an eye on the black-maned giant. Zaporavo drove his ship westward to an uncharted island, where Conan forced a duel on the captain and killed him, while Sancha was carried off by strange black beings to a living pool worshipped by these entities ('The Pool of the Black Ones').

Conan persuaded the officials at Kordava to transfer Zaporavo's privateering license to him, whereupon he spent about two years in this authorized piracy. As usual, plots were brewing against the Zingaran monarchy. King Ferdrugo was old and apparently failing, with no successor but his nubile daughter Chabela. Duke Villagro enlisted the Stygian super-sorcerer Thoth-Amon, the High Priest of Set, in a plot to obtain Chabela as his bride. Suspicious, the princess took the royal yacht down the coast to consult her uncle. A privateer in league with Villagro captured the yacht and abducted the girl. Chabela escaped and met Conan, who obtained the magical Cobra Crown, also sought by Thoth-Amon.

A storm drove Conan's ship to the coast of Kush, where Conan was confronted by black warriors headed by his old comrade-in-arms, Juma. While the chief welcomed the privateers, a tribesman stole the Cobra Crown. Conan set off in pursuit, with Princess Chabela following him. Both were captured by slavers and sold to the black Queen of the Amazons. The Queen made Chabela her slave and Conan her fancy man. Then, jealous of Chabela, she flogged the girl, imprisoned Conan, and condemned both to be devoured by a man-eating tree (*Conan the Buccaneer*).

Having rescued the Zingaran princess, Conan shrugged off hints of marriage and returned to privateering. But other Zingarans, jealous, brought him down off the coast of Shem. Escaping inland, Conan joined the Free Companions. Instead of rich plunder, however, he found himself in dull guard duty on the black frontier of Stygia, where the wine was sour and the pickings poor.

Conan's boredom ended with the appearance of the

pirette, Valeria of the Red Brotherhood. When she left the camp, he followed her south. The pair took refuge in a city occupied by the feuding clans of Xotalanc and Tecuhltli. Siding with the latter, the two northerners soon found themselves in trouble with that clan's leader, the ageless witch Tascela ('Red Nails').

Conan's amour with Valeria, however hot at the start, did not last long. Valeria returned to the sea; Conan tried his luck once more in the black kingdoms. Hearing of the 'Teeth of Gwahlur,' a cache of priceless jewels hidden in Keshan, he sold his services to its irascible king to train the Keshani army.

Thutmekri, the Stygian emissary of the twin kings of Zembabwei, also had designs on the jewels. The Cimmerian, outmatched in intrigue, made tracks for the valley where the ruins of Alkmeenon and its treasure lay hidden. In a wild adventure with the undead goddess Yelaya, the Corinthian girl Muriela, the black priests headed by Gorulga, and the grim gray servants of the long-dead Bît-Yakin, Conan kept his head but lost his loot ('Jewels of Gwahlur').

Heading for Punt with Muriela, Conan embarked on a scheme to relieve the worshipers of an ivory goddess of their abundant gold. Learning that Thutmekri had preceded him and had already poisoned King Lalibeha's mind against him, Conan and his companion took refuge in the temple of the goddess Nebethet.

When the king, Thutmekri, and High Priest Zaramba arrived at the temple, Conan staged a charade wherein Muriela spoke with the voice of the goddess. The results surprised all, including Conan ('The Ivory Goddess').

In Zembabwei, the city of the twin kings, Conan joined a trading caravan which he squired northward along the desert borders, bringing it safely into Shem. Now in his late thirties, the restless adventurer heard that the Aquilonians were spreading westward into the Pictish wilderness. So thither, seeking work for his sword, went Conan. He enrolled as a scout at Fort Tuscelan, where a fierce war raged with the Picts.

In the forests across the river, the wizard Zogar Sag was

gathering his swamp demons to aid the Picts. While Conan failed to prevent the destruction of Fort Tuscelan, he managed to warn settlers around Velitrium and to cause the death of Zogar Sag ('Beyond the Black River').

Conan rose rapidly in the Aquilonian service. As captain, his company was once defeated by the machinations of a traitorous superior. Learning that this officer, Viscount Lucian, was about to betray the province to the Picts, Conan exposed the traitor and routed the Picts ('Moon of Blood').

Promoted to general, Conan defeated the Picts in a great battle at Velitrium and was called back to the capital, Tarantia, to receive the nation's accolades. Then, having roused the suspicions of the depraved and foolish King Numedides, he was drugged and chained in the Iron Tower under sentence of death.

The barbarian, however, had friends as well as foes. Soon he was spirited out of prison and turned loose with horse and sword. He struck out across the dank forests of Pictland toward the distant sea. In the forest, the Cimmerian came upon a cavern in which lay the corpse and the demon-guarded treasure of the pirate Tranicos. From the west, others – a Zingaran count and two bands of pirates – were hunting the same fortune, while the Stygian sorcerer Thoth-Amon took a hand in the game ('The Treasure of Tranicos').

Rescued by an Aquilonian galley, Conan was chosen to lead a revolt against Numedides. While the revolution stormed along, civil war raged on the Pictish frontier. Lord Valerian, a partisan of Numedides, schemed to bring the Picts down on the town of Schohira. A scout, Gault Hagar's sons, undertook to upset this scheme by killing the Pictish wizard ('Wolves Beyond the Border').

Storming the capital city and slaying Numedides on the steps of this throne – which he promptly took for his own – Conan, now in his early forties, found himself ruler of the greatest Hyborian nation (*Conan the Liberator*).

A king's life, however, proved no bed of houris. Within a year, an exiled count had gathered a group of plotters to oust the barbarian from the throne. Conan might have lost crown and head but for the timely intervention of the long-dead sage Epimitreus ('The Phoenix of the Sword').

No sooner had the mutterings of revolt died down than Conan was treacherously captured by the kings of Ophir and Koth. he was imprisoned in the tower of the wizard Tsotha-lanti in the Kothian capital. Conan escaped with the help of a fellow prisoner, who was Tsotha-lanti's wizardly rival Pelias. By Pelias's magic, Conan was whisked to Tarantia in time to slay a pretender and to lead an army against his treacherous fellow kings ('The Scarlet Citadel').

For nearly two years, Aquilonia thrived under Conan's firm but tolerant rule. The lawless, hard-bitten adventurer of former years had, through force of circumstance, matured into an able and responsible statesman. But a plot was brewing in neighboring Nemedia to destroy the King of Aquilonia by sorcery from an elder day.

Conan, about forty-five, showed few signs of age save a network of scars on his mighty frame and a more cautious approach to wine, women and bloodshed. Although he kept a harem of luscious concubines, he had never taken an official queen; hence he had no legitimate son to inherit the throne, a fact whereof his enemies sought to take advantage.

The plotters resurrected Xaltotun, the greatest sorcerer of the ancient empire of Acheron, which fell before the Hyborian savages 3,000 years earlier. By Xaltotun's magic, the King of Nemedia was slain and replaced by his brother Tarascus. Black sorcery defeated Conan's army; Conan was imprisoned, and the exile Valerius took his throne.

Escaping from a dungeon with the aid of the harem girl Zenobia, Conan returned to Aquilonia to rally his loyal forces against Valerius. From the priests of Asura, he learned that Xaltotun's power could be broken only by means of a strange jewel, the 'Heart of Ahriman.' The trail of the jewel led to a pyramid in the Stygian desert outside black-walled Khemi. Winning the Heart of Ahriman, Conan returned to face his foes (*Conan the Conqueror*, originally published as *The Hour of the Dragon*).

After regaining his kingdom, Conan made Zenobia his

queen. But, at the ball celebrating her elevation, the queen was borne off by a demon sent by the Khitan sorcerer Yah Chieng. Conan's quest for his bride carried him across the known world, meeting old friends and foes. In purple-towered Paikang, with the help of a magical ring, he freed Zenobia and slew the wizard (*Conan the Avenger*, originally published as *The Return of Conan*).

Home again, the way grew smoother. Zenobia gave him heirs: a son named Conan but commonly called Conn, another son called Taurus, and a daughter. When Conn was twelve, his father took him on a hunting trip to Gunderland. Conan was now in his late fifties. His sword arm was a little slower than in his youth, and his black mane and the fierce mustache of his later years were traced with gray; but his strength still surpassed that of two ordinary men.

When Conn was lured away by the Witchmen of Hyperborea, who demanded that Conan come to their stronghold alone, Conan went. He found Louhi, the High Priestess of the Witchmen, in conference with three others of the world's leading sorcerers: Thoth-Amon of Stygia; the god-king of Kambuja; and the black lord of Zembabwei. In the ensuing holocaust, Louhi and the Kambujan perished, while Thoth-Amon and the other sorcerer vanished by magic ('The Witch of the Mists').

Old King Ferdrugo of Zingara had died, and his throne remained vacant as the nobles intrigued over the succession. Duke Pantho of Guarralid invaded Poitain, in southern Aquilonia. Conan, suspecting sorcery, crushed the invaders. Learning that Thoth-Amon was behind Pantho's madness, Conan set out with his army to settle matters with the Stygian. He pursued his foe to Thoth-Amon's stronghold in Stygia ('Black Sphinx of Nebthu'), to Zembabwei ('Red Moon of Zembabwei'), and to the last realm of the serpent folk in the far south ('Shadows in the Skull').

For several years, Conan's rule was peaceful. But time did that which no combination of foes had been able to do. The Cimmerian's skin became wrinkled and his hair gray; old wounds ached in damp weather. Conan's beloved consort Zenobia died giving birth to their second daughter.

Then catastrophe shattered King Conan's mood of half-resigned discontent. Supernatural entities, the Red Shadows, began seizing and carrying off his subjects. Conan was baffled until in a dream he again visited the sage Epimitreus. He was told to abdicate in favor of Prince Conn and set out across the Western Ocean.

Conan discovered that the Red Shadows had been sent by the priest-wizards of Antillia, a chain of islands in the western part of the ocean, whither the survivors of Atlantis had fled 8,000 years before. These priests offered human sacrifices to their devil-god Xotli on such a scale that their own population faced extermination.

In Antillia, Conan's ship was taken, but he escaped into the city Ptahuacan. After conflicts with giant rats and dragons, he emerged atop the sacrificial pyramid just as his crewmen were about to be sacrificed. Supernatural conflict, revolution, and seismic catastrophe ensued. In the end, Conan sailed off to explore the continents to the west (*Conan of the Isles*).

Whether he died there, or whether there is truth in the tale that he strode out of the West to stand at his son's side in a final battle against Aquilonia's foes, will be revealed only to him who looks, as Kull of Valusia once did, into the mystic mirrors of Tuzun Thune.

L. Sprague de Camp
Villanova, Pennsylvania
May 1984